Tara's Healing

Janice Holt Giles

With a Foreword by Wade Hall

THE UNIVERSITY PRESS OF KENTUCKY

Published in 1994 by The University Press of Kentucky

Scholarly publisher for the Commonwealth,
serving Ballarmine College, Berea College, Centre
College of Kentucky, Eastern Kentucky University,
The Filson Club, Georgetown College, Kentucky
Historical Society, Kentucky State University,
Morehead State University, Murray State University,
Northern Kentucky University, Transylvania University,
University of Kentucky, University of Louisville,
and Western Kentucky University.

Editorial and Sales Offices: Lexington, Kentucky 40508-4008

3 in 1 ISBN: 0-7394-3237-0

Printed in the United States of America

FOREWORD

Janice Holt Giles was born in Arkansas in 1909 and grew up there and in Oklahoma, but after she moved to Kentucky in 1941 she made her adopted state the setting for most of her fiction. One of the reasons she claimed Kentucky as her literary turf was Henry Giles, a Kentucky soldier she met on a bus near Bowling Green in 1943. They corresponded throughout the remainder of World War II and married when he returned home at the war's end.

For several years Henry and Janice Giles lived in the Louisville area; then in 1949 they moved to Giles Ridge, his home community near Knifley in Adair County in south central Kentucky. It was a fortunate move. Here was the place she renamed Piney Ridge, and here were the people who until her death in 1979 she would transform into some of the most popular fiction ever written by a Kentuckian.

Tara's Healing (1951) is the third novel of her Piney Ridge Trilogy, which also includes *The Enduring Hills* (1950) and *Miss Willie* (1951). Told in the third person from an omniscient point of view, it is the story of Tara Cochrane, a war veteran, a physician, and a burned-out man who describes himself in terms of a bad cigarette: "Like that bitter, dry taste of old smoke, in a mouth dried from fear." Apparently suffering from his war experiences, he is also the product of a broken family and now is a physician who cannot heal himself. After he "cracked up," he left his medical practice and checked himself into the "psycho ward" of a veterans hospital. There he meets one of the enlisted men from his old company of combat engineers. That man is Hod Pierce, who is on leave from his downstate farm for an ear operation. Pierce remembers how well Cochrane treated the men under his command and how he "never slept until they slept, and how he never ate until they ate, and how he got dirty and grimy and filthy right alongside of them."

It is obvious to Hod that his former captain needs help, especially after he discovers that Tara has no family. He therefore offers to share his family and his community with Tara. Moving, even temporarily, into Hod's "backwoods jumping-off place" full of hillbillies will be like sojourning in a foreign land, thinks Tara, but he decides to take the risk. After all, he has nothing to lose. He may even regain his health. So the nervous, taut, fearful, insecure, panic-stricken Tara Cochrane, a man who has "never known the warmth of a sustained and loving human relationship," goes with Hod Pierce to Piney Ridge to rest and recuperate.

Such a remote, backward rural community hardly seems the setting in which a city man can regain his mental stability. But so it proves to be. Tara moves in with Hod and his wife Mary, a cultured, talented woman who practices her own version of tough love in her relationship with her husband's friend. She quickly diagnoses him as "a disillusioned, embittered, unhappy person" and tells him to stop being so self-centered and start focusing on other things. Her truth pill proves to be good medicine.

Tara begins to immerse himself in the life of the community, learning the value of good honest labor as he strips tobacco, splits rails, mends fences, and saws wood. He learns to feel and enjoy the changes of the seasons, and he develops an admiration for the poor earnest people who are becoming his new friends and family. At a Thanksgiving dinner for sixteen of Hod's relatives and neighbors Tara feels at last a part of a family where he is "accepted, honored, and made welcome."

This folk community in which Tara is living is based on Giles's first-hand knowledge, earned as the wife of a man whose family had lived in the region for generations. The dialect and other folkways are depicted with documentary realism. Basing Mary and Hod Pierce on herself and her husband Henry, Giles is able to depict characters and place them in a believable setting with the accuracy of a native and the objectivity of an outsider.

Piney Ridge is a warm and embracing community, but it is no pastoral idyll or utopia. Life is hard, and natives of the ridge have the same virtues and faults as people everywhere. There are marital problems and drunkards who abuse their families. There are many forms of tragedy, from death by natural causes to a distant murder that touches good people in the community. But for Tara it is a community of support as he struggles on his jagged journey to health.

Two people play critical roles in his recovery filled with missteps and pitfalls. From Mary Pierce, with whom he falls desperately and hopelessly in love, he learns the necessity of self-denial and the uses of disappointment and loss. In Jory Clark, a preacher of a small religious group called the Brethren in Christ, he sees the pattern of a man whose faith motivates his life of good deeds. Nicknamed the White Caps because of the head coverings worn by the women, this small Mennonite-related denomination practices pacifism, baptism by immersion, ritual footwashing, and faith healing. Indeed, much of Tara's recovery is due to the influence and example of Jory, "a man who wasn't afraid to be good, " despite a family secret that threatens to destroy him. It seems, however, that everyone on the ridge plays a part in shaping Tara's new life, from the drunkard whose life Tara saves to Miss Willie, the Texas schoolteacher who came to Piney Ridge to teach but found it a good place to live her life and fulfill herself.

But for Tara the ridge is a healing place, not a stopping place. Finally, it is time for him to get on with his life, and he must leave. He must return to the world he fled and resume his own way of healing people as a man of medicine. He must also find his father and be reconciled to the man from whom he has been estranged since his parents' divorce when he was ten. Perhaps the most important lesson Tara has learned at the ridge is that healing of all kinds—physical, mental, spiritual—is interrelated and, like life itself, is a continuing, dynamic process.

During one year at the ridge Tara has learned much. He arrives in the fall a splintered, hopeless man; but the seasons seem to chronicle Tara's recovery, as fall deepens into bleak winter, then turns up into spring's rebirth and summer's fruition.

Tara leaves the ridge healed but not yet whole, for wholeness is what his future life must seek to achieve. Thus *Tara's Healing* is a hallmark affirmation of Janice Holt Giles's belief in the ultimate triumph of decency and goodness among hardworking, sincere men and women of good will. For such a hopeful view of life, she never made apology. And neither should we.

WADE HALL

Tara's Healing

To my sister, MARY HOLT SULLIVAN,
and
To my brother, JOHN A. HOLT
I'm glad we're family!

CHAPTER

1

Tara Cochrane lay on the hard, narrow hospital bed and waited for morning to come. As he had been doing every night for two weeks since he entered the hospital. As he had been doing every night for so long now that he had forgotten what it was like to sleep sweetly and peacefully the whole night through. When had he slept without drugs? Sleeping pills the last two years, and something stronger here in the hospital. He had known when he first began taking the pills where he was heading. Well, a doctor ought to know! But he had to sleep, didn't he? He had to work, and you couldn't work without sleep. He'd known, though, and had pushed the knowledge back of him, that it wouldn't do. He wouldn't have allowed a patient of his to do what he'd done. But he wouldn't do what he would have advised a patient to do. And now, "hoist with his own petard," here he lay in the psycho ward of a veterans' hospital and twittered the nights away just like any other fear-ridden, ghost-haunted fool.

The drug never lasted past two o'clock, and from two until seven, when the nurse brought the insulin shot, he sweated. He sweated for two reasons. One, and the more immediate, was because of the horror of lying alone in the darkness, the thing in his chest crouched like some wild animal ready to spring and clutch and claw if he relaxed so much as one muscle. That had been the beginning of the sleeplessness in the first place. He couldn't now say when it had begun, he had lived with it so long. But he knew it had come suddenly. All at once. One night when he was tired and sleepy and frustrated by a hopeless case. He had gone to bed, and the moment his head had touched the pillow the thing had risen and pounced, and his throat had gone rigid and tight, and his heart had pounded up into the knot in his throat, and fear had swept over him, wave after wave, bringing out the cold sweat and the seizure of trembling and shaking in every limb. He had got up and walked down the hall to the bathroom, and in the normalcy of the lighted room and the familiarity of his surroundings the panic had died down.

But he had been afraid to lie down again. Not without the certainty that the thing would not return. That had been the beginning. And he'd known where he was heading even then. He would have insisted that a patient see a psychiatrist at once. But he wasn't a patient. He was Tara Cochrane, M. D. He was busy. People depended on him. He could handle this thing himself. He was just tired, overworked, strung out too thin and fine. He'd let up a little. Play some golf. Get down to the club to swim more often. He knew he was kidding himself, but he went on doing it. For a long, long time he went on doing it. And he went on taking the pills before he trusted the dark and the night.

The other reason he sweated during these early morning hours was also based in fear. The insulin injection which the falsely cheerful nurse brought at seven induced the very state of panic that he had learned to dread. She came hurrying down the hall at exactly seven each morning, her rubber-soled feet slatting against the floor, as if she couldn't wait to stick the needle into him. "How's my boy this morning?" she'd say, jabbing at him quickly. "Sleep tight last night?"

Fat, gray-haired, nauseatingly jolly, she was as unwelcome as the rack or the boot of the Inquisition. He never bothered to answer her. He simply lay and waited. Thirty minutes. That's how long it took to begin. And he waited for the thirty minutes, and then waited for the next unbelievably terrifying hour to pass. The hour when the insulin deliberately brought on all the symptoms he had learned to dread. The pounding heart. The beating pulse. The knotted throat. The spasms of breath dragging hard in his chest. The feelings of alternate hot and cold. And always and always the sweat and panic and mounting fear. When it was over, he could lie in his sweat, weak, limp, and exhausted. And then they brought his breakfast, and with hands shaking so that he spilled the coffee when he poured it from the pot, he had to force food past the crouched, tightly wound thing in his throat, knowing he could, and knowing he would, but never quite knowing how.

And he was beginning to wonder why. How had Tara Cochrane come to be here? How had this happened to him? And why was he suffering these indignities? After all, he mused in the darkness, there is a certain dignity in death. Perhaps it's the better way. But even as he thought it, the doctor in him rejected the thought. That way out was not for him.

"You're a long way from being really sick," they'd told him when he entered the hospital, forced finally to seek help. "We'll have you out of here within a month."

Well, maybe. Maybe they could break him into little pieces like this and then put him back together again. They'd better be able to. For he sure couldn't do it himself. He had admitted that when he sought help. Admitted he'd reached the bottom of the pit and somebody would have to drag him back up to the top. And if he was a long way from being really sick, if all he had was what they so glibly referred to as an anxiety neurosis, he felt sorry for the poor devils that had worse. In a way it would have been a relief to be sicker. To have been psychotic. He didn't think he could possibly have suffered much worse, anyhow.

He dragged himself up on the pillow and reached for a cigarette. The nerves that twitched so constantly in his hands fretted him now. He lighted the cigarette and pulled the smoke in deep. Then he shuddered at the bitterness of its taste. All his life was like that now. Like that bitter, dry taste of old smoke, in a mouth dried from fear. And he couldn't see any hope that it would ever be different, better, normal, again. The hopelessness was part of the fear. A coward dies a thousand deaths. He remembered that old saying. Well, O. K. I'm a coward. And I'm dying my thousand deaths.

He stubbed the cigarette out and huddled his twittering hands under the blanket, suddenly cold. Once he had been alive. Now he was dead. Walking around dead. He, Tara Cochrane, brilliant young doctor. Fine future. Extremely good diagnostician. Able. He'd make his mark. He was making it. In the psycho ward of a veterans' hospital. Veterans' hospital because he had been the captain of a company of combat engineers during the Hitler war. He wasn't a doctor in those days. Just a budding young medical student who'd been fired with patriotism and had refused his deferment. Veterans' hospital because he knew the man at the head of the psychiatric department here, and knew he was good.

He was making his mark all right. And a fine one it was. Making it with an anxiety neurosis he couldn't handle with all his insight. He knew as well as the psychiatrist that ninety per cent of the neuroses such as his were founded on basic insecurity, and he knew too all too well what had caused his own. What good did it do him when he lay sweating in the dark? You can tell that little frontal lobe that it's all nonsense just so long. It will push down the fear just so many times. But eventually it gets very weary of pushing down the fear and then it doesn't do so well. Not even a doctor's little frontal lobe.

Then the good insight you're so proud of having, and which the psycho men are so proud of your having, doesn't amount to anything but bilge water. Just something to float around in. So Tara Cochrane is basically insecure. So Tara Cochrane has never known the warmth of a sustained and loving human relationship. So Tara Cochrane has tried to make an anodyne of his work. Autohypnosis by way of his pill bag. So what. Here he lies, felled as flat as the next unfortunate guy.

He switched the light on and picked up the book lying on the bedside table. His light would probably bring the nurse, anxious and protesting, but let her come. You had to get through that flat desert of time until daylight somehow. His place was marked by the flap of the jacket. It wasn't a very good book and he took it up wearily. He hoped it would hold his attention enough to get him through the insulin.

It didn't.

But the hours dragged by, the insulin came and was lived through, breakfast came and was choked down, and his bath was taken. Then he grimly wrapped his robe around himself and wandered out into the halls. "Patients are encouraged to get out of their rooms," one of the nurses had told him. And he knew well enough why. You could lie hunkered down into your own fear until you could no longer make the effort to get out of it. So, regularly, he compelled himself to wander through the halls and lounges. He made himself talk to other patients. He sat and looked at the inane television shows. And he hated the halls and the lounges and the patients and the television shows. And he hated himself most of all.

There was one place, a sort of sun porch, that he hated least. It was bright with sun most of the time and it was never crowded. There was no television there, and the crowds followed the television sets. A few men liked it and gathered there. Men who avoided the others, as a rule. Men who, like himself, were locked inside themselves, and he let them alone and they let him alone. He wandered there this morning.

The radio was playing, a soft medley of recorded tunes, smooth, easy-listening tunes. The sun slanted through the east windows warmly, and the quiet tones of a small group of men talking over in the corner did not disturb the peace of the room. He found a chair and dragged it into a corner and slacked down into it to listen to the music. Nice. Velvety. Smooth. He could remember dancing with a tall, beautiful blonde to that tune in San Francisco. When his world was still all in one piece. He remembered the lights from the windows, the low hum of voices lifting and falling around the room, the sweet chill of the gin drink, the moving enthrallment of the music, and the nice long legs of the girl that had followed him through the intricacies of the dance. Nice. Once upon a time it had been very nice. But that had been in another world. And in another lifetime. That was the young, brilliant Tara Cochrane. It had nothing to do with this wreck sitting here now. Nothing to do with him at all. Except that he could remember.

A shadow barred the sunlight on the floor and he lifted his head. A man in the familiar hospital robe had stopped in front of him. "Cap'n Cochrane!" the man shouted, and instinctively Tara got to his feet. He felt his arm pull up in the old salute, and with an effort he brought it back down again. He tried to place the man.

"Don't you know me, Cap'n? Pierce! I'm Pierce!"

It came to him then. Of course. Pierce, the top sergeant of Company A. Sure, sure he knew him! "Pull up a chair and sit down," he told him.

The man pulled up a chair and sat down, leaning forward in his eagerness to talk. "Say, Cap'n, but it's been a long time since I saw you! You're the last man I ever expected to see here!"

Tara braced his hands on his knees. They didn't shake so badly that way. "You're the first man I've seen here that I know, Pierce. What are you doing here?"

The man was tall, angular, and bone thin. Tara remembered his face as having been ruddy, but it was white now. The thatch of unruly hair pushed back from his forehead was just the same though. Like burnt straw. Hod Pierce had never been able to tame that shock of hair. Wet down and combed vigorously, it had always sprung back up again as soon as it dried. Tara remembered all too vividly what had happened the time Pierce had shaved it off! They could have used him to scare the Krauts away, the outfit had said. And they hadn't been far wrong.

"My ears," Hod said now, grinning. "Remember?"

"Haven't they fixed those ears of yours up for you yet? Sure, I remember. You went on sick call and got lost in a mess of hospitals and we had to come get you when Von Rundstedt broke through! 'Lost to hospital,' was the way they had you listed on the records. But I told Jenkins we'd find you tied up with red tape in some repple depot . . . or shacked up . . ."

"Now, Cap'n. You know I never . . ."

The captain laughed. And the sound of it was strange in his ears. Not he . . . laughing! "We found you though, remember?"

Hod nodded. "I never was so glad to get out of a place in my life! Why, I'd of been killed if I'd of stayed in that place much longer. You know what they did? They made a bazooka man out of me! Why, them bazooka men get shot at!"

"Which would have been a new experience for you, wouldn't it?"

"Well, Cap'n, you know a guy has to look out for himself. Come along a real bad detail and there's always a few guns needing cleaning."

"Pierce, do you suppose anyone else in the Army beat your record for gold-bricking?"

"I kindly doubt it," Hod said mildly. But they both knew, these two men, that the kind of talk they were making was

possible only because they had stood together all too often
when neither of them would have given a plugged nickel for
his life.

The captain laughed again. "Long time ago, those days.
Long time ago. Lot of tight places. Remember the Roer?"

Hod's face sobered. "Yeah." The Roer was where they had
lost so many men of the company.

"And Remagen?"

"And the Danube?"

"Rivers!" the captain snorted. "Rivers! Great Caesar's ghost!
Europe is full of rivers, and I think we bridged them all, didn't
we?"

"Might' nigh. If we missed any, I don't recollect it. We must
of got 'em all."

"It was a great outfit, wasn't it? The 291st. Great outfit!"

Their talk went on and on, remembering the summer, the
winter, and the spring when they had swung like a great wheel
across the heart of France into Germany and Austria. Remembering the men and the places and the people and the heat and
the rain and the ice and the snow. Remembering the artillery
and the bombs and the mud and the slush, the eternal and everlasting roads to be built and rivers to be bridged, and over
everything and always with them the sounds and the sights and
the smells of war. Men always remember war so. Nostalgically
and sentimentally. Their finest hour. Which is one reason why
there's always another war.

Tara Cochrane was a big man, and as they talked, Hod was
remembering also his bigness with his men. How he never
slept until they slept, and how he never ate until they ate, and
how he got dirty and grimy and filthy right alongside of them.
He remembered how the captain had asked impossible things
of them, and had gone out and done them with them. How
he never gave an order he couldn't fill himself; how he led
them, never pushed them. How, when things were the roughest,

the captain had cussed until the air turned blue and had slogged it out beside them. He'd been more like a weary old top sergeant than a captain. He'd never pulled his rank to get things easier for himself. He'd figured it was the men that were fighting the war, and he belonged right with them. He'd been a tough old war horse, the captain.

Now he sat in the wicker armchair across from Hod, and he was as lean and brown as he'd been that summer in France. His hair was thinner, but it still cropped up in short, wiry curls, black as night and thick over the ears as if he needed a haircut. His eyes still had a razor-sharp look out of their blue depths, and the wrinkles around them had deepened and scarred permanently. That jaw that had jutted so doggedly in the thick of things still looked square and firm. But he didn't look so good, the captain didn't. He looked too fine and trim and sharp. And his hands were thin and veined and hung limply between his knees, and Hod saw the fingers tremble when he lighted a cigarette.

"What have you been doing since the war, Pierce? I should have remembered you lived in Kentucky. And what about Mary?"

"You've not forgotten all those letters, I see."

"Forgotten 'em! Man, I stamped that censor stamp on more letters to Mary Hogan than . . . why, I didn't write to my own girl as often as you wrote to Mary! You married her, didn't you?"

"Just as soon as I got back. As for what we've been doing . . . we tried it in the city for a couple of years, then moved down to my part of the country. Down in the hills in Adair County. We've been there ever since. Got a little farm down there. Like it fine."

"Any kids?"

"One."

"That's fine. You've got me beat."

"What about you? What have you been doing?"

Here it was. He pulled in his breath to meet it. "I'm a doctor. Been practicing out west." He found he couldn't say it all at once after all, so he waited.

"That old back wound bothering you?"

That would be an easy out. Easy. "No," he heard himself saying. "I cracked up. Nerves shot or something. I'm over in the psycho ward."

Hod Pierce looked at him, disbelief showing in every line of his face. "You! In the psycho ward?"

Tara laughed, a brief, unhumorous snort. "Me. In the psycho ward. Neurotic as a nut."

"They got you in the wrong place, Cap'n. If you're neurotic, I'm buckin' for section eight myself!"

"No, they're right. I'm a doctor and I knew it. Decided I needed some help. It'll all iron out in time, but it's better to let specialists see you through."

"Your wife here with you?"

"I'm not married."

"What happened? You had a girl when we were in Texas, didn't you? Same one wrote to you all time we were across."

"Yes. Things didn't work out when I got back. I dunno. We couldn't even talk the same language. Seemed best just to call it off. You were lucky with Mary."

"Don't I know it! But you'll find one someday. Bet that's mostly what's wrong with you. Nobody to make you take care of yourself."

"Could be. Could be."

"How come you settled out west? Your folks live out there?"

"I haven't any folks. Home's where I hang my hat. I interned out there and liked it. So I just stayed."

Hod was shocked into silence. To a man whose home had been safely and securely in one place for seven generations, and who was surrounded by kinfolk to the fourth and fifth cousins, it was an awful thing not to have any folks, and for home to be where you hang your hat. It made him feel lonesome just to hear it. He'd rather be dead than to be so footloose.

The silence between them grew, and finally, uncomfortably, the captain stood. "Well, I'll see you again. Now that I know you're here, I'll look you up often. Until you leave, that is."

Hod stood also, his hands rammed deep in the pockets of his robe "Sure. Sure, Cap'n. I'll be here another week or two. I'll be seeing you."

He didn't say, and neither did Tara, that the captain might be leaving first. It didn't seem very likely.

They met each morning after that in the sunroom. Met and talked and Hod, at least, mended. He told the captain about his ears, how they had always bothered him since that time in the Hürtgen Forest the winter of 1944, and how they'd flared up one night not long ago after he'd been out planting his winter wheat all one cold, blowy day. And how when Mary and Jory Clark, a neighbor, had brought him to the hospital, there had had to be an operation. "Never had anything to hurt me so bad in my life," he concluded simply. "But they think I'll not be bothered with them any more now."

"What was the diagnosis that time you went into the hospital in the Army?" Tara asked.

Hod grinned. "I sneaked a look at the chart or I wouldn't know. It said chronic otitis. And chronic was the right word for it!"

Tara shook his head. "Should have operated then, I have an idea."

"Well, you know how it was. Too many others worse off. They treated 'em and eased me over it. How're you getting along?"

"I'm not. I think I'm washed up here. Might as well skip it.

Oh, I've got a better appetite and I'm not so shaky. But I've got to handle it myself after all."

"You mean you're going to leave?"

"Pretty soon. In these cases they want you to get out on your own as quickly as possible."

"You going back to your practice?"

"Oh, in time. Of course I'll get back into harness. But I thought I might take a run down to Florida and fish a little. Take a month or two maybe to get back on my feet."

Hod shut the radio off and leaned forward. "Look, Cap'n. I been thinking. Why don't you go home with me? Down to the ridge. We've got plenty of room, and you could rest as much as you like, help me a little around the place if you want. You'd get plenty of good food, and there's Mary and Miss Willie that's your kind of folks to talk to. It might do you a world of good. You needn't stay if you get fed up with it. I don't like the idea of your not having any folks to go to."

"I'm used to it."

"But it's not right for you to be used to it! Why don't you try it?"

"It wouldn't work, Pierce. I'm a city man. Your hills would drive me crazy. I'm used to lights and traffic and crowds of people milling around. I'd just sink farther into my own loneliness down there. It wouldn't work. But thanks anyhow."

"Well you think it over. Hear? I'm not leaving until next Friday."

"Have you mentioned it to your wife yet?"

"No. Just been mulling it over in my own mind. But there's time to write her. And you don't think I'd of suggested it if I didn't know what she'd say, do you? Lord, Mary's got a heart as big as this hospital. She'd be all for it. I think she'd like having you there. It'd give her a change. It'd be somebody new to talk to. You still play the violin?"

Tara nodded. "About the only thing I brought with me here."

"Fine. Bring it on down and you and Mary can have some music. We'll sit around the fire this winter and roast peanuts and pop corn and talk our heads off! Man, it would be wonderful!"

"It wouldn't work."

"Think about it," Hod urged. "Think it over a day or two. It might work better'n you think."

"All right. I'll think about it. But don't count on it."

In spite of himself, however, the idea began to take hold of Tara. It was a backwoods jumping-off place, from all he'd heard of it, among a bunch of backwoods hillbillies. Such a place and such people had nothing for him surely. He'd be bored to death within twenty-four hours. He had always needed life, movement, lights, cities. The only measure of peace he'd ever known had come to him within the movement and sounds of traffic, in the excitement of people, during the busy hours of the day.

But it was when he assayed that tiny fragment of peace that he began to think seriously of going home with Hod. If this was all he had . . . if this was where it had brought him . . . then what did he have to lose? He could always leave if it didn't work out. The door was open, Pierce had said. If he didn't like it, he needn't stay. And it might be that the hills . . . and the lack of people . . . and the quiet . . . It might be if he could take a good, long, deep look at himself . . . It just might help.

It was the doctor, however, who swung the balance wheel. "Go ahead and go," he told him. "Don't stay too long, though. Get back to work pretty soon."

So Tara told Hod he would go home with him, and when Mary Pierce came for her husband the next Friday, the captain's bags were packed and he was sitting on the sofa by Hod. The radio was playing again, the same kind of softened, satiny music—music toned down to the nerves of sick men, silky, smooth, soothing. When he saw the woman come in the outer door at the far end of the corridor and watched her walk the full length of the hall, the thought occurred to him that this woman walked with the same smooth rhythm of the music. That she had a silky grace about her, effortless, easy, rhythmic. Not many women walked so beautifully. He wondered who she was.

And then he knew. For when her eyes found Hod, a glad look swept over her face. It was as if a light had been turned on inside her, a bright light of love and joy, and her mouth widened with her laugh and her walk swiftened to bring her running toward him. "Hod!" she called before she reached him, and then Hod was on his feet and across the room to hide her in his arms. The captain stood and waited.

"This is Cap'n Cochrane, Mary," Hod said, then, drawing her over to the sofa.

"How do you do, Captain." Her voice was low and clear, and he liked it. Women's voices were so seldom nice to hear. Mary's was. He took her outstretched hand. It was cool and hard, and her clasp was quick and done with.

He had meant to ask her if this business was all right with her. But there was no need. Mary Pierce was the sort of woman that didn't fuss about things. He knew just about what had happened. Hod's letter explaining that his old captain was coming home with him. Mary reading it, assenting immediately, and with little or no bother making ready for him. He felt better about going. He swung his bags up and followed them to the door.

CHAPTER

2

THE captain was dreaming. Dreaming that he was trapped in a burning building. The flames ate nearer and nearer, and the heat seared and scorched him, and he struggled to escape. He turned this way and that, and he ran before it and finally was cornered. Then he gasped in the heat and felt himself suffocating.

"Cap'n! Cap'n Cochrane! Wake up, Cap'n!"

The voice came down into his dream urgently, and he knew it for a dream and lunged toward the voice and the light and the room, but the heat was still there and the suffocation. He struggled, wanting to wake from the heat and the suffocation. The covers were laid back and a strong arm slipped beneath his shoulders and lifted him. It was better. Now he could breathe. Now he swam toward the surface of consciousness and took in long gulps of air and felt the heat turn cool around his shoulders and chest. And the air was only warm.

"Are you awake now?"

He opened his eyes. A man, strange to him, was bent over him and his face was troubled and concerned.

"I'm awake. Sorry. That was quite a nightmare!"

He had lain awake, he now remembered, most of the night, unused to the new bed and room, and grimly determined not to resort to a sedative. Along toward morning he had drifted into a light and troubled sleep. Thus the nightmare, he supposed.

The man straightened. The captain saw that he was young. That he was tall, lean, hard and brown and leathery. He stood back from the bed and smiled. The smile flashed quickly across the concern on his face. Quickly, and almost shyly. It sweetened his face unbelievably. It laid his face bare of defenses. It offered the man himself, timidly, tenderly.

"Who are you?" Tara asked.

"Jory Clark."

"Oh, yes. You're the Pierces' neighbor."

The man moved to the open window and pulled it down. "It's cooled off in here now. I'm sorry about the heat. Hod thought your room would be chilly this morning and he asked me to lay a fire on the hearth to take the chill off. I laid too big a one!"

"Was that it? I thought it was a nightmare!"

"You were smothering. You had the blankets over your head, and between the blankets and the fire you were having a time."

"I certainly was! Lucky you came in."

"Mary sent me to see if you were awake. She said if you were still asleep to let you sleep, but if you were awake to tell you breakfast was coming up."

Tara swung his legs over the side of the bed. "I'll be ready in two shakes."

"We thought you might like to have a tray in here. In bed, perhaps."

"Oh, no. I'll dress and eat with the rest of you."

Jory laughed. "We ate hours ago."

"But it's still early!"

"About eight o'clock, yes. But on a farm you eat breakfast around daylight."

"Well, I'm usually awake and waiting for daylight. I'm sorry about this morning. You go tell Mary I'll be right out."

"You were awfully tired last night. We want you to rest and sleep and eat as you like. Don't try to fit into a schedule yet."

The captain was lacing his shoes. He stopped and looked up. "Do you live here with the Pierces? They told me you lived down the hollow."

"I do. But Hod will need help on his place for a few weeks, and I'm helping out until he is strong again. I'll fix your breakfast now."

Suddenly the captain did not want this man fixing his breakfast, helping him, protecting him, gentling him. He felt an irritated need to help himself. "I'll fix it," he said shortly.

"All right, if you want." And the man went out, leaving the door ajar.

When he had gone, Tara felt ashamed of himself and he made an impulsive move toward the door. But he checked the impulse and went on with his dressing. There was nothing wrong with wanting to fix his own breakfast. He wasn't an invalid. Nervous, shaky, burned out perhaps. But he didn't need special attention. It would be good for him to wait on himself. The thing was, he needn't have been so short about it. That was what these frayed nerves did to him. Made him irritable, short-tempered, ugly. His hands trembled over the buttons of his shirt. In disgust he pocketed them and stood indecisively in the middle of the room. His head ached already, and he had that familiar feeling of being separated from reality. As if he had taken passage on a cloud and was floating above and beyond material things. A fuzzy, phantomy feeling that made him quiver with dread.

He shook his head and tried to clear it of the ache and the sense of pressure, and his eyes sought out the boundaries of the room. It was a good room . . . big, square, spacious. The hearth took up one wall, and deep, comfortable chairs were drawn up before it. Bright, braided rugs spotted the floor, whose mirror gloss gave him back an image of himself. The bed he had slept in was wide and high, its headboard reaching almost to the ceiling.

Another wall was given over to tall, floor-length windows, and when he crossed over to them, he found that they opened onto a wide, screened porch. He unlatched the catch and stepped out. Stretched before him lay a field of grass, yellowing and browning in the lateness of the season. It flowed into the curve of a creek under giant sycamore trees, and was lost there in the bend of the water. Beyond rose the hill that marked the rim of the valley, steep and slanted and covered with rocks.

He would like to have had courage this morning. He wished that what he saw now could give him some small measure of it. But it did not. There was a field of grass. There was a creek. There too was a hill. And he was here, still dying his thousand deaths.

He turned and went back inside the house.

Mary Pierce was peeling apples when he entered the kitchen. She looked up when he entered and smiled at him. "Everything is in the refrigerator," she said.

The baby, who had been asleep when they arrived the night before, was playing on the floor. He stared at the captain briefly and then went back to his play. With quiet concentration he was putting small potatoes into the cups of a muffin pan. Putting them in patiently, fitting them quickly, then emptying them to start all over again. "Busy, isn't he?" Tara said.

"For the moment. As soon as it warms up, he'll go outside to play. But he's underfoot temporarily."

Stepping to the refrigerator, the captain found fruit juice, bacon, and eggs. On shelves above the sink he found dishes. Back of the big, shiny electric range he saw a row of copper-bottomed pots and pans. The percolator hummed and sent an amber jet into the glass dome. "I had no idea you had things so convenient down here," he said. "I got the notion you lived very roughly in a sort of primitive way isolated from civilization."

"We did at first. Believe me, it was terribly primitive! But we have improved. Rural electrification has come, and we can have refrigeration and other conveniences. It's made a world of difference, too. I cooked on an old wood stove when we first came down here, and drew water from a well, and washed by hand and ironed with flatirons. You have no idea!"

Tara sipped his fruit juice and slid a skillet over the burner. "Must have been pretty awful."

"No. Not awful. Just hard work. You do what you have to do, and don't let it bother you. But I am grateful, especially since Jeems came, not to have to do it that way any longer."

Tara watched Mary as he ate. She was a tall woman, slender almost to the point of thinness, but slender with a flow of movement as she came and went, bent and straightened, that made every motion beautiful. Her face was tanned and browned from the summer, weathered by sun and wind and rain. A spattering of tiny freckles bridged her nose and upper cheeks to frame the deep, green-gold eyes, and with the dark hood of her hair, the wide, sweetly curving mouth, the high, flat planes of her cheeks, she came close to being a beautiful woman. Tara thought she missed it, probably, only because she did not trouble to be beautiful. You could tell Mary Pierce was a woman who let life have its way with her. Not dowdily and sloppily. Just honestly. It didn't bother her that gray was beginning to show in the dark strands of her hair, that crow's-feet were making tracks around her eyes, that her skin was thickening and browning and her hands were hardening. Mary Pierce didn't make any fight against the ravages of time apparently. Maybe she didn't believe time ravaged. Maybe she thought it left its own imprint of beauty. And on her it did.

When he had finished breakfast, Tara washed up his dishes

and then lighted his pipe and pulled a chair up near the window. "Where's Hod?"

Mary was rolling out piecrust. "He and Jory have gone to look at the fencing on the lower pasture. Jory thought it needed mending in a place or two."

"Who is this Jory fellow?"

Mary's quick hands lined the pie plate and trimmed its edges. "Our neighbor."

"I know. You told me that. But what about him?"

"Well, *what* about him?"

"He's a little unusual, isn't he?"

"How?"

The captain shrugged. "That's what I'd like to know." He blew a smoke ring, and the baby watched it float toward the ceiling. Suddenly he laughed and pointed, getting to his feet and running to catch the smoke ring. Tara blew him another. Entranced, the child broke it with his hands, and then his face drew down in disappointment. "Gone," he said dismally, "all gone!"

Tara watched the child's puckered face. "You're learning young, young fellow," he said. "You can't hold onto your dreams. They're like smoke rings."

"Don't tell him that," Mary said sharply.

"He doesn't know what I'm saying."

The child began to cry. "He knows it was sad and futile," Mary said, picking him up.

"How could he?"

"He could feel it . . . from the tone of your voice."

"Oh . . . now!"

"I mean it. Why do you think he cried?"

"Because he couldn't catch the smoke ring, of course!"

"No. It was your voice. It frightened him. Come, Jeems, outside! Let's go outside!"

The child's face brightened, and he struggled down from his

mother's arms. "Outside," he cried and ran from the room, hunting his jacket and cap. "Outside!"

When Mary came in again, the captain had put his pipe away. "I'm sorry. I didn't think."

Mary peered at the oven thermometer. "They're very sensitive to voices . . . to tones of voices. They're easily frightened and saddened."

"I'll try to remember."

Mary slid the pies into the oven and then, going to a cupboard, she took down a yellow bowl and a bag of dried beans. Sitting down, she began picking over the beans, dropping the cleaned ones into the bowl. They made a hollow, rasping sound as they slid into the bowl.

"You haven't told me about Jory Clark yet."

"I'm not going to."

"Why?"

"The sort of thing you want to know about him you'll have to find out for yourself."

Tara slid his long legs out before him and rocked his chair back. He leaned his head against the wall. "How do you know the sort of thing I want to know?"

"Because you've already sensed that he's an unusual person."

"And you won't tell me what makes him an unusual person?"

"I can't. For me it's one thing. For you it may be another. But you can find out for yourself."

"I may not be here long enough."

"Then it won't matter."

The captain laughed. The beans were filling the bowl now and they no longer rubbed dryly against its sides. They made a full, only slightly rattling sound. "I think," he said, "I've got to find out."

Mary rose and washed the beans at the sink, turning them into one of the copper-bottomed pans. Covering it, she placed it over a burner and turned the heat on. She went to the window and looked out and smiled. "Jeems is digging a hole."

The captain joined her at the window. "What does he want with a hole?"

"You'll have to find that out too. Ask him. He knows."

He raised his eyebrows. Mary Pierce was a very direct young woman. Then he went outside. When he came in, he was laughing.

"He wants a hole to put the dirt in!"

Mary nodded. She was putting up the ironing board and she didn't stop. "I thought it was something like that. My son is a very sensible person. The dirt must go somewhere, so he digs a hole to put it in!"

A ghost of a smile trembled around her lips. She met the captain's eye, and then they both laughed. Laughed until the captain felt the laughter quivering in his chest, and then, to his horror, he felt it turning to tears. He laid his arms across the table and put his head down upon his arms to hide his face. His shoulders shook, but Mary would think he was still laughing. Only she didn't.

She laid a hand on his shoulder. "Tara," she said, and her voice was as gentle as it had been with the child. "How unhappy you must be! How desolately, terribly unhappy!"

He would not lift his head. And she went on after a moment. "It will be all right. You'll see. In time it will be all right."

Fool, he stormed at himself! Fool! And he wrenched himself back under control. He smeared his eyes with his shirt sleeve and straightened. "I didn't know I was that near the edge. . . . I'm sorry."

Mary went back to her ironing, saying nothing.

"It was that digging a hole to put the dirt in, I think. It is so exactly how I occupy myself!"

"Nothing is completely hopeless."

"You don't know!"

"I know *that!*"

Tara drew himself a drink of water from the tap. "What did Hod tell you about me when he wrote saying he was bringing me home with him?"

"Nothing."

The iron smoothed across a wrinkled tablecloth.

"He must have said something!"

"He said you needed rest and quiet. That you were always good to him in the Army, and he'd like to repay you a little if he could."

"Nothing about these nerves of mine?"

"I've told you."

"Didn't you know?"

"It wouldn't have mattered."

"To him or to you?"

"To either of us."

"Is Jory here to help me?"

Mary's head jerked up. "Certainly not!"

"I'm not dangerous, you know. At least, I don't think I am!"

"No one else thinks you are. Jory is here to help Hod. You aren't the only one who has just been released from the hospital, remember?"

The captain smiled. "Of course. But that's part of it, you know. This everlasting thinking of myself!"

"That will pass too."

He set the glass down in the sink. The words came from him edged with irony. "You're very certain, aren't you?"

The iron went on smoothing. "I'm not certain at all. But I am hopeful."

"That's more than I am!"

Mary upended the iron and turned to him with a quick, impatient gesture. "Look. Whatever's wrong with you, part of it —most of it, perhaps—is just a good, strong case of feeling sorry for yourself! But you needn't go off the deep end in such a sea of self-pity. There are a great many sick people in this world. A great many who are sicker than you are. What makes you think you have a monopoly on pain and suffering and fear and hopelessness? You're a thousand times better off than most people. Why don't you think of that once in a while? I doubt if there's much wrong with you that forgetting yourself won't help a lot!"

Her words hit him like hard stones, graveling, biting, stinging, and he wanted to dodge them and tell her to stop. He felt affronted by the brashness of her daring. She didn't know what she was talking about! How could she? Anger against her rose in him, floating a kind of oily nausea into his mouth. Shut up! Shut up! he wanted to cry out at her. You don't know anything about it! You, with your love and your child and your home. All safe and cozy! What do you know about fear and horror and panic? What business have you got talking about it? Shut up! And the nerve ends in his hands quivered and set his fingers to jerking. Shut up!

He didn't know what else she said or when she stopped talking, for he quit hearing her. He stopped his ears against her and stood stonelike and unfeeling. But he knew when the room was quiet again. For the quiet beat the echo of the words into his mind, over and over again. And his heart piped the blood up into his face and temples where it hammered in thin, painful thuds against the skin.

Mary turned back to the ironing.

He found his voice. "You don't like me, do you?"

"I don't know you. I don't know whether I like you or not."

"And it doesn't matter."

"Yes, it matters. I hope I may like you. You were good to Hod during those bad times overseas. I'd like very much to like you."

"That's got nothing to do with it." He was impatient. "Don't try to like me for Hod's sake!"

"That's the only reason you're here."

The logic of that stopped him. "Of course. I forget. . . . But

still you think I'm a selfish, egotistical person, don't you?"
There was no answer.

"Don't you?"

"I think you're a disillusioned, embittered, unhappy person."

"You left out lonely."

"Lonely . . . , yes."

"And what do I do about it?"

"Well, forgetting some of it would help."

Suddenly there were no sparks flying. Mary smiled at him and the tension was gone. The stillness grew between them, but it was a comfortable stillness. The captain rose and moved toward the door. "I'll try."

He went out of the kitchen into the living room. The grand piano which took up one entire corner of the room loomed large before him. Without thinking he went to it, opened it, and sat down. Also without thinking, he found his hands thundering into a polonaise. The walls shook with the fury and the violence of the music. He played it all the way through . . . crashingly, terribly, hungrily. And when he had finished, he closed the piano and went into his own room.

In the kitchen Mary went on ironing. But her face was frightened. Who was this man they had brought into their home so thoughtlessly? this man of storms and tensions! this man of heights and depths! How were they to understand and live with him? And she found herself almost wishing that he would not stay!

CHAPTER

3

Now in November the trees began to lose their leaves and shake them down. The nights were cold with frost, and in the morning the leaves hung whiskered and rimed. The sun mellowed the days and dried and crisped the leaves, and slowly, regretfully, great branches trembled free and stood forth black and sharply bare. The sides of the ridge, which had been soft and hidden behind green screens, emerged rocky and steep and ledged with eroded cliffs. Little by little all the softness went away . . . and all the fluffed veiling of the swollen leaves. And what remained were the ribs, the vertebrae, the rocky spines, the sharp, angled bones.

But like all things clean and stripped they had their own gaunt beauty. There was the chiseled angle of a limb where it joined the tree; the slender, unmittened fingers of topmost branches against the sky; the sturdy trunk, rooted in the hillside, groined and lined with years. There were the jagged, sawn teeth of the rocks, sharp, bare, clean. There was the fragile sereness of the broom sedge, rattly, dry, brittle in the wind. There was an undressed and a stripped look to all things—an etched and whittled look.

Tara Cochrane watched daily as this revelation took place. Never before had he been brought so close to it. Of course he had known the seasons of the year. He had noticed spring and summer, fall and winter, and he had reacted to them largely by a change of dress and activities. Light clothes when it was hot. Heavy clothes when it was cold. Golf and tennis in the summer. Bridge, shows, and parties in the winter. But between air conditioning and central heating weather had made very little difference to him, and one season was as good as another. He had not actually paid attention to any of them.

You can't ignore the seasons in the country. You're too close to them. So now each day he sat on his veranda and watched the autumn days pare down the countryside in preparation for winter. The cottonwoods in the bend of the creek lost their leaves rapidly, and with delight he watched the pale, whitened trunks shine forth as if they had been newly enameled. The path that wound up the side of the ridge had been hidden by the heavy undergrowth. Now it was unraveled from the green and it curved, cleanly penciled, against the hillside, a winding line drawn by the seeking feet of men coming and going.

The maples and beeches were quick to shed their leaves, but the giant chestnut oaks were like old, bearded men, clutching their green whiskers, afraid to be shorn. They were the last to bare themselves, and each morning Tara looked quickly at the hillside to see the change in them. There was a swift-mounting excitement in him, fresh each day, as he watched them shaken loose from the tough fiber of their foliage, and he felt a sorrow for their slow acceptance of the inevitable.

But when the rains began and beat down the last of their leaves, he felt a great sweep of exultance at the nobility of line and structure that was then revealed. Somehow he had known those giant old trees would stand the tallest and the strongest of them all. And there was in him, along with them, a sense of battle won instead of defeat accepted. Bareness they must accept. But it would be a noble bareness.

He had decided to stay on awhile. He had liked the big,

quiet room, and he had liked the casual way he had been accepted into the house. No one pressed him. No one sought him out. No one questioned him. No one suggested anything for him to do. He was let entirely alone. When he went into his room and shut the door, he was never disturbed. When he came out and joined the family, he was cheerfully welcomed. There was nothing in this place that pushed in on him and made him guard his privacy. Instead it was guarded for him. There was nothing to rub him into the familiar friction of annoyance.

He walked every day, sometimes up the hollow into the narrowed neck, where there were places to sit in the sun and watch the tiny stream that flowed forth from a rock-bound spring. Sometimes down the hollow through the flat meadows, where thin, slender little blue-tailed lizards ran frantically under stones before his footsteps. He had never seen so many, and when they froze in their panic, and the sun shone on them, they reflected the whole prism of colors. Sometimes he climbed the ridge and stood resting under the white birch that marked the top of the trail. Rested and looked across the hollow and down upon the house with its weathered, shingled roof.

He read a lot, from Mary's books, and he spent much time sitting on the veranda that opened from his room. He sat there, lethargically . . . idly . . . willing his mind to blankness and his body to stillness . . . watching the trees and the hills, feeling strange and alien most of the time, but no stranger or more alien than he had felt everywhere.

He was sitting there one gray morning when the rain hung a sheer scarf between him and a ridge. The chill ate through his coat, and he was thinking he should go inside and build up a fire. It was a damp and uncomfortable chill. The living room door opened and he looked up. It was Jory Clark.

He had had no further conversation with the man since that first morning. There had been little opportunity to talk with him, for Jory spent the nights at his own place down the hollow and came to help Hod during the day. Tara had seen him coming and going with Hod, but he rarely came into the house. Always he seemed busy. Sunk as he was in his own misery and unhappiness, Tara felt irritated by something about the man's industry, and he spoke to him now out of that irritation. "Well, do you actually have an idle moment? I thought you never stopped work?"

Jory crossed the porch. "We stop for a breath once in a while. We're getting ready to strip tobacco, but Hod has something else to do first, so I'm waiting."

"Sit down. Smoke?"

Jory shook his head. "I don't smoke, Cap'n." He hooked a heel under a chair and pulled it up. "You feeling any better?"

The rain sifted through the screen and Tara watched it run down and make a small flood of water along the edge of the porch. He shifted his look to Jory's face. It was quiet, still, almost devoid of expression except that his eyes were pleasant and friendly in their look. Tara saw that there were fine lines spraying out from the corners of the eyes, crinkling deeply at the inner edges. He saw too that there were lines riven around the mouth—as if, for some long time Jory had needed to hold his mouth firm. Tara felt his interest in the man spring up again. "I can't say that I'm any better," he said. "But I'm not really physically ill, you know."

"No. I didn't know." There was even a quality of quietness and stillness in the voice. Not that it was flat or level. Rather it was in the timbre of the voice and in the unhurried manner of speaking, in the simplicity of the man's words.

"Well, I'm not. There's not much wrong with me actually. I'm nervous, moody, out of sorts. Just a psycho case."

"Most of us are at one time or another."

"Not you! Don't tell me you were ever jittery and half nuts!"

"Plenty of times. Until I found salvation."

Salvation! The captain stared at him. One of those religious fanatics! He flung around in his chair impatiently. "I'm
afraid that's one of those pious words that has no meaning for
me."

Jory rubbed his chin slowly. "No. I reckon it wouldn't. Unless you'd say that finding a body's health and strength is a kind
of salvation."

"Oh, certainly. If you're going to define the term technically.
I thought you meant it in a religious sense."

"I do. I'm a preacher, you know."

Tara stared at him. "No, I didn't know. Well, we can't all
find salvation like you."

"You could. But it may be you won't."

The captain shrugged. "You a Baptist preacher? Methodist?"

"Brethren in Christ."

"Never heard of them."

"Probably not. We're a rather small group."

"New?"

"No. One of the oldest in Protestantism. Actually we're de-
scended from the Mennonites. We go back to the Pietists in
Reformation days. We were brought to this country in the late
eighteenth century by an old Mennonite preacher from Switzer-
land. We are largest in Pennsylvania, I suppose. Our national
headquarters are there. There are only a few of us in Kentucky."

"Interesting. I'll have to come listen to you preach sometime.
If you can find me enough salvation to get me on my feet again,
I'll be everlastingly grateful to you!"

Jory laughed and stood up. "Why don't you come help us
strip tobacco?"

"Me? I don't know how to strip tobacco!"

"You can learn. Hod needs another hand."

"Oh. Well, sure, then. I've not been paying much attention to
what goes on around here. He should have told me."

"He wouldn't do that. But it would help him a lot. You have

to strip when tobacco's in case, and these damp days may not last. Put on old clothes, though. It's not a very clean job."

When they went through the kitchen, Mary looked up. "I'm the hired help today," Tara told her. "I'm going to help strip tobacco!"

"You've not let Jory talk you into a nice job, then," she laughed. "You'll freeze to death out in that cold, damp barn, and you'll break your back and your arms, to say nothing of gluing your hands up with tobacco gum! You'll regret it!"

"You're not very encouraging!"

"What's encouraging about stripping tobacco! Jory, you've not done him a good turn!"

Jory opened the door. "We need him, Mary. I appealed to his conscience."

The captain looked curiously around him when he stepped inside the barn. He had never seen a tobacco barn before. It was full of tobacco, hung on sticks racked in tiers crowded close together. It went up and up into the top of the barn, and he craned his neck to count the seventh tier. The tobacco had already cured to a ripe, golden brown, and now it hung limply, moist and lifeless in the damp air. It had to be stripped in damp weather so the leaves would handle without breaking.

At the far end of the barn there was an open space with a long table reaching across it. A powerful light hung over the table, and Hod was at work there slipping tobacco off the sticks. He piled it high on one end of the table. He looked up when Jory and the captain came in. "Hey!" he said in surprise, "what you doing out here?"

"Gonna help."

"Well, whaddya know! We can sure use you!"

"That's what Jory said. What do I do first?"

"Ever strip any tobacco before?"

"No."

"Well, we grade it as we strip. See these lower leaves on the stalk? Crushed and sort of broken? We call that trash. Up to about here where the good leaves begin. These first, heavy leaves we call red. Then about here the cream of the crop begins. The bright . . . these big, yellow leaves. Then these last ones at the top are called tips. You stand up there and strip the trash. Pass your stalk to Jory and he'll take the red. I'll take the bright. We'll do the tips later. When you get a handful, take a long leaf and tie it. Like this. Pile your hands on the floor near you. See?"

Hod had been stripping as he talked, ripping the leaves from the stalk cleanly and quickly. When he finished, he showed Tara how to tie a hand. Tara nodded. "Looks fairly simple."

"It is. The only difficult part is grading red and bright. But we're old hands at that and we'll not let you try it today."

"Do we start now?"

"Better. It's liable to fair up by noon and we'll have to quit."

It took handling only a dozen or so leaves for Tara to know what Mary had meant about tobacco gum. The sticky, resinous flow from the stalks coated his hands at once, and he worked with the stuff accumulating and hardening into armor over his fingers. He noticed Hod and Jory bending to rub dust on their hands and when he tried it he found it helped cut the viscous stuff for a time.

Steadily they worked, with little conversation. Lift a stalk, strip, pass it on. Another stalk, strip, pass it on. About every tenth stalk stop and bundle a hand. His arms felt heavy as lead within fifteen minutes. But Hod and Jory worked mechanically on. And he was determined to keep up. Once he glanced up at the endless tiers still hanging overhead. At the rate they were going he thought it would take months to get it all stripped!

He was saved by the sun. It shone weakly through the mist at midmorning, and by noon it had rolled the clouds away.

Rapidly the tobacco leaves dried out, and when the men went in for dinner, Hod said that would be all for today. Another morning, another misty rain, more tobacco stripping! The captain moaned, "My aching back!"

Hod laughed at him. "This ain't near as bad as those Bailey bridges across France, Cap'n!"

"Yeah, but that was war. And I was in condition then. I didn't know I was so soft!"

"Time we get this crop stripped you'll be in condition again."

"If I should live so long!"

But even though he groaned over his back and moaned over his stiffening arm muscles, he felt a sort of pride that he had kept up. And he derided himself even as he felt the pride. "Stupid," he jeered, "what's there to be proud of! Any lug with two arms and a backbone can do it! What's gained when you've stripped five hundred sticks of tobacco!"

The derision, however, did not banish his feeling of satisfaction. It was good to be as tired as he was now. It had been good to stand there with Hod and Jory doing his part. He had felt like he was part of a team again. Almost, he and Hod could have been getting up an advance detail, placing the guns, hauling and pulling them around, shoveling the mud down to the level for their bases. One of a team. Important in his place. The team not whole without him. Others counting on him.

There was a blister inside his thumb and he eyed it ruefully and held it up. "Mark of toil," he said, showing it to the others. "In five years I've not had a blister on my hands! I have to come to Wishful Hollow to get it!"

Jory touched it lightly with one finger. "It will callous," he said, "when it has been covered many times with other blisters."

Tara stared at him, and then he laughed shortly. "Salvation by blisters, huh?"

Jory smiled at him and took up his cup of coffee. He shook his head at Tara. "Maybe."

When he had gone the captain said, "He's a queer duck, isn't he?"

Mary was stacking dishes. She paused and looked at Tara. "Is he? Did you know that his religion forbids him to grow or to use tobacco? And tobacco is the only cash crop we grow around here. All of us depend on it for money."

"How does he live then?"

"He has a large garden each year, and he has a cow and chickens. He gets the freewill offerings from his church, which amount to eight or ten dollars a month. And he also gets the princely sum of fifteen dollars a month from his Church board."

Tara stared at her unbelievingly.

"Yes!"

"Well, if he's not allowed to raise tobacco, what's he doing helping Hod with his?"

"His religion also commands him to help his neighbor. But he'll not take one penny for helping. He *is* a queer duck, isn't he?"

Tara fingered the blister on the inside of his thumb. "Yeah," he said, rising, "mighty queer."

CHAPTER

4

A̲t noon on Saturday of that week Tara appeared at the dinner table dressed finely. Hod looked up at him and hooted at his white shirt and pin-striped suit. "Where you think you're going?" he wanted to know.

"I'm going to a love feast with Jory."

"Lord help us to get right! What's a love feast?"

"I don't know. But I'm going to find out. He's coming by for me around one thirty. It starts at two. Don't expect me home until you see me. I understand there's supper at the church and another service in the evening."

When he had gone, Hod and Mary looked strangely at each other, a little embarrassed. "The cap'n is sure taking to Jory, isn't he?" Hod said.

"It pleases me, Hod. Jory will be good for him."

"Yeah, I know. But I wouldn't have thought of the captain going to one of their services."

"It won't hurt him."

"No." But Hod was still uneasy. "What you reckon he wants to go for?"

Mary was sharp suddenly. "Hod, what's the matter with you? What difference does it make? It's strictly none of your business!"

Hod shrugged his shoulders. "Sure . . . sure. You don't reckon he'd kind of make fun of 'em . . . or say something . . . might hurt Jory's feelings, do you?"

"Jory doesn't go around getting his feelings hurt. He's too big a person for that."

Hod took his hat down from its peg. "Yeah . . . that's right." He lifted Mary's face as he went by. "You liking the captain any better?"

"Much better. He's nicer these days."

"That's good. He's all right, Mary."

"Yes. Hod, bring some potatoes up from the cellar before night. I'm completely out in the house."

"O. K.," and the door slammed gently behind him.

Jory's Ford was even older than Hod's, and it shook and clattered over the graveled pike and threatened to lose all its insides. Jory didn't apologize for it, but he laughed as he explained its origin. "Fellow over at the Gap give it to me. He'd driven it so long they wouldn't allow him much on a trade-in when he went to buy a new one, so he said he'd just keep it. I heard about it and went to see what he'd take for it. He knew I needed it in my work, I reckon, for he told me to take it and welcome. And taking it was mighty welcome, I'm telling you!"

"You couldn't get along very well without a car, could you?"

"It would be right unhandy. The churches are scattered through the county, and days like today when all the congregations meet together it's a help. Then there's folks to go to see, and the Bible schools in the spring at the different churches, and there's always folks to take to town to see the doctor. I could manage, if I had to, and I did when I didn't have a car. But it's easier with one."

"Cost you much to keep it up?"

"I'm a pretty good mechanic, or it would. Hasn't anything come up yet I couldn't fix, though."

Tara watched him nursing the old car over the rough spots in the road. It was the first time he had seen him dressed. Usually he wore blue denims and faded old work shirts, like Hod. Today he wore a dark gray suit—a thick, heavy, plain suit —and the erect collar of the high-buttoned vest gave it a clerical look. The shirt, which was buttoned out of sight by the vest except for an edge around the collar, was spotlessly white. Today, somehow, Jory was a stranger. His manner was the same . . . easy, gentle, slow-spoken. But he had taken on dignity with his preaching clothes, and they set him apart from the commonness of every day. Tara felt a little uneasy with him.

Jory's church was a plain little white chapel which sat back off the road in a grove of cedar trees. This grove gave it its name, Cedar Grove. A few people were gathering and Jory introduced him quietly. "This is my friend, Cap'n Cochrane."

But Tara noticed when the people spoke to Jory they called him brother. "Brother Jory," they said, or "Brother Clark," and Jory called them brothers and sisters.

The superintendent came, and Tara met him. Jory left him with him while he went across to speak to some others. "Fine man, Brother Clark," the man said to Tara, "fine man. Only native preacher among us, but he can do more with the people in five minutes than the rest of us can do in a month. Seems to understand them better."

"Because he's one of them, perhaps," Tara said.

"Perhaps. It doesn't always work out that way, though. Sometimes a native raised up among the people antagonizes them. It takes a fine talent of humility to do otherwise. Brother Clark has it."

Tara noticed immediately the uniform dresses of the women, different only in their material and color. None were bright. None were rich. A few were made of material with a small, neat-flowered print, but most were solid colors . . . blue, gray, lavender, and black. All had round necks with small round collars. All were long-sleeved, gathered into wristbands. All were sufficiently long to cover the calf of the leg. And all had a double thickness over the front to the shoulder.

All the women had long hair, he noticed, and the sheer, beautiful little white caps, which they themselves called their prayer veilings, were pinned like pure white wings on the back of their heads. Jory had told him this signified four things. First, it was a recognition of woman's position under grace. It signified that she, who suffered most by sin, was redeemed and enjoyed equal privileges with man in approach to God. Second, the veiling was woman's visible sign recognizing man's position as social head of the race. Third, it was a recognition of the interest and the care of the angels. Fourth, the veil was to cover her own natural covering, because there was a difference between man's hair and woman's. And a woman in the Lord must cover her hair.

The veiling symbolized woman's holiness, purity, undivided love and devotion to Christ, and the preservation of her glory, charm, and grace, as well as her person, for him. So Jory had explained. The theology meant little to Tara, but he was enchanted by the aesthetic beauty of row on row of the small white caps bent humbly before the Lord. Indeed their prayer veilings did set them apart, he thought. And he wondered how many of the women thus kneeling were entirely unconscious of the loveliness of their heads so veiled! If he were a woman, he would be tempted to join this faith if only to wear that sheer, beautiful bonnet!

Inside, the chapel was bare, clean, plain. The benches were handmade, but they had been finished by a deft craftsman who had smoothed and polished them lovingly—Jory, very likely. Up front was a low platform which formed the pulpit, and directly before it was placed a long, low bench. This was the prayer bench . . . the altar, the heart and the center of the church.

Jory in his pulpit was even stranger than Jory in the car. He had explained to Tara that the afternoon would be given over to examination and preparation for the observance of the ordinances in the evening. He had said that the Scriptures for both services were proscribed. Now he took his place behind the altar, and his lean, brown face was alight with tenderness and love. Slowly he looked out over the congregation and his smile lingered sweetly upon them as he took up his Bible. He read from the fourth chapter of Ephesians, and there was in his voice beauty and majesty:

"Let all bitterness, and wrath, and anger, and clamor, and evil speaking, be put away from you, with all malice. And be ye kind one to another, tenderhearted, forgiving one another, even as God for Christ's sake hath forgiven you."

The closing words lingered over the room and were amened by a chorus of voices. Tara felt the absolute simplicity of the words entering his heart. But he was made sad by his own feeling of the utter impossibility of the injunction. It was a beautiful ideal. But it could never be attained. It was impossible to purge the human heart of bitterness, anger, malice, and evil. So long as the heart was human, it could not be perfectly good. So long as the heart was human, it would hold such things. But it was an imperishable ideal that Paul had held up, even though it could not be attained. And he had worded it beautifully!

Someone raised a hymn then, and following it there were testimonies, witnesses to the glory of the Lord. Some of the testimonies were given in calm, assured voices. Others were tremulous with emotion, tearful in expression, repetitious in phrasing. But all were testimonies of joy in the Lord.

Jory was standing with his eyes closed, his face rapt and adoring. His deep voice rolled a heavy amen to each testimony, rolled and reverberated through the room and came to rest in benediction. Tara felt his stomach quiver. And he felt a squiggle of embarrassment. His emotional reactions were always so controlled, so restrained, so bounded by dignity and silence, that inevitably he had this squirming embarrassment for others when emotion was released. And emotion was beginning to release these people. It began with one woman who, in the midst of testimony, flung her arms high and began to shout and scream, long, high, piercing screams. Others joined in immediately, crying, praying, shouting, sobbing. There was swaying, moaning, weeping. "Yes, Jesus," a bearded old man cried over and over, "Yes, Lord . . . precious Lord!" And the amens mounted and rolled, and the women covered their faces with their hands.

Some of Tara's embarrassment faded before his curiosity. He studied the face of a white-haired old woman as she stood, brokenly giving her testimony, the tears furrowing her cheeks and dropping onto the bosom of her dress. "I was in sin," she wept, "in sin . . . buried deep in sin, until the Lord came and set me free." Her hands were knotted, twisted before her, the joints swollen with rheumatism. "Yes, Lord!" the people shouted. "The Lord sets me free!"

And then Jory spoke quietly and calmly from the pulpit, and the congregation seated themselves and the tears were wiped away. Jory spoke of the joy of witnessing for the Lord. Joy? Tara wondered. Joy. Emotional release . . . autohypnosis . . . religious enchantment. Maybe it was joy at that. But now when Jory spoke, the spell was broken. Tara took out his handkerchief and wiped his face. It was wet with sweat and his hand shook as he lifted the handkerchief. He felt let down and unkeyed, but he was thankful there were no more testimonies.

When the afternoon service was over, the women unpacked the huge baskets of food and spread it on benches in the back of the church. Tara ate hungrily of baked beans, potato salad, fried pies, and homemade pickles and relishes. The people urged him on hospitably. They were friendly, soft-spoken, accepting him unquestioningly as Jory's friend, making him welcome gladly. He watched them laughing together, at ease with one another, bound closely together by the smallness of their group and by their separation from others. That they loved Jory was evident. They clustered about him, the women plying him with food, the men talking familiarly with him about crops, the weather, the market on calves and hogs.

And Jory was at home with them, moving about among them, stopping to talk with Aunt Mahaley, the old blind woman, about her chickens; listening carefully and patiently to the old bearded man, Uncle Jake, tell about the great blizzard of 1888. Tara was sure Uncle Jake had told this story of the blizzard to Jory hundreds of times before, but Jory's face betrayed no impatience. Tara felt a swift impulse of love toward Jory. He himself could not have been so kind. The old man would have bored him, made him irritable. But he was grateful to Jory for being thus kind. It went with Jory, somehow.

After the supper when the congregation gathered for the evening service, Tara noticed that seats had been arranged in opposite corners of the room. Two long benches in each corner faced each other and there were basins of water and stacks of towels nearby. Now was to come the feet-washing, one of the ordinances. Jory did not officiate at this service. As the pastor of the church, he took his place beside the superintendent, who was here to administer the ordinances.

There were hymns and then the reading of the Scriptural injunction—the description of Jesus washing the feet of the disciples: "He . . . took a towel, and girded himself. After that he poureth water into a basin, and began to wash the disciples' feet, and to wipe them with the towel wherewith he was girded."

The congregation separated, the men going to one corner, the women to the other, and seated themselves thus on the long benches facing each other. The steward poured water into a basin, and the superintendent came down from the pulpit and removed his shoes and socks. Tara felt repugnance at the sight of the bare feet. Feet were so ugly, so essentially private! But the steward girded himself with a towel and knelt before the superintendent and washed and wiped both his feet. Finished, he rose and the men clasped hands and exchanged the kiss of fellowship. Then the superintendent girded himself with the towel and knelt before Jory and repeated the washing of feet and the wiping. Jory then took the towel, and so the washing and the wiping went from one to the other until all were washed and all were wiped and all were shod once more.

Not knowing what to expect, Tara had watched with curiosity and with the queasy feeling of revulsion sitting heavy in his stomach. This washing of feet publicly . . . even in the name of religion! How could such a service be religious? But so quietly was the service conducted, so earnestly, so humbly, so tenderly was all of it done, that a sense of wonder took possession of him. The revulsion remained, but it was purely personal. His own dignity would have been affronted by participation in such a ceremony. But with a flash of insight he knew that was because of his own lack of humility. He could not wash another's feet tenderly. But these people could and did. With dignity and beauty and humility. And he wondered if all things done humbly, done gently, done tenderly, did not hold dignity and beauty. He felt a pang of envy for the mind that could accept literally and simply this admonition to humility, and he knew remorse that his own complex and sophisticated mind could never do so. This was what the intellectual mind forfeited, he thought—this peace, this humility, this love.

After the Communion service, which followed, Jory and Tara drove home. They were both quiet for a time, then Tara spoke. "Jory," he said, "mind if I ask you some things?"

"Depends on what things, Cap'n."

"Well, for instance, how did you happen to join the White Caps?"

"That's a long story."

"I'd like to hear it." And it struck him as funny that he meant it. He did want to hear it.

"Well, I reckon it commenced when I got home from the Army. I was out in the Pacific, and when I first got back to the States, I was restless and pretty unhappy and couldn't get settled down anywhere. I didn't want to come back to the ridge, for I'd not found much here to commence with, and my pa's house was always full and running over. He's been married three times and there's a lot of us kids. So I rattled around here and there, never satisfied but not knowing what I wanted. I worked at first one thing then another, spent my money, fooled around, and got nowhere. Then I just got homesick for the hills one day and packed up and came home."

He drove slowly, his eyes on the road, carefully avoiding the worst of the chugholes. "Something happened then that come mighty close to driving me out of my mind."

Tara waited.

"I'm the oldest, but I had a brother just a couple of years younger than me. He'd married just a few months before I come back to the ridge. I'd not seen Rose Pierce since she was a little kid. Don't reckon I'd ever give her two thoughts. Tay brought her over home the first Sunday after I got back, and the minute she walked through the door I knew she was the only one for me. Knew why I'd never been in love enough to get married before, and knew I'd never be able to love anyone else. And she was my brother's wife. And happy with him as far as a body could tell."

The captain struck a match to light his cigarette. In its glow he sneaked a look at Jory's face. There was no grimness on it. It had the same steady, quiet look it usually wore. This telling, then, was not harrowing him, Tara thought. "That," he said, "was a pretty big order, wasn't it?"

"It was," Jory agreed. "Might' near too big for me. For the worst was, Tay was a wild, wayward lad, always handsome and swaggering and lawless. It was bad enough to love her and to stand aside and watch her married to someone else. But it was worse to think of the harm Tay could bring her and likely would."

The car rattled across a wooden bridge and Jory waited for the noise of their passing to die away. "It was during that time that I went kind of wild and crazy myself. Took to drinking too much and roistering around. Seemed like that was about the only way I could find any peace. And then one night I wandered into a White Cap revival meeting. Went just for something to do and with more of an idea of stirring up some mischief than anything else. The White Caps have always had a pretty hard time in these hills. When they first came, around thirty years ago, their meetings would be broken up and their property destroyed and their fields and gardens ruined. It was a bad place to live in those days. The law was generally a man's gun and his quickness to use it. And while there's more peace now, still there's gangs of boys like to make trouble at their meetings. I was one of them."

"How did they come to be in Kentucky in the first place?" Tara asked.

So Jory went on to tell how a wandering preacher came looking for his brother, and how he was amazed and distressed by the need he found in the hills. How he convinced the home group in Lancaster of the need to establish a mission in Kentucky, and how he himself took charge and administered it for years. How a few converts had been made, and how, while they had never been a sizable group, they had remained a constant group, going about among the hill people, ministering to them, preaching to them, and praying over them.

He told how they had, in time, established seven congregations, all in Adair County. Small bands of zealots, ascetic, ardent, self-sustaining. How they established a small clinic at the Gap, and brought on a registered nurse to conduct it. And how at another small settlement they placed another nurse. For the White Caps, if they themselves are otherworldly, still recognize the sorrows and griefs of this world and do what they can to ameliorate them for the people.

He told how something of this was known to all the ridge folks of course. But how, in the main, they remained in ignorance of the White Cap beliefs and doctrines. And were content merely to use the nurses, when all else failed, and to regard the white-capped women and the soberly dressed men with curiosity and a tinge of contempt. They were different. On the ridge that was the ultimate sin. Everything unfamiliar, unridgelike, different, went plumb foolish. The barrier of hill ways is rocklike, and the prejudice of set and settled people is always complacent. It was like battering with a thin rod against a stone wall.

"At the revival that night," Jory went on, "I don't know how to explain what happened. Something kept pushing me to go up to the altar, and I was more ashamed of it than anything else. I felt towards the White Caps like everybody else felt. That they were queer. Not my own folks at all. I fought it two or three nights, but I kept wanting to go back. So I did. And when I got up to the altar, it was like a white light shining, and I knew I was through wasting my life. I knew this was the way for me, and I knew I wanted to preach the way. It was like a clear light, or a plain call. And something inside me was willing and made answer."

There was silence between them and Tara waited, feeling Jory had not done. But the silence grew until Tara spoke. "Was that all? Was it that simple?"

"No. It wasn't simple at all. It took a powerful lot of praying and studying and examining of myself. I had to learn the doctrines and everything they believed. And I had to be sure I believed them too. But I did. You couldn't help believe. Listen . . ." and his voice repeated the sonorous words of the creed: "We believe that the work of Calvary is made effective to the believer through justification (forgiveness of committed sin), and sanctification (heart-cleansing and empowerment); and that the work of grace thus wrought in the heart will effect a transformation of life and conduct. . . .

"We believe that the ordinances, namely, baptism by trine immersion, washing the saints' feet, and the Communion or partaking of the emblems of the broken body and the shed blood of our Lord and Saviour Jesus Christ, the holy kiss, and the devotional prayer veiling for women are enjoined in God's Word. . . .

"We believe that the Scripture teaches that Christians should not be conformed to the world, but that they are a separate people; and we believe that it teaches nonresistance in a qualified sense, that it is not the Christian's privilege to take up the sword or to fight with carnal weapons; yet it is his duty to be strictly loyal to the Government under which he lives in all things that do not conflict with or are not forbidden by the Word."

"It made me," Jory said, finishing the majestic words, "want to live like that . . . going the second mile, lending to the borrower, saluting them outside the household of faith. It made me want to toil with my hands so I might have that with which to give my brother, and it made me want to live clean and in unity, with fellowship and love, with my neighbor."

"Yes," Tara said. He couldn't understand it, but no one could listen to this man and not know what his religion meant to him. And every integrity in any man demands respect. Is worthy of respect. "What about your brother's wife?"

"You'll see her someday. She's living with her folks, Miss Willie and Wells Pierce. Miss Willie is Mary's aunt, I reckon you know. Rose is Wells's girl. Tay got killed in a raid on his still a couple of years ago."

"Oh. So everything is going to be all right."

"Well, not exactly. You see, now I'm a preacher of the faith, I can't marry except in the faith. And Rose don't hold with the White Caps."

"You mean your religion now stands between you? Man, you don't really love that girl!"

"I love her more than any other human being in the world. But I can't go against my faith. I wouldn't have anything left to give her if I did that. And until she comes of her own free will into the fold, it wouldn't be right for her."

He turned the car off the graveled road into the old dirt road that wound up the hollow. When they came to his cabin, Tara touched his arm. "No need taking me on home. I'll get out here and walk the rest of the way."

"Be glad to take you."

"No, I'd rather walk. Thanks for taking me today."

And Tara got out of the car and walked down the road, out of the spearing lights spread by the lamps of the car. There was enough moon so that he could keep in the road, and he walked rapidly, following its curves through the trees and the fields.

Inevitably his mind was busy with what he had seen and heard this day and night. Never before had he come into such close contact with such a faith. It was a good thing, he thought. A very good thing. There was so much healing in such a community of faith. And he wondered if the loss of faith, for to him it seemed one had to admit that faith had been lost in this generation, weren't responsible for many of the world's ills. And, he conceded, for many of the ills of the individual.

With that thought the old loneliness returned with renewed sharpness and he felt left out and barred from something warm and good. What the something warm and good was, he couldn't say, but the feeling was one of being lost in coldness when the rest of humanity had found warmth. How? And where? He shivered and walked on, a symbol, even to himself, of man walking alone.

CHAPTER

5

THE time drew on to Thanksgiving. Each misty, damp morning the men went to the barn and stripped tobacco. Day by
day, little by little, they reduced the high-mounting tiers until
finally there were only the lowest racks remaining. Tara felt a
personal victory when he could stand and look across the barn
and see only an emptiness overhead. And as they bulked it
down and it rose higher and higher from the barn floor, he
thought he would always have a new respect for the stuff he
smoked! Stripping was only one small part of the whole job of
making a tobacco crop. But it had convinced him that raising
tobacco was no easy way to make a living.

He had put new blisters on top of the old one, over and over
again. Neither Hod nor Jory told him that stripping tobacco
wouldn't put blisters on any farmer's hands . . . it was too
easy a job for that. But Tara's soft hands had rubbed and
blistered under the small friction of the leaves almost daily
until finally, after a couple of weeks, a calloused knot had
formed. He took pride in that callus. He showed it to Jory one
day. "No blister today, see!"

Jory took his hand and looked at it. "He'll be in shape to
split rails for the new fence after Thanksgiving, Hod," he said,
laughing.

Tara groaned. "No, sir. I'm too beat up to split rails!"

Jory pitched him a stalk of tobacco. "You'll get over that," he said comfortlessly.

Thanksgiving week there was hustle and bustle in the house. On Monday night Mary sat worrying a pencil between her fingers. "Hattie and Tom," she said, writing down their names, "and Miss Willie and Wells. Rufe, Abby, Rose and Taysie. That's eight. Irma and John and Susie. Eleven. And Jory . . . and we four. My stars, Hod, that's sixteen!"

Hod was tinkering with an old clock. It worried him when things wouldn't work. They didn't need the clock, but because it was there he was determined to make it run. He didn't look up. "Sixteen what?"

"Sixteen people for Thanksgiving dinner!"

"Pretty good crowd."

"Well, I can't leave anybody out!"

Tara was slumped down in a chair, nursing his pipe. He had been sawing wood that day and every joint in his body felt pulled apart. When he moved he moaned. The muscles in his back and arms were sore and stiff, and to lift his hand to his pipe made him wince. "You can count me out, Mary. I'll go to town to eat. Maybe Jory would like to go with me."

"You'll do no such thing," Mary retorted. "I'm not complaining. I'm just figuring."

"I wouldn't mind."

"No. I'll manage. This is a family affair and no one is going to be missing."

Tara looked at the dark head bent over her list. At the full lower lip bitten softly between her teeth. A softening, warming glow crept over him. Family affair! It was good to be counted in the family. Even a temporary family, an adopted family. It was good to be where an old-fashioned Thanksgiving was the custom. Interest grew in him. "What's the problem?"

"Nothing, really. I was trying to plan the table. I'll just put the small fry at another table. That'll take care of it. Now," she said briskly, "now you guys can just count on giving me a couple of days to get the house cleaned, and another one to run errands!"

Hod looked over at Tara and his eyes twinkled. "There goes the week, Cap'n. Shot to pieces! Can you still spit 'n polish?"

"Under compulsion . . . I suppose I can."

"This is compulsion," Mary said, and she rose and slid her list into the table drawer. She moved by Hod on the way to the kitchen, and in passing she reached out and rumpled his hair. Hod ducked out of her way, but as she went by he slapped her thigh affectionately. She whirled and hugged him so that his arms were pinned to his sides. Laughing, she bent and kissed him.

Tara watched them and a deep-drilling pang of envy went through him. They were so close . . . so deeply in love . . . so content with one another. Family? No, he wasn't part of the family. He never would be. He was just a guy they were being nice to. Trying to make him feel good. Trying to help him. They felt sorry for him. And his old pride stirred against such pity. But then, he thought, pity is very akin to love. Real pity, that is. Whatever you feel for someone when you feel sorry for him, it's a genuine feeling . . . and any feeling is better than none.

So he rejected his pride and accepted the pity. They didn't need him. But he needed them. And that would do just as well. But he felt an awful emptiness at times like this, when the love between the two showed itself. At first they hadn't. They had been careful around him. And he knew it was a mark of their affection for him that had relaxed that care. For, anomalously, while it indicated their increasing regard for him, it set him more definitely on the outside . . . on the edge of the circle. They were fond of him, accepted him, so they could now show their love before him. But the showing brought them together before him, in a place and feeling where he could not go. It kept him an outsider. He stirred in his chair. Well . . . that couldn't be helped.

For two days they cleaned house. Rubbed down the walls, washed windows, cleaned and waxed floors, polished furniture. Hod grumbled. "I don't see why having company for one meal always brings on a regular upheaval! Nobody's going to look at the house! Nobody cares if there's a spot on a windowpane, or whether the floors are slick as glass! All this stewing and fussing! But this happens every time we have company! Cap'n, you wait until you're married! You'll see!"

Grimly Mary prodded them on. "This is a good time to put up the storm windows, Hod. Take the screens down and wash the outside of the windows!"

"See!" Hod said triumphantly. "She'll end up having me mend the fence before they come!"

Mary turned in her tracks. "That reminds me! The gate *is* sagging!"

Wordlessly Hod went after his hammer and tools, his indignation complete, and Mary looked at Tara and chuckled. "He doesn't mind, really."

Tara knew that. The grumbling was just part of loving it all. In Hod's place he wouldn't have minded either. To have his own home! To have someone like Mary ordering him around! To have a family coming for Thanksgiving dinner! No indeed, he wouldn't have minded!

Then the day before Thanksgiving they went into town for the things the farm didn't provide for the dinner, leaving Mary behind busy with her cakes and pies. Carefully they prowled through the market, checking their purchases against Mary's list. Suddenly Tara wanted to have a more personal part in all of it. "Hey!" he said, "how about me getting some sherry or wine or something for the dinner?"

Hod laughed. "You'll learn. In the first place Adair County is dry. So is Taylor County. You'd have to drive plumb to Marion County to get anything to drink. In the second place, you'd shock the eyebrows off the folks. It's a sin to take a drink on the ridge. A mortal sin, that is!"

Tara looked at him in amazement. Cocktails, highballs, social drinking, had been a part of his life as long as he could remember. It was part of being a gracious host. He couldn't imagine a party without it. "Doesn't anybody drink?"

"Oh, sure. The stills would go out of business if they didn't. Lot of men keep a bottle hidden out in the barn and tip it a little every day. But they don't bring it out in the open. Pa does, for instance. But you think Ma'd let him fix a drink in the house? Not on your life! It's a sin!"

"Well," Tara said, giving the grocery cart a shove, "that's out then. But I want to do something for this party. What could I get?"

They puzzled over it and Tara tried to remember the dinner tables at which he had sat. China . . . silver . . . glass . . . flowers. Flowers! That was it! "Is there a florist in this town?" he asked.

"Yeah."

"We'll stop there, then, and I'll get flowers for the table. You think Mary would like that?"

"I know she would."

He chose tall-stemmed baby chrysanthemums, coppery ones, sultry with dull red fires and flame at their hearts, and he bought a copper bowl to put them in. They looked like autumn and harvest and Thanksgiving, he thought. When he came back to the car with them, Hod looked. "Fall roses," he said. "Mary loves 'em."

Fall roses. Tara had never heard them called that. But he
liked it better than chrysanthemums.

Thanksgiving morning brought the first snow of the season
slanting down against the windows. The sun came up grayed
over by lusterless clouds, and by the time breakfast was over,
the snow, falling slowly, feathered as goose down, was filling
the air. They all rushed to the windows, excited, to see. Mary
lifted Jeems and he wiggled and squirmed and squealed. "I'll
take him out if you'll dress him," Tara said.

Jeems looked like a small, red Teddy bear in his snowsuit,
and he ran wildly around, lifting his eager, shining little face
to let the snow wet it. Tara showed him how he could hold his
arm still and the flakes would fall against the cloth and boldly
outline themselves for a moment before melting. He stood
transfixed and rigid then, catching snowflakes. He reached for
them, and when they crumbled under his touch, he frowned,
puzzled. "Gone," he said, "all gone."

And Tara was reminded of his reaching for the smoke rings.
He chuckled. "You're always reaching for intangibles, young
fellow," he said. "Smoke rings . . . snowflakes. You better
learn to grab hold of something solid."

But the chuckle that accompanied the words disarmed the
child and he looked up at the man and squealed gleefully, and
then he ran in widening circles, flinging his arms and whirling
dizzily. The child looked a lot like Mary, in spite of his fair hair
and blue eyes. The shape of the face was Mary's, the fullness
of his mouth was Mary's, and, Tara thought, the dream in his
eyes came from her. In so many ways he was all Mary's son. He
felt a great tenderness for the child. He wished he had a son.
And then Jeems fell in a rosebush and Tara went to untangle
him. "That's the way tail spins usually end," he cautioned him.

About the middle of the morning the folks began to arrive.
Tara was curious about them. He was looking forward to this
family gathering in one way, and in another he thought it

might be very tiresome. He had stayed pretty close to home since he had arrived, and had gathered his knowledge of the other members of the family entirely from the conversations of Hod and Mary. Some of the talk had interested him, some of it had bored him. He expected it would be like that with the people.

Hattie and Tom came first, with Sarah, Hod's little sister. They made a great stamping on the porch, shaking their feet free of snow, and brought some of the damp freshness of the morning in with their cold faces and hands. Tara saw that Tom was simply an older Hod, the structure and design of their faces being identical. He was tall too, like Hod, stooped a little now, with a gaunted neck. But the eyes had the same mischievous glint, and the face had the same expression of content. Where Hod's hair was a thick straw thatch, Tom's had thinned and grayed, but Tara knew that in his youth he had been as Hod was now. He spoke to Tara with a chuckle hidden in his voice.

Hattie was a thin, browned woman, small, shoulders bowed and rounded, stomach paunched, her face a sharp peak between parted wings of graying black hair. Her mouth was sunk over badly fitting false teeth, but under it her chin firmed and squared, and directly in its center lay the deep dimple that she had passed on to Hod. Jeems had that same dimple. There was a look of suffering on her face, and a look of patience with the suffering, as if she had been friends with it a long time. Tara had seen that look on the faces of patients in the wards sometimes.

Hattie was cordial, but shy, with him. "Pleased to meet you," she said, without extending her hand. "I've heared a heap about you." Then she ducked into the kitchen, murmuring something to Mary about bringing mince pies.

Sarah was a beautiful surprise to Tara. He had heard Hod and Mary speak often of this youngest sister of Hod's, and

Mary had said she was lovely. Hod had told him how Sarah had come in his mother's middle age, after he himself was a grown man, and how he had resented her coming. But even in the telling of it, now, there was love and pride. Both Hod and Mary spoke of Sarah with a special affection, as if she were set apart in their thoughts. She was now in the ninth grade, and it was they who were sending her to high school over at the Gap.

He could see why they loved her so much when he saw her. Sarah Pierce was as beautiful as a porcelain figurine. Every feature was delicately molded, fine, perfect. Her bones were small and exquisitely proportioned. Her hair tangled in a mass of silvery curls over her head, soft, corkscrew curls which danced springily when she moved. Her eyes were wide and blue, childishly eager and curious just now, framed by yellow lashes so long and thick that they seemed too heavy for the thin-veined lids that drooped under his gaze. Oddly enough, her skin was not the milky fairness you would expect with such hair and eyes. Rather, it had the smooth, rich thickness of new cream, faintly gold with the warmth of red in her cheeks. Her figure was already womanly, her hips broadened slightly, her dress tightened across her breasts, which pushed impatiently and boldly against the imprisoning fabric. All the guys that can't have you, young lady, he thought, are going to have some pretty rugged heartaches! Trouble. That's what as much beauty as Sarah Pierce had would spell. She bobbed her head shyly and sidled past him into the kitchen.

Then came Miss Willie and Wells Pierce and their family. There was a glad confusion at their entrance, voices excited and high, and a great laying off of wraps and general milling around. Then Mary brought her aunt over to Tara. "This is Miss Willie, Tara," she said, and to Miss Willie, "Captain Cochrane."

A small, hard, firm hand met Tara's and he looked down into the face of the woman who had reared Mary. He knew the history of that from Mary herself. He saw a bright, eager, in-

tellectually curious face, with a keen, clear, direct look out of
her eyes. The eyes were blue, a beautiful, clear blue that had
not faded with the years. He knew she was around forty-six or
seven, that she had been a teacher of the ridge school for one
year, and that she had married Wells Pierce at the end of that
year. She looked like a schoolteacher, he thought. A little dusty,
a little dry, a little brittle. But he knew she belied her looks,
because he knew that in her wifehood she had also acquired
motherhood, and that she did a good job of both. "I'm so glad
to know you, Miss Willie," he said sincerely.

"And I'm so glad to know you," she replied.

And then Mary was back. "Tara, this is our cousin Wells
Pierce." And she laid her hand fondly on the arm of the man
she was talking to. He was a short man, not much taller than
Miss Willie, dark-skinned by nature and browned to the shade
and texture of shoe leather by the sun. His black-haired head
sat on a short, strong neck which rose stoutly from his shoulders. And his eyes, small, brown, deep-set, were enfolded by
the creases of merry laugh lines around their corners. His hand
was as rough and hard as a cob of corn, but the clasp was firm,
strong, friendly. "Howdy, Cap'n," he said, "I been meanin' to
git over to make you welcome to Piney Ridge. You're not less
welcome on account of me not gittin' here, though. Hit's jist
I've been busier than common."

"I can understand that, sir, at this time of year," Tara said,
taking his hand, liking this man at once. "We've been pretty
busy around here ourselves."

"Got yer tobacco all stripped?"

"Finished last week," Tara said proudly, "all bulked down
now, ready to go."

"Well, it's a good feelin', once the crop's made an' done with.
Sort of winds up the year, like. I allus want to set an' stretch
in front of the fire a coupla weeks when I git through. Jist to
think on it an' admire myself fer gittin' it over."

Tara laughed. "We're not going to get to sit and stretch very long, I'm afraid. We've got the winter wood to saw up and rick, and then Hod says the fences have to be mended. He's got me ticketed to split rails."

"We," he kept saying. "We." He liked to be saying it. It gave him a good feeling inside. Although he borrowed his part in it, it still gave him a good feeling. Wells laughed with him, and then turned to the boy who had come up beside him. "Cap'n, this is my boy, Rufe, and," laying his arm around the shoulders of a young woman who was near, "this is Rose."

So this was Rose Pierce—Tay Clark's widow. She was like her father. Brown, plump, partridgelike. The same crinkly-cornered brown eyes, the same short, stout neck holding her head well up, the same crisp, dark hair. She held her child, Taysie, on her arm and tried to get her to look at the captain, but the child hid her face in her mother's neck and refused to have anything to do with him. "Let her alone," Mary said, taking her. "You come with me, Taysie. There are lots of lovely things in Jeems's room."

There was little to tell what sort of person she was, this woman Jory loved. She was composed in Tara's presence, not shy as Hattie and Sarah had been, and her face had an open, honest, pleasant look. She laughed quickly and easily, he saw, when she answered some quip of her father's, and doubtless she was brimming over with the energy of good health and youth. But he shook his head over that statement of Jory's, that the moment he saw her he knew she was the only one for him. Still, if every man found the same thing to love in women, he thought, the world would be in a sad state of confusion!

Mary came back into the room. "Where's Abby?"

Miss Willie answered her. "She went to Wells's sister's for the holidays. Where Veeny is, you know."

And then there was another stamping on the porch and another inrushing of people. This was Hod's sister, Irma; her husband, John Walton; and her five-year-old daughter, Susie.

Jory came last. He had honored the occasion with his clerical vest, and he looked, as always, scrubbed and clean. He was a fine-looking man, Tara thought, one who would feel at ease anywhere. His poise came from his lack of self-consciousness, from his concern and interest in others, and from some serious, inherent dignity which had been implemented with the finding of his own place in life. It would never forsake him, Tara thought. No matter what the occasion.

This, then, was the Thanksgiving family and Tara took his place among them, feeling not very sure of what was expected of him, but learning soon that nothing at all was expected of him. He was accepted, honored, and made welcome.

The day was confused, but it was a happy confusion. The women came and went from the kitchen, and there was a clattering and a chattering and a general bustling about. Good smells drifted over the house . . . the smell of turkey baking, the rich, heavy odor of coffee, the spicy thinness of sage in the dressing . . . all of them smells that stimulated and tantalized the appetite.

The snow stopped and the men went out to the barn, fingered Hod's tobacco, commented on it, ambled around the barn lot looking at his cows and mules, making small, comfortable talk among themselves. Tara went along, listened, took it in, feeling the content of these men among familiar things. There was Hod, Wells, Tom, and John. Their way of life was patterned and ruled by the seasons. They shared a common bondage to the plowing, planting, and harvesting of their crops. Whatever their individual peculiarities, in this they were all alike. They were all slow-talking, tall-standing men. Bound to the soil, but free in their bondage.

Tara pulled on his pipe and listened. Year after year their talk went thus, varying only with the seasonal changes. Tobacco, cows, mules, fences, pastures . . . these were the boundaries of life. They were fundamental things, solid, real. But so narrow, he felt impatiently. Here they were, these men, shut in by the hills, content never to lift their eyes beyond them. Treading daily the same dull paths. Rarely lifting their eyes either to the beauty of the hills or to the skies that rose above them except to consider the weather. He wondered what kind of nature it was that could be placid in the dull, ever-changeless life they lived.

Almost as if he too had been wondering, John Walton spoke. The men had wandered out to the pasture and were standing, feet propped on the bottom fence rail, looking over Hod's stand of winter grass. He was experimenting with fescue, and the men were interested. But John Walton stood apart, his eyes on the gray haze blanketing the top of the ridge. "I been thinkin'," he said slowly, "I been thinkin' some of goin' over to Indiany this winter."

Hod shot him a startled look. "Sell out and move over there?"

John shook his head. "No . . . leastways not jist yit. Thought I'd work out over there this winter. See if I like it. Might sell out then."

"Why, that goes plumb foolish to me," Wells said frankly. "You got a nice place fixed up down the ridge. Got yer fields in good shape. Got a purty little house. How kin you better yerself over there?"

John moved his hands restlessly. "I dunno. I jist feel a discontent here on the ridge. Thought mebbe things'd be better out there."

"Where would you aim to work?" Tom asked, shifting his tobacco from one side of his mouth to the other.

"Oh, one of them factories, I reckon. Or the railroad. They's a heap of places to work. So I've heared."

"You mean the city?" Hod asked incredulously. "You and Irma move to the city? Why, John, you'd hate it!"

Bitterness crept into John's voice. "I couldn't feel no more discontent anywheres than I do around here!"

"But why? What's come over you? You and Irma have a good life here. You've been a farmer all your life! I thought you liked it!"

"I do. Ain't nothin' wrong with farmin'."

"Then what's the matter?"

John rammed his hands into his coat pockets. "I reckon you'd best ask Irma that," he said.

Hod stared at him, and his face mirrored his amazement. Jory was standing near John, his hands braced against the fence. His face was quiet, thoughtful, shuttered. "It might be," he said, "that you would do well there. But it might also be that you would take your discontent with you. A sore cures itself best from the inside."

"Not this sore," John said shortly, and he walked away from the group of men into the house.

Hod picked a dried stem of grass and bit absently at it. "He'd never like it in the city. John's a farmer. He'd die by inches in town."

"He's dying by inches now," Jory said.

Hod flung the grass stem to the ground. "What do you mean?"

Jory rubbed his hands together and their hard palms scraped out a dry sound. A silence settled over the little knot of men, and Tara Cochrane was conscious of an apprehensive tension in them . . . a stilled, quieted feeling of waiting. He felt it himself. They were all, he included, waiting for Jory to speak.

"It's something gone wrong between Irma and John, Hod. Likely they're the only ones to know what it is. But whatever it is, it's come between them. And they take no joy in one another any more."

Flatly Hod replied, "I don't believe it!"

Tom moved then, one slow foot, only mildly restless. "I've thought some they wasn't as happy as they used to be. Seemed like when little Johnnie died . . ."

Hod looked at him sharply. "That! That foolishness of Irma's! Nobody can blame John for being put out with her . . ."

"It's their life, Hod," Jory said quietly. "They'll have to work it out."

Rose Clark stepped out onto the porch then and called: "Dinner's ready! You all come on!"

Her voice lifted over them, clear and young. Tara saw Jory turn toward the girl and saw his face go gentle and sweet, as if the sound of her voice had reached out and laid itself over some rough place in him and had smoothed it out. He does love her, Tara thought. He loves her very much. It's there for all to see, when he is least aware of it. There for her to see if she has eyes to see it. And he wondered how a man could live with a love he couldn't have.

The dinner was a feast of good things, and the noise around the table was a merry, laughing noise. Plates were heaped, the food disappeared, and there was passing of more. Once Hattie sighed when the platter of turkey went by. "I wisht I could eat like I used to! Ain't nothin' I'd like more'n jist to set here an' taste of ever'thing!"

"Hattie, does your stomach still bother you?" Miss Willie asked.

Hattie laughed. "Oh, now, let's fergit my stummick! Hit does right well if I don't put nothin' in it but milk an' bread!"

"I get so provoked with her," Mary said. "If she'd just listen to us and see a specialist!"

"Hit wouldn't do no good," Hattie said apologetically. "My people's allus had stummick trouble. Ain't nothin'd help it as I know of. I'm used to it."

Tara said nothing, but his practiced eye looked her over.

Ulcers, probably, he thought. If not worse. Stupid of her not to have it looked into. Used to it!

Rose, from down at the end of the table where she could see after the children, laughed suddenly. "Why don't you git Jory to heal you? The White Caps believes in faith healin', don't they, Jory?"

Jory answered quietly. "Yes. For some."

Irma spoke up quickly. "They ain't the only ones believes in faith healin'. I believe in it too. An' I ain't no White Cap."

"You might as well be," John said acidly.

"Them white bonnets," Rose sniffed. "The day'll never come when I put one on my head!"

She slanted a look at Jory, and Tara knew she had spoken brashly especially for his benefit. Ought to be spanked, he thought.

Jory crumbled a piece of bread. "Religion is a thing that all people must decide for themselves. None of us has got a right to try to make others believe our way. And the ways of one religion may seem queer to another. I think the white caps are pretty. You think they're queer-looking. But I can't help thinking if you knew what they stood for, you'd think they were pretty too."

Rose's chin went up in the air. "I know what they stand for. You've told me. Prayer veilin's! I kin pray without a bonnet on my head!"

"Yes . . . of course you can. But it might be the bonnet would remind you to pray oftener. And if you took a pride in your faith, the wearing of the cap would be like a bright flag flying for all the world to see."

"Not me!" Rose said defiantly.

"An' I've had my truck with that faith healin'," John put in. "I want no more of it."

Tara remembered that Irma and John had lost a little boy a year or two ago. And that they had quarreled over calling a doctor, Irma standing firm in her faith that he would be healed, John frightening and weakening, and too late hurrying for the doctor. More stupidity, he thought. He had no patience with it! Hod was right. It was just foolishness.

Jory spoke again. "We believe that there are some who can be healed by faith. I have been myself. I know others who have been. But we believe also that it is not open to all. That's why we train a few of the women in each church community to be nurses. That's why we have medical missionaries. It is not given to all to be healed divinely."

Irma was quick to speak. "But hit says in the Bible that if you have faith as a grain of mustard seed!"

"How are we to measure faith, Irma? How are we to know?"

Irma looked at Jory queerly. "I don't know." Her mouth quivered. "But I believe it! I do believe it!"

"So do I. But I would not want to test the faith of any other man. I believe. I cannot say what another must believe."

Tara had a shuddering sense of curious and tactile awareness. It was as if his whole body had suddenly sprouted antennae, feeling out sensitively the undercurrents of complexity in this gathering of people. There was Hattie and her illness. There were Irma and John and something that lay coldly and at the same time hotly between them. There was Jory, his heart turned toward Rose and she not receiving it. People, he thought. People! Bones and flesh and blood and hanks of hair . . . all with eyes and mouths and ears, made in a common image. And all stewing and boiling inside, with their own feelings, frustrations, illnesses and health. Their own hopes and desires, their own bitter tastes in their mouths, their own wails of disaster, their own mountain peaks of happiness and troughs of despair. What did he know about people? What did he know about how they felt? Here was a family of people, bound together by ties of blood, and set cross-grained by currents of tension and fear. And he, among them, set apart by his own currents of tension and fear. Each man alone, he thought, unable ever to know or understand the man who lived beside him, but always hurt and suffering so long as any other man anywhere was hurt and suffering too. He felt the old strangeness. The old loneliness. The old hopelessness.

After dinner, when the dishes were done, they gathered in the living room. They were replete and drowsy. And for a time the talk wandered aimlessly around general subjects. Then Miss Willie asked for some music. "Mary, play for us," she said.

"I have something better in store for you," Mary said. "Tara, will you get your violin?"

Together they played then, and Tara knew he had never played better in his life. This was an unsophisticated audience, uncritical, undemanding, but they gave him the great compliment of their close and undivided attention. He felt as if they waited for every note, and that they heard it individually. He made each one beautiful for them.

When he and Mary had finished, Mary turned to Sarah. "Sarah, sing for us, won't you?"

The girl ducked her head and shook it. A scarlet wave began at the base of her neck and flowed up into her face, and she would not lift her eyes. "Come on, Sarah," Mary insisted, "you do those old ballads beautifully, and you know it. Don't be shy."

"I'd ruther not," Sarah said, and her voice was barely more than a whisper.

"But I want Captain Cochrane to hear you!"

Sarah shifted her eyes across the rug to Tara's feet, and she giggled. "He's why I'd ruther not!"

Tara laughed. "Now, look, Sarah! I don't know a thing about your ballads. Just go ahead and sing them. The way you sing them will suit me fine."

Persuaded, Sarah tuned Hod's guitar and pulled a chair to

the center of the room. Her touch on the guitar was light, pulling thin shadows of chords from it, fingering an attenuated tune and losing it in the mesh of strings. Once she made up her mind to sing, she had lost her shyness and she handled her guitar easily and with poise.

"This is the 'foggy, foggy dew' song," she said. Mischievously she picked one trembling note from a string and tossed it like a stone into the pool of their attention, then she lowered her fabulously lashed eyelids and hooded the blue of her eyes from them and eased her back against the chair.

Laughter struggled to escape Tara. The girl was a consummate actress, he thought. She knew exactly how effective that modest, hooded look would be. Then when she began to sing, he amended the thought. "Why, she can sing!"

The song was plaintive, minor, amusingly doleful. About a weaver lad who loved his girl in the summer, and loved her in the winter. But all he ever, ever did was to keep her from the foggy, foggy dew! Now he had a son who looked just like the girl he had kept from the foggy, foggy dew! Sarah treated it mockingly, her voice clear, birdlike, lyrical. She let her voice move lightly from note to note, using them like steppingstones across the stream of chords from her guitar. Her eyes crinkled with hidden laughter, although she never lifted them, and at the last she drew her mouth down in a woeful parody of distress and rue.

Tara led the group in applause. He looked across the room at Mary and nodded. He had seen and heard what Mary wanted him to see and hear. What a talent the girl had!

She sang two more songs . . . the long, sad English ballad about Lord Lovel, and she made it as haunting and as full of grief as the words themselves. Heartbreak and the death of love were in each note. Then, deliberately, she shifted to a nasal whine, twanged harsh chords from the guitar, and clowned her way through the Red River Valley. Tara was

laughing helplessly by the time she had finished. Wonderful!
Wonderful!

But that was all she would sing. And when she laid the guitar
down, she slipped timidly across the room to her place in the
corner of the sofa and fixed her eyes on the floor once more.

The day was over, filled up and brimming, and the Thanksgiving family took their leave. "Hit shore was nice, Mary,"
Hattie said.

"It's been grand," said Miss Willie.

"Jist go with us," invited John Walton.

"We'd better stay here," came Hod's reply. "Thanks for
comin', everybody!"

And Tara felt like echoing the words. "Yes. Thanks. Thanks
for coming, everybody!"

It was only by accident that Tara overheard Mary and Hod
talking later. They were doing the dishes, weary now of the
day and anxious to set the house right. Tara, in scuffs that made
no noise as he went to see if he could help, heard Mary say,
"They haven't lived together since Johnnie died."

"How do you know?"

"Irma told me. She moved into the front room the day after
the funeral. John sleeps in the back room alone."

"Well, that's a fine way to do a man! And my own sister! I
thought Irma had more sense! John ought to just up and leave
her!"

The dishes rattled indignantly under his hand.

There was a splash of water as Mary slid them into the dish-
water. "They'll surely work it out. Someway. They used to be
so happy!"

Noiselessly Tara went back to his own room. In the happiness of the afternoon he'd forgotten the trouble that lay hidden.
But it was there, and Hod and Mary didn't need his help in
holding a post-mortem over it.

CHAPTER

6

I T WAS late on the Saturday afternoon after Thanksgiving that Tara went over to the village with Jory to have new tires put on his old car. "Got to get ready for winter," Jory told him. "These old tires are worn so thin they won't do anything but slip and slide when the roads get muddy."

While the tires were being put on, Tara wandered from store to store in the village, buying a little red truck for Jeems, a pair of small pliers he'd heard Hod say he needed, and a carton of cigarettes for himself. The stores were all alike. A counter down each side and one across the back. Groceries, dry goods, farm implements, feed, and a few sundries occupied the bulk of the space. But in each one he noticed that a goodly portion of the shelf space behind at least one long counter was given over to row after row of patent medicines. He looked at the names on the bottles. There they were, offering their cure-alls for stomach ailments, for headaches, for that tired, run-down feeling. For rheumatism, cuts, bruises, and burns. For heartburn, indigestion, for pains in the kidneys, the back, and the side. For every ill under the sun, he thought ironically. Hopefully people bought and tried one, and then, hope not daunted by its failure, bought and tried another. "It done me good fer a time," he heard one woman say to another, "but then seemed like hit jist got so's it made my pains worse. So I quit takin' it. I'm takin' this here now. An' hit's helpin' me a sight." The wishfulness of all humanity to find a panacea. If not this bottle, then that one there. If not golf, then swimming. If not Wisconsin, then Florida. If not the city, then the country. Around and around the mulberry bush, that elusive, perishable, fragile thing called . . . what? Life? Happiness? Peace? But anyway, it's always just one step ahead. Just out of reach. Just around one more corner.

He left the last store thinking thus futilely. Across the road was the little building that housed the White Cap clinic. One room, very small. Couldn't be much of a clinic, he thought. But if the girl who ran it was a registered nurse it was better than the bottles on the shelves. He walked over as if to go in, but he changed his mind. He didn't want to see the appurtenances of medicine just yet.

The time dragged on, and as it grew dark, the blinking, unshaded electric bulbs in the stores shed a dim, spectral glow over the counters and shelves. On Saturday night the stores stayed open until nine o'clock. Tara hoped Jory would soon be through. He had exhausted the village long ago.

Eventually the job was done, and they were headed back to the hollow. He felt tired and dispirited by the jaunt. It was such an ugly little village . . . the Gap. Its name was apropos. For it huddled down in a narrow gap between the hills, bordered on one side by a rushing stream which made it damp and cold in the winter and muggy and steamy in the summer, and by a succession of ever-narrowing farm lands stretching back up the hollow on the other side. The road split it down the middle, leading from one hill to the next. There were three or four general stores, a church, two garages, the little clinic, and a very dejected-looking small restaurant. Tara wondered who ever ate a meal there. He was very quiet on the ride home. And

Jory, probably, he thought, thinking of his Sunday's work, was quiet too.

As Jory turned the car into the road that led up the hollow, the headlights flashed briefly on a form lying in a ditch by the side of the road. Both of them saw it at once. Tara sat bolt upright. "What was that?"

Jory brought the car to a sudden stop. "Looked like a man," he said. "Bring that flashlight out of the door pocket." And he moved back down the road as he spoke.

Tara followed him with the light. Jory turned the man over and lifted him up. Tara held the light on his face. "It's Ferdy Jones," Jory said sadly, "and he's drunk again."

Ferdy's face was bloated and his breath was sour. Tara stepped back. "Oh, well. He'll sleep it off, I guess."

Jory brushed the lank hair back out of the man's face. "Cap'n, we can't leave him here. He might rouse up and wander out onto the pike and get killed. Besides, Corinna will be uneasy with him out all night. You mind if we load him into the car and take him home?"

A burr of irritation pricked at Tara. He was tired and he wanted to get on. But of course the man might come to grief, and it was Jory's car after all. "Sure," he said, "sure. Here, let me take his feet."

So they loaded him into the back of the car and Jory turned around and headed back toward the road that climbed the ridge.

The house was dark when they drove up, but a light gleamed through the windows before they had Ferdy onto the porch. "Corinna wasn't asleep," Jory said softly.

She met them at the door with the lamp. Her face was crimped and her mouth was thin and sour. "Bring him on in," she said bitterly. "Jist dump him on the bed there. I'll bed down with the kids an' he kin have it to hisself! Where'd you find him, Jory?"

"At the mouth of the hollow."

"I knowed in reason what he was up to. He's been out all day. An' I missed the walnut money outen the teapot."

"Was it very much?"

"Clost to ten dollars. Me'n' the kids has been pickin' walnuts fer two weeks to git it. Hit was to buy shoes fer the littlest 'uns." Acidly the words ate through her lips. "Reckon now they'll go barefoot a time longer!"

A bleak anger flared in her. "Why'd you bring him home? Whyn't you let him lay? Mebbe he'd of got run over by a car on the pike! Mebbe he'd of froze . . . only it ain't cold enough. Mebbe with him outen the way I could do fer these young'uns in peace!"

"Corinna!" Jory laid his hand on her arm.

She brushed at her hair with the back of her wrist. Its limpness told how tired she was. And if she wasn't pregnant, then she had a worse paunch in front than the rest of the hillwomen Tara had seen. Her shoulders sagged. "Oh, I know. Hit's a sin to talk so. But they's times when I could kill him myself! I could take a meat cleaver to him! You don't know, Jory Clark! You don't know what it's like! Workin' till yer ready to drop fer all these young'uns. An' then him atakin' ever' penny fer moonshine! Hit's enough to make a body lose their mind!"

Tara stood and watched. There were no tears in the woman's eyes, nor even in her voice. It was flat, harsh, dry, but vehement with her anger. She didn't scream the words at Jory—she pelted them at him, as if they were rocks she'd picked up from somewhere down deep in her own darkness to hurl at anyone passing by. Tara looked around him at the bleak room, the bleak, filthy, pigsty of a room, and then he looked at the sodden man sprawled on the bed, still snoring drunken bubbles from his mouth. He didn't wonder at the anger in the woman. And he thought she was right. She'd be better off if the man would die. At least she could work her fingers to the bone in peace.

Jory bent and pulled the shoes off Ferdy's feet and tugged the thin old quilt higher around his shoulders. "Will he be all right by morning?"

Corinna opened the door for them. "He'll be all right. He'll be ill an' cross-grained, but he won't miss his breakfast. He ain't never missed a meal yit!"

"We'll get the shoes for the kids, Corinna. I'll figure on it."

"Jist git me some more walnuts to pick out. I kin git the shoes. An' this time I'll hide it where he can't find it!"

"All right. I'll hustle up some more walnuts for you."

And then they said good night and drove off down the ridge. Out of their silence Tara spoke suddenly. "A guy like that ought to be shot!"

Jory sighed deeply. "Sometimes I think so too. Sometimes I wonder why the Lord doesn't strike him dead for his wickedness!"

Tara snorted. "The Lord helps those who help themselves!"

"Yes. But he also moves in mysterious ways his wonders to perform."

"Jory, you're a fool!"

A deep chuckle rumbled up from Jory's chest. "I may be, Cap'n. I may well be a fool. But the Lord isn't!"

Hod and Mary were still up when they reached the house in the hollow. An icy wind was blowing down Wishful Creek and Tara shivered when he came into the warmth of the big, comfortable room. Hod was hunched over a book by the fireplace, his pipe curling smoke wreaths around his head. Mary was at the piano, making soft music which lay gently over the room.

"Come in," Hod said, laying his book aside, "come in and close the door! Man, I think it's blowing up a norther! How was the village?"

Tara laid off his coat and hat and moved to the fireplace to warm his hands. "I wouldn't say it was doing a rushing business, but there seemed to be a right smart stirring around."

Hod shouted with laughter. "Mary, the cap'n is catching on fast to our way of talking!"

Mary smiled at both of them. "I'm going to make some coffee, if anyone is interested."

"Count me in," Tara said quickly, tasting already the good, hot strength of the brew.

"And me," Hod nodded. "See anybody we know?"

"No. Just Ferdy Jones. We picked him up drunk out of a ditch and took him home."

Hod clucked his tongue. "He's goin' to get hisself killed one of these days!"

"Saw one thing interested me a lot. Over in the village."

"What was that?"

"Enough patent medicine to stock a medicine show! People must take it by the gallon around here!"

Hod sucked on his pipe, found it dead, and lighted it again. "They do. Depend on it a heap. Any harm in it?"

Tara shrugged. "None at all sometimes. Deadly other times. Take a woman like your mother . . . stomach probably raw with ulcers. She oughtn't to be taking any of the stuff."

"She don't," Hod said quickly. "She's got that much sense anyhow."

"Why don't you run her up to the city to see a specialist, Hod?"

Hod sighed. "I wouldn't know the times we've tried to get her to go. She won't do it."

"Why? For heaven's sake, why?"

"I don't know. They can't afford it for one thing, and she knows Mary and me'd have to pay for it. Not that it would matter to us. But she wouldn't like that. And then for another thing, folks around here don't like going to strangers. If Jory

Clark ever gets his doctor settled here he's always talking about . . ."

"Is he dreaming about a doctor for the settlement?"

"Has been for a time and a time. Says the folks won't go to town in time, and won't do what the town doctors say, and if we had a man of our own here, they'd come to trust him and put their dependence in him, and a lot of 'em would maybe be treated in time. There's a lot of stomach trouble in these hills. Bound to be when all they eat is beans and corn bread. And there's a sight of t.b. Things like that need to be caught in time. Cap'n, would you take a look at Ma?"

"It wouldn't do any good, Hod. I couldn't tell anything. There'd have to be X-rays and a complete gastrointestinal. It can only be done where they have the facilities. But it ought to be done. That much I can tell you."

Hod uncrossed his legs and stretched them. "Well . . . she'll not do it, so I reckon there's nothing to be done."

Mary brought the coffee and set it on the low table in front of the fire. "You were talking about Hattie?"

"Yes. I was telling Hod he should have her see a specialist."

"And he was telling you she wouldn't."

"Have *you* tried?" Tara asked.

"Yes. She won't."

"Well . . . I could give her a diet list, and prescribe a mild sedative, perhaps. Does she have any pain?"

Mary's eyes were warning Tara, but he saw it too late. Hod was quick to answer. "Of late. She doesn't complain but little, but you can't help knowing when she's hurting."

So . . . Tara thought. And, answering Mary's warning, he said no more. They sipped their coffee and the men smoked.

Tara put his empty cup on the table and wandered across the room to the piano. He ran his hands over the keys, his fingers finding chords absently. He ran a scale, and then he said: "Could we have some music? Would it wake the baby?"

Mary came eagerly to the piano. "Of course it won't wake the baby! Get your violin and let's play some together!"

For an hour they played. Tara was a real musician. His hands which, idle, were so trembly were firm and sure on the strings, and his violin was a musician's instrument, responding richly to his touch. Mary's accompaniment was light and certain, following deftly where he led. After the first few moments Tara was lost in a world of his own making. The room and the people blurred and faded, and he stood alone, high and apart, he and his music made one, his soul singing through the strings. The notes lifted and fell, swelled and faded, and the walls of the old log room took them in and gave them back softened and mellowed.

It was a time of lonely ecstasy for Tara. Lonely, because any time he played he was always transported to that high hill of solitary awareness of beauty. Ecstasy, because music always filled him with some singing, nameless longing that went beyond joy. Then at the last Mary began the somber, beautiful notes of the *Moonlight Sonata*. She played the opening slowly and strongly, as it should be played, and then Tara took up the theme, exquisitely sustained, choosing the lower octave to give his violin the cello tone. A wild exultance ran through him. No note, he thought, no note in all of time is as beautiful as the lower G. It's like worlds turning in space. Like stars singing in the night. Like wind crying in the trees. The note sang under his bow, and obediently Mary muted the accompaniment. It's like, he thought, everything good and fine and promising and eternal and forever lasting. It's like love beating in the blood, never dying . . . and then he looked down and saw the dark wings of Mary's hair, the clear, clean line of her cheek rounding into the thinned jaw, the long, slender fingers tan against the piano keys, mobile, gentle, useful. His bow faltered as his heart skipped a beat, and the breath in his chest drew in harshly. Suddenly he couldn't bear this beauty they were making together. Only love should make such beauty. Only love should make it and hear it and share it. They were trespassing on love. And then he knew that he, Tara Cochrane, was not trespassing on love. He, at least, was not. It was singing all through him, through the strings under his fingers, through the bow bent under his hand.

When he faltered, Mary looked up quickly, questioningly. The lamp laid a golden light over her upturned face, broadening its planes, deepening its shadows, sparking golden glints from her eyes, and Tara felt all his strength drain weakly down his body to his knees, and felt them quiver and tremble under him. He felt a wild, crazy yearning to throw aside his violin and his bow, and to kneel and lay his face against the one lifted in question.

Mary smiled and turned back to the music before her. The moment passed. With the greatest effort of will, Tara swept his bow across the strings in a recovery of the theme, renewing its depth and richness, strongly sustaining it to the end when its beautiful, exquisite sadness lingered even after the last note had died away. Then he let his bow fall limply to his side.

"Beautiful," Mary said softly, "beautiful. Nothing else tonight, now. Nothing else, after that."

"No," Tara agreed, and he laid his violin on top of the piano. He picked up his coat and hat from the couch where he had left them and went toward his room. At the door he turned. "Thanks, Mary. Many thanks."

But when he closed the door behind him, he leaned wearily against it. Thanks, he thought bitterly. Many thanks!

CHAPTER

7

H E UNDRESSED slowly, every motion made with an effort. He let his clothes lie where they fell, although he was as a rule precise and meticulous about his clothes. He got into his pajamas, found his robe and tied it about him. Then he walked over to the fireplace.

The room had grown chilly as the fire on the hearth had died down during the evening. The backlog was almost burned through. Mechanically, he pulled it forward with the tongs and heaved a new log into place. Then he drew up a chair, pulling it close to the hearth. He propped his chin in his hands and watched the flames catch on the new log. The flames took on form and shape, and they were Mary's face, upturned, questioning; her eyes, glinting in the lamplight, depths of green veined with gold; her hair, dark, smooth, drawn back from the broad band of her forehead; her hands, slender, long-fingered, browned, quick-moving, light-touching. He groaned and reached for a cigarette.

All I need, he thought wearily, all I need to make this misery complete, is to fall in love with Hod Pierce's wife! That will make it just perfect! That will complete the whole vicious circle of frustration! He lighted the cigarette and flicked the match in the fireplace. I ought to get out of here, he thought. Ought to get out right now, before any harm is done!

Then his mind went as sour as vinegar. Some people have all the luck! Here is Hod Pierce with everything he wants in life . . . a home, Mary for his wife, a youngster . . . his whole life settled and safe stretching out ahead of him. No turmoil, no torment, no inner strife. Nerves like steel, peace of mind, happiness. How does it happen to a guy? Why can't it happen to me? Why can't I control these jittering nerves, these palsied hands, this bleakness that settles over my mind? This everlasting feeling of futility! Why isn't there someone like Mary for me? Why do I run all over the face of the earth, escaping one dark time only to exchange it for another? How am I different, and what have I done?

As he searched himself, Tara Cochrane went back through the years to his childhood. His mother and father were divorced when he was ten—old enough to feel the loss of his father, old enough to know the insecurity of living with his mother in hotel after hotel, old enough to hate the other men who had trailed after her, but too young to understand any of it.

His mother, Lossie Cochrane, had been a beautiful woman, spoiled by too much money, a husband who had at first adored then ignored her, and an empty and idle life. She had not been a bad woman; she had been simply a bored one.

Her husband had been a quiet, introspective man, interested only briefly in his beautiful wife. Inheriting his money, he had had to give no thought to earning more, so he had immersed himself in his studies. He wrote better than average poetry, which he never troubled to have published, but his great love was history. Tara could remember his father's library, the high-reaching shelves of books, the wide, cluttered desk, and he could remember, also, the immolation of his father within that library. "Your father is studying," his mother would warn him, when the door was closed, and Tara had memories of the tall, studious man bent over his desk, with maps spread all about him and volumes of heavy books stacked near.

For years John Cochrane had been working patiently on a history of the Aztec Indians. Frequently he was away on long trips to lower Mexico and Central America, doing research on the book he was writing. It never seemed to progress very far, but he was constantly at work on it. Perhaps this concern with the exotic, the beautiful, in history, explained the attraction the young and beautiful Lossie had had for him. Whatever it was, it hadn't lasted long, and when it faded in disillusionment, he had closed himself in his study, climbed back into his ivory tower, and refused steadfastly to be drawn into the mad race of the social life which Lossie required.

Tara could not remember ever feeling very close to his father. The relationship between them had always been thin, tenuous, only faintly outlined. There was his mother's constant warning, "Your father is busy," and there were only his father's infrequent and shy attempts to talk with him to offset them.

Thin as the relationship was, however, it had sufficed to round out a family feeling for Tara. An orthodox, traditional feeling. There was his father, remote, engrossed in study, closed off, but still his father. There was his mother, beautiful, young, gay, and exciting. And there was himself, timid, shy, sensitive, and bookish. The three points of the triangle framed his world. He knew no other, and found nothing wrong with what he knew. Thus when his mother took the easy way by divorce to new adventures, new excitements, new loves, Tara had felt uprooted, lost, insecure. One point of the triangle, however fragile it had been, was now missing, and he felt its loss. The frame was weakened. He had gone with his mother, naturally.

She had left her husband, still young and vital, and had dragged her small son from one resort to another, smothering him with love and attention at times and neglecting him at others. She had asked little of him except that he be well-behaved, well-dressed, unobtrusive when she didn't want him around, and lovingly attentive when she did. He had learned

early to sense her moods, and because she was all that was left
of the familiar frame of his life, he had set himself always to
make her happy with him. Eagerly, wanting desperately to be
loved, wanting to satisfy her, wanting to fill his life with the
only thing that offered itself to him, he had made himself into
what she wanted him to be. He had been by nature a charm-
ing, courteous, thoughtful child, and he deliberately cultivated
the things in himself that brought approbation from her.

When he had been sent, at fourteen, to military school he
had accepted it without question, for Lossie had told him it was
best for him. She wanted him to make the Army his career. She
could see him at West Point, handsome, attractive in the uniform, manly in his bearing. She could see herself, still young
and lovely, the center of an admiring group of his friends and
classmates. Frequently she dreamed of his graduation, and the
honors that would be his, and always she was at the heart and
center of it.

The years at school he had lived through as best he could,
always looking forward to the holidays with his mother. One
great fear had lived with him: that in his absence from her,
without him to guard her, she might meet some man and be
sufficiently drawn to him to marry again. He didn't think he
could bear that. Wherever she was, men gathered around her,
but she liked to draw Tara to her side and laughingly tell them
that he was her best beau! That she would never find a man
who could take his place! He was terribly afraid during his
school years that she might forget that, and he didn't think he
would be able to live if she married again. He was deeply
jealous of any man who gained her attention beyond the
ordinary, and he had suffered through her spasmodic and oc-
casional light loves anxiously and achingly.

The truth was that Lossie Cochrane had no intention of
marrying again. She was much too selfish to give up her free-
dom and independence, to take on new responsibilities, to tie

herself to one man on whose whims she would have to wait, whose advice she would have to heed, and whose demands she would have to meet. She loved her own way of life too much. There was money enough for comfort and ease, even for luxury, and it was much too satisfying to gather her own small court around her, to dress beautifully, to travel leisurely, to lay her affections lightly on first this man then that one. But she had liked to threaten Tara coquettishly with marriage.

When he displeased her, she would smile sweetly at him and say lightly: "It isn't wise of you to be difficult, dear. Mother may not be entirely yours always. There *may* come a time when you must please another person too. I have been seriously thinking that you really need a father. Sometimes you almost get out of hand!"

And she would sigh, and Tara would fling himself into her arms and promise not to be difficult again. "Only don't marry, Mother! I don't need a father, Mother. Truly I don't. I'll not be difficult any more. Let's just stay the two of us, always!"

He had not gone to West Point after all. Shortly after he had finished the years in the military school, during the summer when he was just eighteen, he and his mother had been traveling to the west coast. The car was new and he was driving. Very fast, on a wide, flat Texas highway. They were very gay and happy over their plans for the summer. They were talking, lightly, amusingly, about some of the people they would see, when, without warning, a front tire blew out and the car careened out of control. Tara had been too inexperienced a driver to know how to manage the wild, plunging car, and it had gone over the end of a culvert, turning end over end three times. His mother had been gravely hurt and had lain for weeks in a Dallas hospital. Her spine had been injured, and she never again walked without help.

Strangely, Tara had not been hurt except for scratches and bruises. But because he had been driving he never forgot that he had almost killed his mother . . . and in her own sweet, affectionate way she never let him forget it. She allowed him to put aside every plan they had made for his future and to devote himself entirely to her. She spoke of it often to her friends. Of his unselfishness, of his tirelessness, of his adoring solicitude. "Poor boy," she would say gently, "he feels so badly about the accident. He blames himself entirely too much. He never thinks of anyone but his mother. Never even looks at another girl!"

Not once in the six years she lived after the accident had he left her side, and when finally she died, still assuring him that it had not been his fault, still absolving him of all blame for it, he had gone almost crazy with his grief and feeling of guilt.

But her death had done one thing. It had released him to do the thing he wanted to do. All his life he had wanted to be a doctor. He had never said so. He had accepted military school, and West Point to follow, because that was what his mother had wanted for him, and he was too keenly aware of the necessity for pleasing her to go against her wishes. So he had never mentioned it at all. Never. Not to anyone. But when she died, he was determined to study medicine.

It was wonderful, and at the same time it was terrible. For so attuned was he to his mother's desires that even after her death he felt a heavy burden of guilt to be doing what he wanted to do, rather than what she wanted him to do. He never really got away from that feeling of guilt. And there were times when he felt it so deeply that he thought he must give it up.

One of those times had come when the war began. Lossie would have wanted him to go into the Army. As a matter of fact, had her plans for him worked out, had he not crippled and finally killed her, he would have been an officer by now, a graduate of West Point, and on active duty automatically.

So, although he was deferred, he had enlisted immediately and had thrown himself into it with all his heart . . . to appease . . . to assuage . . . to atone. And he had liked the

Army, partly because he could finally lay aside his burden of guilt, and partly because its precision, its organization, its regimentation, appealed to him. It had taken over his problems and solved them for him by keeping him busy, by leaving him no time to think, by giving him a purpose he need not figure out for himself. In truth he had a talent for the Army. His years in military school had seen to that.

It was while he was in officers' training school that he had met Edith Towner. She looked very much like his mother had looked. The same fair masses of hair, deep blue eyes, thin white skin. The same sweet, light, affectionate ways, the same clinging to him, which he so much missed. She had not stirred him particularly deeply, but he had thought he loved her. He had felt protective toward her, as he had done toward his mother, loving her helplessness and wanting to give her happiness and safety.

When he had gone overseas, she had written him faithfully at first, long plaintive letters, missing him, longing for him, grudging his absence, fearing for him, hating the war. He had seen nothing wrong with her letters. They were the kind he had received from his mother all during his school years, lightly chiding, strongly binding.

But it was during his time overseas that something had been drawn up out of him. That guarding protectiveness that he had felt first for his mother, then for Edith, had transferred itself to his men. It was manifested in a tough concern for them, a hardened, steeled sense of responsibility for them. This plus his talent for the Army made a good officer out of him. Unbearably sensitive always to beauty, he had learned to live with ugliness, drawing the beauty his soul needed out of the brotherhood of his men. He had been a reckless, tough, tireless officer . . . strong where strength was needed, reliable where dependability was needed, brave where courage was needed.

He had not known where the sources of these things were in

him. Had he thought of it then, he would have given the credit to his mother. For, remembering her long years of invalidism, he thought of her as one of the bravest persons he had ever known. He had no reason ever to know the tensile, stubborn strength of his father. His mother had taken good care that he should not know it.

During the last year he was overseas he had known he and Edith were drifting apart. When he tried to summon up concern over it, he had not been able. He thought he was too tired, too exhausted and fatigued, to feel any other emotion, and even when he returned and they broke their engagement, he had felt nothing more than relief that his obligation to her was ended. It never occurred to him that something in his overseas years had broken his bondage to the type of woman she was. He only knew that Edith bored him, that he was grateful to her for releasing him, and that life, in general, had little to offer him now.

The war over, he had gone stubbornly back to medical school. He was beginning to have a little knowledge of himself now. Not much, but a little. Uncomfortably he found that instead of thinking fondly of his mother and remembering with affection their years together, he was putting her more and more out of his mind. Only by not thinking of her at all could he dig into the hard work that lay ahead of him. Only by not thinking of her could he exorcise the ghost of her displeasure with him. Only by not thinking of her could he find any purpose for his life.

He had finished medical school, had served his internship, and had been practicing two years in a fairly good city on the west coast. But almost as soon as he had set up his practice, he had been struck down. And he had had to take the memories of his mother and of his life with her out of hiding and look at them. He had had to face the fact that he had never loved his mother at all. That she had never loved him. That, instead, there lay between them the most devastating hate, and that it had carried over even beyond her grave for him. Anxiety, guilt, and fear. They had lived with him too long. Oh, yes. He had good insight into his problems now. He knew what had caused them. And it did him no good. He would rather, he knew, go back into the thralldom of his memories than to face the emptiness of the present truth. If he could! If only he could have gone on fooling himself!

Not once since his mother took him away from the tall brick house that set well back from the sea had he seen his father. Not for years had he even thought of him. Actually he did not know where he was, or even if he was still living. His mother had carefully sponged every thought of John Cochrane out of her son's mind.

Then Hod had found him in the hospital. He was at this ragged end of the rope, and he had not known with what hopelessness he had snatched at any way out of it. Now, here he was. This was Tara Cochrane!

And here was this sudden, startling uprush of emotion for Mary. What was he to do with it? He hovered his hands over the flames of the fire, feeling cold and chilled and as if he would never again be warm. The form and the shape in the flames were gone now. He began to rationalize. I don't know the woman, he thought. I don't know a thing about her actually, except that she's Hod Pierce's wife. That she's warm and human and sensitive to beauty. A guy doesn't just fall in love like that!

He remembered how she had looked walking down the corridor of the hospital that day . . . tall, slender, straight. Walking with that free and easy grace that was so much a part of her, and how he had thought her beautiful even then before he had known who she was. Well, he told himself, you've seen dozens of women walking freely and easily with that same kind of grace. Hundreds of women possess it. Mary Pierce doesn't have a monopoly on it. You've seen it and appreciated it before.

That means nothing. Any man likes to see a woman walk
beautifully.

He thought of the other things he knew of her. Her obvious
love for Hod. Her gentleness with the baby. Her understanding
of Jory. He summoned up the daily pictures of her around the
house . . . the clean neatness of her dress, the quick, efficient
way she went about her work, the warm response she made to
any person near her. He remembered her sympathy . . . even
her pity that day in the kitchen when he had broken down. And
he shook off the memories impatiently.

What am I trying to do, he thought, catalogue her? What
difference does it make? So she's loyal and thoughtful! So she's
lovely to look at! So she's gentle with Hod and tender with her
baby! So she loves music and plays the *Moonlight Sonata* with
me! So what! She's still another man's wife! And she's not for
me!

Abruptly he got up and flung his robe off and got into bed.
He made a great effort to lay his thoughts aside. But it was another white night.

It was strange, he thought, that it should be the very next
morning that Mary asked him about himself. No one had asked
questions before. Hod was outside, and Mary and Tara were
sitting by the fire, Mary sewing and Tara watching the flames
moodily. There was no contentment in it for him, and he was
thinking he'd better get out, wondering how to say it, when
Mary spoke. "Tara, tell me about yourself. Where were you
born? What were your parents like? How were you reared?"

So he told her. She drew him on until she had his whole
story . . . all the facts. How his father had been a scholar and
a poet. How his mother had divorced him and what his life had
been like with her. Even the truth about Edith and the flatness
of their parting. He left out none of the facts. But he told
nothing more.

"And you've never seen your father since?" she asked when he had done.

"No."

"Haven't you even wanted to?"

"No."

Mary folded her sewing and rose. "What a pity!"

"Why?"

She looked at him quietly. "I think your father must have been a man well worth knowing. And I think you've lost a great deal by not knowing him."

Tara flushed. "He never bothered to know me!" He stood restlessly. "Yes, he must have been quite a man. Well worth knowing, as you say."

Mary passed him on the way to the kitchen. "It's time for Jeems to come in. Will you get him for me?"

CHAPTER

8

H<small>E DIDN'T</small> leave. He was indecisive and vacillating in his
moods, one day determining to get out, the next deciding
no harm would come of staying. So he stayed. But for a few
days he kept pretty much to himself. He didn't want to be
around Hod and Mary. Especially in the evenings when there
was such a family feeling in the big room, with Mary on one
side of the fire and Hod on the other. It made him feel extra,
unneeded, unwanted. So he stayed in his own room those
nights. He never had to explain anything to them, but for some
reason he felt he must explain this hibernation. "Got an article
to do for a medical journal," he told them. "Been putting it off as
long as I can. I'm digging into it."

It got by. He wasn't sulking, he told himself. He was just
getting used to this new thing. He'd been feeling better. Now
he was thrown back down in the pit again. He'd have to think
it through. That's what he told himself. And he built up the fire
in his own room and sat, lonely, before it.

One night he had been sitting there, glooming, when the
room began to feel chilly to him. He glanced at the wood box
and then he swore softly. He'd forgotten to bring in any wood.
He stepped out into the night, around the corner of the house
to the woodpile.

A new moon, silver-sickled in the sky, hung thin and frigid over the rim of the ridge. Like a crescent of boreal and illuminated frost, its curved ends tapered to the barely visible wire of the full circle and pointed, hornlike, to the shape of completion. The stars were far away and cold, distant in time and light, iced, frozen, and unsparkling. They were like diamonds in their purity and in their hardness, small pin points of light caught and held, transfixed in atmospheric cold. There was frost in the air, and when Tara stepped on the grass, it crackled underfoot. It was December, and winter had set in, casing and hardening the earth with layer on layer of cold.

He took a deep breath of the thin air and gulped its sharpness down inside him. Suddenly he had a wish not to go back inside his room, not to sit housebound on such a night, brooding over a fire. He wanted, instead, to walk briskly, quickly, under the new moon and the indifferent stars. Walk with long strides down the hollow, filling himself with the frost-laden air. Why not walk down to Jory's? He had not yet been inside Jory's cabin. This would be a good night to go. Jory would make him welcome, he knew.

He went inside to get his coat and hat, and, opening the door into the adjoining room, he called to Hod and Mary that he was going down to Jory's. He slipped on the warm, lined jacket left from the war years, and closed the door behind him.

The tang of the air bit at him immediately, and he flung his head up, taking the frostiness full in the face. It felt good, clean, cold against his skin, and the blood swiftened in his veins and pulsed strongly in his throat. He stepped off the distance rapidly and covered the mile and a half within twenty-five minutes. Not bad, he thought, for a guy soft from illness and easy living! Time was when he could have done it in less . . . but even so he had raised a tingle in his toes and fingers and his breath came hurriedly.

Jory's cabin stood at the mourth of the hollow, where Wishful

Creek swelled and gentled and flowed more serenely toward the river. It was a tiny cabin, hugging the foot of the last, rounding hill of the ridge. Jory had one acre of ground with it, which he had bought from Hod, and on this he raised most of his food and kept his one cow and little flock of chickens. When he had become a minister of the White Caps, he had built this cabin and moved into it to live alone.

There was a light in the cabin, and when Tara knocked, Jory came to the door. He flung it wide. "Why, Cap'n! Come in, come in! Something wrong up at Hod's?"

"No. Everything's fine as far as I know. I got restless and decided to go for a walk. Thought you'd make me welcome."

"That I will," Jory said gladly. "That I will. Take off your jacket. Let me build up the fire and put a pot of coffee on!"

Tara laid off his jacket and looked around curiously. The cabin was plain and monklike. It allowed its occupant no luxuries. There was a bunk built in one corner, with a shelf nearby to hold a lamp and books. There was the hearth and a table and two chairs. On shelves near the hearth were a few dishes and some pieces of cutlery. But the hearth itself held all Jory's cooking utensils—an oven, a long-handled skillet, a pot to be swung on a crane. Evidently Jory Clark lived very austerely, Tara thought.

"Were you busy, Jory?" he asked, looking at the books on the table. He walked over and picked one of them up. It was the Augustine *Confessions*. He laid it down.

"Just got in a minute ago." He spooned coffee into the old gray granite pot, filled it with water, and swung it over the fire on its crane.

"Read a lot?"

"Pretty much. Of evenings."

Tara looked at the *Confessions* again. "Jory, where were you educated?"

Jory straightened from the fire and smiled at him, his face

red from the heat. "Wasn't. Not what you'd called educated. I went to the Big Springs school as far as the eighth grade . . . like most the other ridge kids. Never thought about going further. But I had a lot of time in the Army . . . spare time. I was in the ground force of the Air Corps and work came in fits and starts. The chaplain loaned me some books to read, and got me started studying. And I took some of those Army courses . . . English, history, literature. Didn't amount to much, but they sort of straightened me out on my grammar and gave me an idea of what I'd been missing. I've kept up some kind of reading and studying ever since."

"And you like Saint Augustine?"

"I don't to say like him. I don't actually understand him most of the time. But when I do . . . it's . . . it's, well, it's like a bright star shining. Clear and clean and white."

"Yes."

"That's the superintendent's there. But I'm going to get me a copy as soon as I can. Have you had supper yet?"

"Long ago. Haven't you?"

"I've been over to Ferdy Jones's place. Just got back. You care if I fix me up a bite? I'm pretty hungry."

"Go ahead. Pour me a cup of that coffee, though. What's wrong over at Ferdy's? Drunk again?"

Jory set food out on the table and pulled up his chair. He nodded.

"What do you bother with them for? What can you do for them? People like that will always be a drag on society. They ought to be exterminated!"

Jory had the cup of coffee halfway to his mouth. It poised there and he looked at Tara over the rim. "You talk like they were animals."

Aren't they? Not even as clean as some animals. Dirty . . . soiled with living. That house was like a pigsty, and they were like hogs living in it! Lying in their own filth, rooting in it, living on swill!"

Jory set his cup down. "You sure don't mince words."

"Why mince words? If it's there to be seen, it's there. Why ignore it? Why whitewash it? I say people like that have no business in the world. They go on breeding more people like themselves. More Jukes and Kallikaks. More filth and disease and dirt and shame. The world would be better off without them!"

"But what about them? You've condemned them for the world's sake. What about their own sake? You don't give them anything to live for!"

"What have they got to live for? They're so far down they'll never come up! I haven't condemned them. They've condemned themselves. I've just told the truth about them!"

"The truth . . . without mercy, and without hope!"

"Truth isn't necessarily merciful. Neither is it necessarily hopeful . . . for the individual. Truth is merely truth. Abstract, logical, reasonable."

"But people are more than animals! They live and suffer and feel things. People aren't abstract. They love and they get married and they have kids and love their kids. They aren't logical. Most times they don't make sense. But they hope and they dream and they work and they hurt and they fail. And they die."

"What dreams did Ferdy Jones ever have? What hopes? Beyond filling his belly and avoiding work and sleeping with his wife? How much does he love her, or his kids?"

Jory wiped his mouth. "I don't know, Cap'n. But he must have. When he was young, maybe. When him and Corinna was first married. What do we know of him? How can we say what he dreamed and wanted? Or what happened to him? And maybe started him drinking when it happened. They're people, anyways. And they need help and they need love."

Tara spoke with heat. "How can you love the kind of people they are?"

Jory shook his head stubbornly. "Well, I can. I don't look at the kind of people they are. All I see is what they need. There's nobody who doesn't need love. I don't mean the kind of love that's between a man and woman, nor even the kind that's in families. But . . . the kind that sort of spreads out from one person to another, and lets 'em know that no matter what they've done, or what they are, or how they live . . . no matter what, they're still worth loving. You take love away, and there's nothing left. Someone's got to let folks know they're important. Everyone's important. Everyone's worth something. And worth saving. And I don't know of but one way to save folks . . . and that's to love them . . . and to let them know they're loved."

"Are you talking about saving them for the Church now?"

"No! I'm talking about saving them for themselves! Saving them for the good that's inside of them! Saving them for usefulness! Saving them for another chance!"

"And can you go around spreading that kind of love everywhere?"

"No. But I can go around spreading it up Wishful Hollow and the ridge! I can go around spreading it on Hod and Mary Pierce, and Hattie and Tom, and Becky and Gault, and Ferdy Jones and Corinna!"

"Don't forget me," Tara said softly.

"I'm not. You've got your share. A big, big share too."

Tara blinked. Unreasonably his eyes were pricked with wetness. This guy. This guy that believed all this about love! But for some reason it made him feel good to know some of it was for him. And it embarrassed him. He stood up. "Finish your supper. All right, Ferdy Jones is worth saving. But you'll get no thanks for your pains."

"Why should you want thanks?"

Tara shook his head. "I'd better go. We're miles apart." He picked up his jacket.

"Wait a minute," Jory said, "I'm through. I'll walk piece the way with you," and he pulled an old cap over his ears and took a leather Air Force jacket off its peg.

The moon was down and the night was dark, but strangely enough it seemed warmer to Tara. Perhaps the lack of that frosted moon in the sky made it feel warmer, or perhaps it was the closeness of the dark. They walked along, silent for the most part, but it was a comfortable silence, in spite of their disagreement.

They were about halfway home when they saw the flash of a light through the woods, and then they heard the yelp of a dog. "Hod must be going hunting," Jory said.

"I'd like to go!" Tara said.

"So would I!" And Jory lifted up his voice. "Hey, Hod! Can you take two more?"

Hod's voice came back at once. "Sure. Come on."

They caught up with him where he waited in a clearing, the dogs milling around him. "Thought there might be a coon or possum out tonight," he said when they came up.

"Might be," Jory agreed. And they climbed the far side of the ridge, the dogs sniffing, yelping, circling ahead of them. They followed where the dogs led, down another hollow and across a stream. Across the stream the dogs suddenly ceased their milling and sniffing and took off up the hollow, their voices bugling, excited, eager, high, and free.

"They've trailed," Hod yelled, and he forged ahead into the dark, his flashlight beaming a short path before him. Tara and Jory stretched their legs to follow.

It was rough going, through thickets, up the steep hillsides and down them again. Saw briers and dry blackberry canes cut across the way, and often they clambered heavily over rocks and ledges. The dogs stayed out in front, their voices distant and thin. They came out on another ridge top, circled an abandoned field now high with brush and broom sedge, climbed an old stone wall, and then pitched steeply down the other side of the ridge. Tara's legs began to waver, and his breath hurt in his throat. He wondered how much more of this wild chase he could take!

At the bottom of the hill the dogs followed a stream that cut narrowly down the floor of a boxed ravine opening off to the right. So narrow was the canyon that there was no room for a path on either side of the stream. The men, perforce, took to the stream bed itself. Thickets closed in around them, hanging dried and deadened over the narrow creek. Logs choked the stream and they climbed over them, slipping and sliding. Tara had the feeling that they were climbing, that the ascent of the creek here was very sharp. Then they clambered up over a small rockfall and came out in a wide, circular level.

When Tara had pulled himself up over the fall, he came up to Hod and Jory, who had stopped. The dogs had stopped too. They huddled close around Hod's feet, whining, whimpering, growling.

"Have they lost the trail?" Tara asked.

Hod flashed his beam all around. From its reflection Tara could see the puzzled look on his face. "I don't know. I never saw them act like this before. Jory, do you know where we are?"

Jory took the flashlight and made a circle of the clearing. "I never saw this ravine before, Hod. Didn't even know it was here. That was Bear Hollow we came up the main stream, wasn't it?"

"Yeah. I thought I knew every inch of it. I've hunted Bear Hollow and the Springer spur of Sawtooth all my life!"

"So've I. But I sure never saw this ravine before."

Hod moved restlessly. "Don't reckon we could both be wrong."

"I wouldn't think so, though places look different at night. But that opening is so narrow and so clogged with thickets we must have missed it times without number." Jory laughed. "I could have swore there wasn't a hill or a hollow within ten miles of home I didn't know!"

"I'd have gone you one better than that! I'd have laid money on it! Doggone, it sure gives you a funny feeling!"

One of the dogs suddenly lifted up his voice in a long-drawn-out wail, a wail that was like the cry of a lost soul keening down the wind, high, sustained, haunted. Tara felt the hairs rise on the back of his neck and a swift shudder shook his spine.

The other dogs stirred uneasily about Hod's feet, crouching warily against him, their voices whimpering in their throats. "Shut up, Coon!" Hod barked shortly. "What in tarnation's got into these dogs!"

"They hear or smell something we don't, Hod," Jory said, "you know a dog . . ." but the sentence hung suspended in mid-air, uncompleted. Out of the night around them came the sound of a bell. It sounded far away, timeless in the distance, tinkly and thin. On the clear, cold air it carried distinctly, a high, silvery tone, lifted as light as the frost and as brittle. It had a ghostly sound, unreal, otherworldly. It tinkled and at the same time it tolled. The sound was evenly spaced. Three times it tinkled, then it paused. Three times and another pause. Three times and another pause. Tara's flesh pimpled along his arms and his knees grew weak under him. "Let's get out of here," he whispered.

"Wait," Hod said, putting out his hand. "Jory! What is it?"

Jory was listening. "Sounds like a sheep bell."

Hod let out a long breath. "Why, sure. We're beyond Sawtooth, and some of the folks over this way raise sheep. Likely one has wandered off and got lost."

"Yes," Jory said.

They turned to go then, making their way with difficulty

back down over the fall and along the stream. The bell was quiet now. "Just a lamb, or an old ewe wandering around," Hod said again.

The dogs had struck out swiftly down the stream, silent and shadowy. Jory laughed. "Those dogs are sure glad to get away from there," he said.

"Ain't they, though," Hod agreed. "They didn't like that place at all!"

"Neither did I!" Tara was emphatic.

And then the bell tinkled again. Nearer this time, clearer. Three times and then a pause. Three times. A pause. The men stopped and listened. Hod turned his light off. The bell stopped. No one spoke. They waited, not knowing for what they waited, their breathing quiet, their ears sharp. The dark was close around them, still, quivering, empty. "Jory!" Hod said suddenly, his voice coming as if it had been punched out of him, "I know where we are now!"

"Where?"

"Bethel graveyard's up on top that ridge to the left! It's just on beyond that level. That's why the dogs behaved like they'd lost their senses!"

"Why, sure!" Jory said, and Tara could hear the relief in his words. "Sure!"

Tara's teeth were chattering, and he knew it wasn't entirely the cold that was shaking him with such a clammy ague. "The bell?" he said, "what about the bell?"

"Oh, it's just a sheep bell," Hod answered. But Tara knew he was evading any talk of the bell. "Come on. Let's go."

He whistled for the dogs, but they were gone. He flashed his light on again and they started down the stream. The bell tinkled immediately, and its tone was urgently nearer. "I never thought there was anything to that old story," Hod said, but he didn't pause. He led the way hurriedly, and the others followed in equal haste. They scurried down the stream bed, fighting rocks, the thickets, the down logs, and the bell tinkled behind them, urging them on, hurrying them. Every step of the way down the narrow, boxed ravine the bell followed them. Three times and a pause. Three times. A pause. Clear, silvery, brittle, its tinkling sound accompanied them until they came out in the main hollow. Then it left them. And the silence that followed was a great, gaping hole in the night! Tara found himself still hearing it, but when he listened, it was gone. It had vanished entirely, the sound, the ghost bell, the following tinkle. It was gone.

They stopped then. And Hod frankly wiped off the sweat that had poured out on his face. Jory ran his sleeved arm across his forehead and pushed his cap back. Tara leaned against a tree, trembling, weak, scared so badly that the tree shook with him. "Now," he said when he could finally control his voice, "what's it all about?"

"You tell him, Jory," Hod said. He pulled out his cigarettes and lighted one shakily. Tara took one too.

"Well," Jory said, "there's an old story about a belled hant. I reckon it's nearly as old as Hod and me. Way it's told is, there were two brothers thought a lot of each other all their lives. Might' near inseparable, they were. Then they had a falling out. Wouldn't speak to one another. And finally one of them killed the other, and then killed himself. They were buried side by side up there in Bethel graveyard. And not long after, folks passing late of a night heard a bell. A bell that sounded like a sheep bell. And it would follow them until they got out of sight of the graveyard. Nobody ever liked to go near there at night. Folks said it was the ghost of the one did the killing, grieving over his sin, condemned to wear a bell, haunting the graveyard. But there's nothing to it, of course. Just an old story."

"Of course there's nothing to it," Tara said grimly. "We never heard any bell, did we? There's not a thing in the world to it!"

"Well, there's not!" Hod said hotly. "I don't believe in ghosts, do you?"

"No," Tara said, "I don't believe in ghosts! But I sure as Christmas heard that bell. And I believe in bells when I hear them!"

Jory's voice was quieter. "There's some simple explanation for it. There has to be. We're reasonable men. We *know* there's no belled hant. We ought to go back and find out!"

Tara snorted. "*You* can go back if you want to! Me, I'm putting just as much distance as possible between me and this place! That thing scared the living daylights out of me and I'm not making any bones about it!"

Hod and Jory laughed. They confessed that they didn't feel any too good about it, and they said nothing more about going back to investigate. They took up their way down the main hollow. Each kept his thoughts to himself, and silence lay heavily over them. They didn't see the dogs again. "They've lit a shuck," Hod said. "They'll be at home when we get there."

And they were, bedded down and quiet.

Mary met the three men at the door. "It's your mother, Hod," she said. "She's had a hemorrhage."

CHAPTER

9

Hod's glance flew to Tara. "I'll go, Hod," Tara promised and his mind instantly canvassed possibilities. He cursed himself for ever having come off without his bag. With nothing. Man oughtn't even to go into the hospital without it. "Mary?" he asked questioningly.

"No," she said quietly, "Becky's with her, and Irma's coming. I'll stay here with the baby."

Hod backed the old Ford out and the three men crawled into it. "I've been afraid of this," Hod said.

"If we just had a doctor of our own out here," Jory said. "Our folks won't go into town until it's too late oftentimes. And the doctors don't know their way of living. If a doctor lived here . . . knew the folks and understood them . . ."

"That's just a foolish daydream of yours, Jory," Tara said sharply. "You can't get a good doctor to come back here in these hills and practice! Be realistic! The man would have to live, wouldn't he? And the settlement's so scattered he couldn't make a living. Even if you found someone willing to bury himself out here!"

"I know," Jory admitted. "He'd have to love the hill folks more than money. He'd have to be a missionary in more than one sense."

"You'll never find a man willing to do it!"

"If it's the Lord's will, the man will be found," Jory answered quietly. "I never cease thinking about it . . . and praying about it."

They were quiet then, and Tara felt the quick prick of irritation that Jory sometimes aroused in him. The man was so full of ideals. So impractical. His head was up in the clouds when he talked like this! No doctor was going to give up a chance of a good practice in town and come out here and bury himself in these hills. That was as plain as the nose on your face. People didn't do things like that! Every man was out for himself, and the hill people could get along the best way they could. Money was what talked nowadays, and not even Jory could say that a man could make money ministering to the hill people. Why, the guy would starve! But this impractical, visionary man kept hoping. And the hope ran a stab of exasperation through Tara. He hated to see people blind themselves to reality.

When they drew up in front of Hattie's, light was streaming from the windows. Becky let them in. "I'm shore glad you've come," she whispered to Hod. "She's bad off, I'm afeared."

Tara looked curiously at the dwarfed, shriveled little woman who stood aside to let them pass. Her clothes hung from her shoulders like a bag, scarcely touching her anywhere. Her head, with straight, coarse hair slicked tightly back over her ears, was small and set like a hard, round ball on her neck. Her eyes were beady and sharp. Becky! Tara had heard about her. She was Hod's aunt, having married his father's brother, Gault. Long years they had been married, and remained childless. Becky had worn rusty black garments and had gone through her days like a shadow, grieving over her barrenness, hiding herself in guilt. No one knew why. And then Matt Jasper, a feeble-minded epileptic, had gone crazy one day and had killed his wife, leaving a house full of children and a new baby. He had died after his fit of insanity, and the children were left both motherless and fatherless. The older children had been parceled out among relatives, but Becky had asked for the baby and had got it. And a great change had been wrought in her.

Hannah was two now. And Becky lived and breathed and had her being in the child. She left off her black dresses, ceased her grieving, and her voice was lifted in song. This was Becky who opened the door to them.

Hod went straight to his mother's bedside, where his father sat. Hattie lifted her great, haunted eyes to him. "Ma," he said, and she reached out her hand.

Hod spoke then to his father. "Can she be moved?"

"We've sent fer the doctor," Tom replied. "Gault went. Best wait an' see what he says, Son."

"I'm sorry I wasn't at home."

"You couldn't be knowin'." Tom's voice was gentle . . . without blame.

"What happened?" Hod asked then.

"She waked up from her first sleep, chokin' an' gaggin'. I heared her, natural, an' come an' lit the lamp. She was all over blood, an' the bed, so I knowed hit was bad. When hit sort of let up, like, I went fer Becky, her bein' the clostest. Then when she come, I went fer you. When I got home from yore house, Gault said he'd go. He's jist went. Reckon they's nothin' to do now but wait."

"I brought the cap'n," Hod said, and he motioned to Tara.

"I clean fergot the cap'n was a doctor," Tom said. "Not used to havin' none handy. Wisht we hadn't of sent now."

"It's just as well," Tara said. "I haven't a thing with me. Nothing. But I'll ask a few questions and take a look at her if you want me to."

"Wisht you would."

They stood back and let Tara sit by the bed.

When he had finished, Hod asked again, "Can she be moved?"

"Better let your own doctor tell you," Tara answered. "But I should think he would want her in a hospital. Is there one near?"

"At Campbellsville."

Both were thinking of that rough twenty miles. But neither said anything.

Hattie was resting now. The hemorrhage had checked and she wasn't suffering. So they left her to sleep and pulled chairs up before the fire and wearily dropped into them. It was a very long night!

The lamp sent a flickering light around the room, probing into corners, darkening sharp edges. The woman on the bed lay very still, her breath coming softly. Outside, the wind rose and blew past the corners of the house. It was a small wind, crying grievingly. A small, lost wind, lonely and forlorn, and it cried about the eaves and soughed down the chimney. Tara shivered, and Jory bent to lay another log on the fire.

The night passed and morning had come, stealthy and gray, before Gault came with the doctor. Tara had dozed and nodded in his chair during the night hours, but he waked at their entrance, his mouth dry and ashy, his eyes prickly and hot, and his body stiff and sore.

The doctor didn't take long. "Get her to the hospital," he said.

"Now?" asked Hod.

"Now."

Becky packed a small bag and wrapped Hattie in a clean blanket. Then Hod and Jory lifted her as easily as they could and shifted her into the back seat of the car. It was the doctor's car . . . larger, roomier, springier than either Hod's or Jory's. Jory got in with Hod to hold her, to brace her against the jolts and the ruts. Careful as they tried to be, they saw a thin stream of blood seeping out of the corner of her mouth, and the doctor muttered under his breath.

"Tara," Hod called, "I hate to ask you—you're worn out—but reckon you could bring my car along? We'll be needing it in town."

"I'll bring it," Tara promised. And the doctor meshed his gears and drove away.

Tara went home first. Mary would want to know, and he felt the need of a shave and clean clothes. The night had been interminable.

"They're taking her to the hospital in Campbellsville," he told Mary. "Hod and Jory went with Tom and the doctor."

Mary nodded. Her face bore the marks of the night's strain. "It's a pity," she said. "A pity. She's not an old woman yet. Only fifty-odd. Too young to die."

"She may not. I've seen people live through much worse hemorrhages . . ."

Mary put the coffeepot over the burner. "You're hungry, I know. And tired. I'll fix breakfast for you right now."

"I've got to take Hod's car to him," Tara said, "but I *will* take time to eat. And I'm going to shave and change. I feel about a hundred years old."

Hattie was in the hospital only three or four days. Then the doctor told Tom and Hod to bring her home. "There's nothing we can do for her here," he said. "I think she has cancer. But to be certain you should take her to Louisville, where they can do a complete examination and operate if necessary. We don't have the facilities here."

Tara was standing near when the doctor told them, and he saw Hod's face whiten and his shoulders droop. He also saw Tom's eyes go bleak. Hod's voice cracked when he spoke. "That's your best opinion, then."

"That's my best opinion." The doctor was not impersonal or cold. But too many of these hill people had been brought to him at the last moment for him to have any hope of their doing what he said. They came, watched his face while he examined them, listened to his words, and then went home and died. As if the effort to come to his office, or the small hospital, exhausted their resources, few of them ever went farther when he so advised. He said what he had to say. That was his duty. But beyond that he could not push them.

Hod turned to Tara. "Is that what you think too?"

Tara hated to answer him. "No one can know positively, Hod, without complete examination. But it's what I was afraid of."

Hod said no more. He went about the business of getting Hattie home.

When they had her settled at home again in her own bed, Hod told her something of what the doctor had said. "Ma," he said gently, "the doctor thinks you should go to a hospital in Louisville for examination. Maybe for an operation. Mary will go with you and stay right by your side. We think you should go right away."

Hattie smoothed the sheet over the blanket and waited a time to answer, as if she were considering his words. "No," she said then, "no." And the word had the power of finality in it. It was an end, full stop, unappealing.

Hod told Mary and Tara that night at supper. "She'll not go."

Mary spooned a mound of mashed potatoes into Jeems's wide-open mouth. "I didn't think she would."

"Is it the money, Hod?" Tara asked.

"Partly, I reckon."

Tara fingered his fork and looked down at the food on his plate. With some hesitation he spoke, then, a little embarrassed, feeling more than a little unsure. "Hod, I've got some money stashed away. Don't need it. Probably never will. If she knew

. . . well, if she knew it wouldn't burden you, would it make any difference?"

Neither Hod nor Mary spoke for a moment, and the stillness around the table grew heavy. Tara wondered if he had hurt them in some deep, secret place. He had meant well . . . but the pride of some people was so great. Maybe . . . maybe he should have kept quiet.

When he lifted his eyes, he saw that Mary was blinking hers, and she ducked her chin to keep from meeting his glance. Hod's mouth was working. He reached out his hand and laid it on Tara's arm. "I misdoubt it would," he said, "but thank you, Cap'n."

It made no difference in Hattie's decision. That was irrevocable. But Tara's offer made a difference to him. Impulsively, not reasoning why, he had offered it. Compelled by something enkindled within himself, some pity, some generosity, some stirred feeling near to love, he had made his offer. It had taken him by surprise. But it made him feel fine. Not the offer. The way Mary and Hod had taken it. As if a brother had held out his hand, they had taken it. As if family stood by. He felt as if they had sort of opened the circle and let him in.

Now came the difficult days of nursing Hattie. For she could never be left alone, and she needed the tedious care of constant attention. Mary went. Miss Willie went. Becky, Rose, and Irma. All gave their time. But all had duties and responsibilities at home. Tara suggested a nurse. But Hattie, again, would have none of it. In her illness she could not discern between economies. She could ask, and take, the patience and time of her ridge people, counting no cost. She thought she was being considerate. She saw nothing of the release a nurse would have brought, and those who loved her would not press her. And she might live for months yet, spendthrift of the energies and strength of the women who gave her as much as they could. It could go on until they were all worn out.

It was Jory who, saying nothing, brought relief. One morning Mary returned from her daily visit. "Jory has moved to the folks'," she said, a queer, still look on her face. "He's going to take care of Hattie."

Hod and Tara said nothing for a moment. And then, "Will she let him?" Hod asked quickly.

"He didn't ask her. She isn't entirely helpless, you know. There's much she can do for herself. And what another man shouldn't do, Tom will do. Jory means to do the cooking, the cleaning, the washing, the chores. So Sarah can stay on in school, and so Hattie won't worry."

So that's the way it was worked out. Jory wouldn't discuss it beyond saying that he was the freest of them all. He had no family, no ties. He could bring his stock to Tom's and take care of them. He was the logical one to go. What a blithering idiot the man is, Tara thought. What a blithering *noble* idiot! But he knew Jory well enough by now to know that Jory didn't feel noble at all. There was a thing to be done, and he was the right one to do it. In Jory's mind it would be as simple as that.

But Tara was impatient with it just the same. The woman should have had a nurse. Hod and Mary should have insisted on it. There was no use giving way to a sick person's whims. This was a time when she didn't know what was best for her, and the family should have stepped in and taken over for her. It was all very well for Jory to play the good Samaritan, but it shouldn't have been necessary.

Tara himself went fairly often up the path that wound along the side of the ridge climbing up from Wishful Hollow. He went with Mary, to carry Jeems or a basket of food. He went with Hod, to help Tom with the work. Or he went alone, to inquire politely after Hattie.

One day when he had gone alone, he was sitting in the kitchen talking to Jory. Jory had a washing in tubs by the stove, and dinner was cooking over the same fire. Tara watched him scrub at the clothes, then stop, dry his hands, and stir something boiling in a pot. He noticed too that Jory kept watching the clock, and when Jory saw that he had caught him at it, he grinned. "Dinner's going to be late today. What with this washing and all, I'm running behind."

Tara stood up. "I can't cook, Jory, but I've done many a washing, in the Army. I'll finish that job."

Gratefully Jory surrendered the washboard into his hands, and Tara scrubbed out the sheets and towels, Hattie's garments, and Tom's overalls. Scrubbed them clean too. He hadn't done his own laundry in all the rivers of France for nothing! When he hung the clothes outside in the winter sun, he looked at their immaculateness with pride. It had been quite a time since he'd bent over a washboard. But he hadn't forgotten how.

Several times a week he climbed the ridge after that and lent a hand where it was needed. He ironed the clothes he had washed. Awkwardly and not too well, but they passed muster. He washed dishes, mopped the floor, eased Hattie in and out of her bed, and once, in a crisis, he cooked the noon meal. It was just scrambled eggs and bacon, and he burned the toast, but Hattie ate it and vowed it was right good.

Then one day when Hattie was restless and in pain, he picked up a farm magazine lying near and read aloud to her. She listened and forgot her pain for a while. Jory had come to the door and stood there looking on. When Tara glanced up, Jory smiled at him. "You got a good voice for reading," he said.

After that Tara went every day, taking books up the path with him. Instinctively knowing that Hattie would like the old things, he had gone to Miss Willie and borrowed *David Copperfield, Pride and Prejudice, The Return of the Native.* Each afternoon he settled Hattie into the big chair and read to her. She would sit quietly and listen, her eyes fixed on him. Sometimes she would comment. "That's jist like folks, ain't it?"

Or: "That's jist how folks are when they're wearied an' sad. Oh, them's the *best* books!"

Sarah, who rode the school bus daily to the Gap, got home each evening around five. That was dark these short winter days, and the thought of her walking the two miles from the pike alone fretted Hattie. "Hit's too fur fer a little girl," she said, "by herself. Tom, you'll jist have to meet her ever' day."

Tom had never learned to drive a car, never having owned one, so he walked. But ever since a serious illness he had had years ago, his legs had given out under him when he pushed with extra strain. He didn't say anything, but Jory noticed him rubbing them occasionally and he noticed also that he limped when he walked. "One of us had better meet Sarah," he said to Tara. "That two miles down to the pike, and two miles back, every day is too much for Tom."

"What next?" grumbled Tara.

But he took his turn driving Jory's old Ford to meet her. She was always shy with him, quiet, never chattering about school or anything else. She sat on her side of the seat, and after her first awkward hello she rarely spoke.

At home, when Jory and Tara were around, she was equally quiet. She helped with getting supper, and she usually did the dishes afterward. Then she disappeared into her room to study. Except for her coming home each afternoon and except for her silent presence at the supper table she might almost have not been a part of the family.

When Christmas came, Tara and Jory put their heads together to make it a lovely time for Hattie. The others helped—Hod and Mary, Irma and John. But it was Jory who went out and got the little pine tree and brought it to stand in the chimney corner, and it was Tara who drove Jory's old car to town and bought bright ornaments and shining tinsel ropes for it. He found candles to light it, and it was the two of them who festooned the tree with beauty for Hattie.

That same day in town Tara had looked for gifts. For Hattie there had been a warm, fleecy robe; house shoes lined with a gay plaid woolen material; and for foolishness, yards and yards of red, yellow, and blue ribbons to tie her braids with.

For Jory he got books, half a dozen, one of them being the *Confessions*. For Hod there was a new pipe, handsome in a fine leather case. For Jeems there was a boat to sail down Wishful Creek, a boat with real sails! And for Mary—he had searched long for it—there was a small head of Chopin, whose music she loved so much.

He hesitated about a gift for Sarah. What would a girl her age like? Especially a girl he didn't know, and couldn't get to know. Books? He had no idea whether she liked to read or not. Clothes? Well, that would hardly be appropriate. After all she wasn't exactly a child. Music? But what kind? He looked and he looked. Finally in desperation he bought a small portable radio. Maybe she would like to have one in her own room.

When the family gathered around Hattie's tree on Christmas Eve, there was laughter and happiness for a time. Hattie was awed by her gifts, opening them carefully and saying they were too fine for her. But she snuggled into the robe and slipped her feet into the slippers, and she tied bows of ribbon in her hair and asked for a mirror like a young girl.

Jeems squealed over the boat and sailed it back and forth across the floor. Hod lighted up his pipe, and Jory ran his hands lovingly over the binding of his books. Mary sat with the bronze head in her lap where her fingers could smooth its rounded shape.

But when Sarah opened her gift and saw the small radio, she gasped and looked at Tara with a wild, startled look. "For me?" she said, "for me?"

"For you," he assured her.

She scrambled out of her chair and ran with it to her own room.

"Sarah!" Hattie called, "Sarah! Well, I never! She never even said thank you! Sarah!"

"Let her alone," Tara said. "She said her thanks all right."

When the others would have thanked him for their gifts, it annoyed him and he brushed them away. "I just spent a little money, that's all," he said curtly. He felt like a fool now, having done it. And he didn't know why he had.

It was when the evening was over and they were all making ready to leave that John told them he was going to Indiana right after the first of the year.

"You're going then," Hod said.

"Yes."

Irma said nothing, but her lips set tightly and she bundled Susie roughly into her wraps.

"Might as well," John went on to say.

"How are you going to manage alone, Irma?" Mary asked.

Irma's answer was brusque. "I'll git along. If John kin go off an' leave us, we kin manage."

CHAPTER

10

THERE was no sun on New Year's Day. Like a gray sail the sky stretched over the ridge and the hollow, cracked here and there, patched with dark and lowering clouds. Toward noon the clouds built up into a solid mass and the sail sagged and tore under its heavy burden, and the rain came down and was as gray as the sky had been.

When Mary called Tara to dinner, the rain had settled into a steady sluice. Not the heavy downpour it had been at first, but a patient, enduring falling, straight down, wet and penetrating.

"Got a slicker, Cap'n?" Hod asked, "and boots? Be pretty wet going up the ridge today."

"I'll have to borrow the boots," Tara said. "I'll buy some the next time I'm in town."

"No need. There's three or four pairs around here. You're welcome to 'em. If they'll fit."

They stuck their feet out and decided they were nearly enough the same size. Mary was standing at the stove, lifting hot rolls onto a plate. When she turned suddenly, she stumbled over Hod's feet. The plate crashed to the floor and she twisted, falling into Hod's lap. "Hey!" he yelled, easing her fall and cradling her.

She lay laughing across his knees. "My soul, Hod! You'll give Willie Belle a real jolting up if you're not careful!"

Hod was serious immediately. "You hurt?"

She pulled herself up off his knees. "Of course not! But you keep your big feet under the table! I might have been!"

"I'm sorry," he said, and then to Tara: "Willie Belle's the little sister that's due about the middle of May. Have to be careful with her."

Tara's stomach cramped with a painful spasm, and his hunger left him. A sick tightness seized his throat, like a hand closing around it, and he swallowed hard against the lump.

What was the matter with him? Of course there would be Willie Belle! There might be a dozen Willie Belles. It was nothing to him! It *had* to be nothing to him!

He laid his hands on the edge of the table and gripped hard until the knuckles whitened and his fingers ached. With effort he forced his breath to come slow and even. With effort he swallowed his nausea and lifted his head. With effort he made his voice light and careless. "We'd better measure our feet in the barn from now on, Hod."

The sweat broke out on his forehead and his back went limp, but he achieved the appearance of normalcy. "You sit down, Mary. I'll get the rolls."

But his mood was as broody and dark as the day when he climbed the ridge after dinner. His feet slopped heavily in the mud, and the wet branches that hung over the path slapped at him and showered his shoulders wetly. He slogged along, sunk in his thoughts, seeing nothing, hearing nothing, trying, desperately, to feel nothing. Once more he wished to escape. "I'd better get away from here. Better go at once."

But even his thoughts were indecisive and unconvincing. They were framed in irresolution, longing on the one hand for escape, and dreading on the other hand to turn loose from the meager store of safety he had achieved in this place. There was no place to go. There was no one to turn to. There was nothing away from here, now. He even knew, actually, that he would not go if given a good reason for going outside himself. He would not willingly break the bonds that had come to bind him here. He knew he did not want to go really. And that he would not go.

He came out on top of the ridge at the white birch tree that marked the trail down to the hollow. It was a huge tree, spreading widely over the path. Its trunk was cut deep with many initials, record of passing generations of ridge folks. Once Tara had examined it closely, and he counted forty different sets of initials. Hod's had been there, and Tom's. Gault's, and scores of others he didn't know. And he had found the entire name "Mary" chiseled under Hod's older and indelible scars.

Tara rarely passed the tree without tracing the name with his fingers. It had become a habit with him, and today as he stopped to catch his breath after the climb, he reached out his hand toward her name. He caught it halfway. No, he thought. Not even that much of her belongs to me. I'd best forget it. And he made a fist of his hand inside his pocket. There was a dull, sodden ache in this renunciation. But he made himself do it.

He had turned to start on when a sound, a sort of stifled, smothered groan, reached him. It came from the other side of the great tree. He circled the tree and stopped short, almost stepping on a man crawling crazily in the mud and wet. He knew instantly that it was Ferdy Jones again. Drunk. Blind and crazy drunk, unable to stand or walk, but trying to crawl wherever he had started. The man weaved, even on all fours, crawling a step or two, then sprawling face down in the mud, and he kept up that soft, stifled moaning all the while. Tara stood and looked at him, and a curious numb envy crept over him. "That's one way out, brother," he said gently, "that's sure one way out."

Well, what to do now? He considered the sprawling man and prodded him with the toe of his boot. Ferdy collapsed and his face scraped into the muddy gravel beneath him. The fool will drown himself if he gets to the road, Tara thought. He'll fall in a pool in one of the ruts and never know it.

Suddenly deciding, he leaned down and hefted the man like a sack of meal over his shoulder, letting his legs dangle behind and his head in front. Sour slobber drained from Ferdy's mouth and Tara's nose wrinkled in disgust. But he slogged out into the road and stumbled heavily along toward Hattie's house. From there, Jory could take over. Jory was the professional good Samaritan!

"Where'd you find him?" Jory wanted to know.

"Under the birch tree at the head of the path."

Jory nodded. "Been on a New Year's spree, I reckon." He sighed. "Well, take the car and take him on back to Corinna."

"You take him! I'm not having any more to do with him!"

"Oh, yes, you are! He's your baby today. You found him!"

"Now, Jory . . ."

"I've got work to do. Besides, Tom's gone and we can't both leave. One of us has to stay here with Hattie."

"Then it'll be me."

"No!"

But Tom came in just then and Tara laughed at Jory. "O. K., friend. Now who has to stay with Hattie?"

Jory grinned and lifted his coat off the peg. "All right. Reckon it'll take us both anyhow if he starts coming to. Hattie, we'll be back in a little."

Hattie sniffed. "If hit was me, I'd of left him lay! Good riddance of bad rubbish if he had of drownded!" Hattie had no patience with those who drank strong liquor. They were beyond the pale of her tolerance.

Tara crossed to her and tucked one of her braids behind her

head. "You're pretty today, Hattie. I believe I like the red ribbons best, after all."

Easily the words came to him. Like reaching down into the past and pulling them, spared and left over, from those he had used so constantly with his mother. "How clear your eyes are! And you've got more color today."

And Hattie laughed at him and told him to be gone. "We'll read some when you git back, won't we?"

"We'll read. I promise. And we won't be gone long."

But he was wrong. They were gone a long, long time. And a part of the time Tara wondered if they would ever get back!

It was Jory who lifted Ferdy this time and shouldered him into the car. When he touched Ferdy's face, straightening him on the seat, he turned to Tara, startled. "He's awful hot. Feel him."

Tara laid his hand against Ferdy's forehead, and the hot, dry skin burned his palm. "Good grief, he's burning up with fever! He's not only drunk—he's sick!"

"He's sure worse than drunk this time. Wonder how long he's been out?"

"No telling. His clothes are soaked."

"Well, he wouldn't have to be out in this kind of a rain more than half an hour to be soaked. Reckon there's no way of knowing. Come on."

There was no smoke from the chimney when they drove up, and the shutters had been closed, giving the place a deserted and alien look. No children peered from the windows and a voiceless silence hung loud with quiet over the house. It was a dissonant silence, harsh with probabilities. It struck Tara like an unorchestrated theme, discordant, wayward, reasonless. He didn't know why he felt a foreboding of evil.

Corinna did not meet them at the door today. Instead, they found it tightly closed. "She must be gone somewhere," Jory said. "The door's probably closed with a button. We've got to get him to bed. Heave, Cap'n!"

They put their shoulders against the door and heaved. It gave, but it held, and they heaved again. Under their combined strength the crude latch on the other side gave way and the door was flung open, spilling them into the room. It was dark inside.

They picked Ferdy up and carried him into the room and laid him on the bed. "Open the shutter, Cap'n," Jory said. "It's so dark in here I can't see what I'm doing."

Tara moved to obey.

"No!"

The voice came from a corner of the room, as cold as death and as expressionless. Its intonation was flat and level, deliberate, quiet. "No. This is a house of death an' mournin', Jory Clark. It has need to be kept dark!"

They could not see Corinna. Only her voice came out of the darkness. "It needs to be dark for death. Dark and black. Dark for the deed. Black for the death!"

The voice rose and shrilled. Outside, the rain dripped from the eaves and the limbs of the trees scrubbed against the roof, and the scrubbing sound scraped into the room, through the shuttered windows, and mixed with the voice shrilling in the darkness. "It needs to be dark! It needs to be dark!"

"Corinna!" Jory spoke, making his voice steady. "Corinna, Ferdy's sick. We must get him to bed."

"I know he's sick. An' I'm sick! An' the kids is sick! We're all sick, Jory Clark. From the sickness he got an' give us!"

Tara had stood paralyzed, fear and horror racing through him. But Jory ran quickly across the room and flung the shutters wide. The woman screamed and threw herself toward the bed, the knife in her hand glancing silver in the sudden light. Jory sprang at the bed, yelling at Tara: "Cap'n! Get her!"

Even as he moved, Tara saw Jory fling himself across Ferdy's body, protecting it with his own, shielding his own head with an upflung arm. Tara saw the knife bury itself in the pillow, only inches from Jory's head.

A keen, wild thrill flooded him and he went into action fast, his paralysis gone in his swift movement, and a wary, cautious bell in his mind telling him: "Get the knife. Get the knife!"

When the arm swung back up again, he grabbed it, but with the strength of a wild animal Corinna twisted free, frantically jabbing at him. "I'm goin' to kill him," she screamed, "kill him dead! I'm goin' to! I've got the kids latched in the loft room. An' I'm goin' to kill them too! An' I'm goin' to kill myself! We're all sick . . . sick . . . sick! An' I'm goin' to kill us all!"

She fled to the corner of the room and crouched there, her hair torn loose from its pins and hanging over her face. Spittle drooled from the edges of her mouth, and blood, where she had bitten her lips. Tara inched toward her carefully. "Give me that knife," he said, "give me that knife!"

"No!" she shouted. "No!" And she circled warily out of the corner and beyond his reach. He followed her. Slowly she backed around the room, Tara edging closer. Jory eased off the bed. Out of the corner of her eye she saw him, and whirled toward the bed again. Quickly Jory had to move to intercept her.

Then she flashed on Tara behind her, and whirled between him and the bedposts to the other side of the room. Around the bed he went after her, she backing and stabbing before him. Shrewdly, she allowed him to close the distance, then she ducked, and as fleet as a rabbit was under his arm and across the room.

Jory guarded the bed and tried to ease toward them. Each time he got more than a few feet away, however, she threatened the bed again. It seemed impossible that she could hold two men at bay thus. Twice Tara caught hold of her, and twice she bit and twisted and flailed at him, eluding him. She was so insane with fear and anger that she was as strong as ten men, as slippery as an eel, and as cunning as a fox. And always there was that flashing blade to be wary of.

If I can get her in the corner again, the captain thought. Corner her. Get her back against the wall.

Changing tactics then, he tried edging her into the far corner of the room. Picking up a chair to use as a shield in front of him he narrowed the distance between them, hedged her, meeting the thrusts of the knife with the slats of the chair. Confused, she gave ground and backed inch by inch into the corner. Once more Jory eased off the bed and flanked Tara on the left. The two of them advanced on her. She slashed violently at them as they closed in. Tara dropped the chair and the blade of the knife scraped the back of his hand as he clutched her. A second later he had the hand that held the knife, and he tightened his hold like a vise. Jory bound her arms to her side. Even then she struggled and screamed, bit and kicked, and fell clumsily to the floor, rolling them with her. They sprawled, lost their hold, struggled to regain it, and then suddenly it was all over. Corinna went limp in their arms and sagged, crying weakly. The knife fell to the floor, and Tara kicked it across the room, not daring yet to loose his hold on her wrist. The woman shielded her face with her arm and wept bitterly. "I'm all right now, Jory," she said. "I'm all right."

Slowly Jory sat up and raised Corinna with him. "Corinna, Corinna!" he said softly. "What got into you?"

She shook her head and burrowed it against his shoulder. "Hit jist come over me, Jory. I reckon I went clean outen my mind. Hit jist come over me that hit was more'n I could bear." Her voice was muffled by the cloth of his coat and it came through the folds indistinctly. "Hit was knowin' we all had the sickness done it."

Jory held her away from him. "What sickness, Corinna?"

She hid her face in her hands. "The bad sickness. That nurse over at the Gap says we all got it. Me an' the kids an' all. She says we got to have the shots."

Jory's eyes met Tara's. They looked clouded and bewildered. Suddenly Tara's knees gave way beneath him and he sagged to the bed. "My aching back," he said, "my aching back!"

"What does she mean?" Jory asked.

"Don't be so naïve, Jory!" the captain snapped. "You've been in the Army!"

And then Jory understood. With infinite tenderness he pulled Corinna's head to his shoulder and smoothed the wild hair out of her face. Quietly he cradled and held her. Wordlessly he comforted her until her weeping ceased. And then he spoke softly to her. "It's all right, Corinna. It's all right. The shots will make you well so quick you'll never know you've been sick. It won't take long."

"I've allus heared it wasn't to be cured."

"Oh, but that's wrong. They've found a new drug that cures it quickly . . . and completely. There's nothing to be afraid of. Five or six days, maybe a week, I don't know exactly, but not long."

Fresh tears overtook her then, but they were tears of relief. "O Jory, I was so afeared! So skeered! Hit seemed like the only way out was to kill us all! Ifen you an' him hadn't of come! Jist think, what if you hadn't of come!"

"But we did," and Jory rose to his feet and lifted Corinna to hers. "Now. Ferdy is very sick, Corinna. On top of everything else he's got pneumonia or something very close to it. The captain's here and he's going to help him all he can, but we'll have to send for the doctor and you'll have to pull yourself together."

She shoved her hair back and straightened her shoulders. "I'm all right," she insisted, "an' I know what to do for lung fever. I'll make a plaster of grease an' camphor an' turpentine. I've broke up lung fever with it many's the time. I'll take keer of Ferdy."

Jory turned to Tara. "Would that be all right?"

"It'll do as good as anything else until he can have penicillin. Lord, I'm beginning to think I was the biggest fool in the world to come off down here without a thing! You folks need a doctor every time you turn around!" He laughed shortly. "I came here to rest. Rest! All we do is take care of sick people!"

Jory looked at him steadily. "That's what I been trying to tell you."

Tara turned to the bed. "Let's get his clothes off and get him covered, and Corinna can put one of her plasters on him. You better get someone to come, though. I'll help Corinna."

They set to work while Jory made the twenty-mile trip into town.

About Ferdy they were encouraged. "His lungs are congested, of course," the doctor told them, "but he doesn't have pneumonia, yet." He shot him full of penicillin and told Jory to get more from the nurse at the Gap if he needed it. He laughed over Corinna's poultice, but knowing she believed in it more than she did in the penicillin, he told her to keep on poulticing him. "I aim to," she said. "Hit's what I allus do fer any that's got the lung fever."

The children were milling uneasily about, getting in the way, and Tara herded them all into the kitchen. Between the rain and the early winter dark a lamp was needed. Then, having nothing else to do, he built a fire in the cookstove. The lamp and the warmth from the stove made the room more cheery, and the children huddled around the fire, staring at him and hugging close to one another. All but the oldest boy and girl. They eyed him with curiosity and silence and kept their distance.

Tara was always ill at ease with children. He never knew what to say to them or how to behave. They made him uncomfortable. These children were especially unattractive to him, large-eyed, thin, swollen-bellied. And on the bare legs

of the youngest two he noticed great sores, putrescent and running. Those two, at any rate, he thought, were infected. What a
rotten mess the whole thing was!

The least one, satisfying himself about Tara, and losing his
shyness before another urgent need, took his finger out of his
mouth and came toward the captain. He wedged himself between Tara's knees and looked up at him. He had a shock of
touseled yellow hair, and when his small, wizened face turned
up to Tara's, Tara was surprised to see that it would have
been attractive had health glowed in it, and soap and water
cleaned it. In spite of himself, Tara reached out and ran his
hand over the yellow curls. "What do you want, young fellow?"
he said.

The child ducked his head instantly and mumbled something.

Tara looked at the oldest girl. "What did he say?"

"Milk. He's hungry. We've not had nothin' to eat all day."

"All day?"

The girl nodded. "Ma shut us up in the loft room this
mornin'."

Tara stood the child away from him. "Well, great day! Come
on and let's get something cooked here!"

The girl helping, he found potatoes and eggs and milk. He
peeled the potatoes and put them on to boil; then he set the
eggs to boiling in another pan. There was no bread except cold
biscuits left from breakfast, and he was baffled for a time. "I
kin make bread," the girl offered, and with relief he turned that
chore over to her. He shuddered when he saw her mixing the
dough with her hands, but then, he supposed, it was too late
to worry about germs between them now. And they had to
eat!

Within an hour he set the children down to a hot supper, and
when Jory and Corinna came into the kitchen after the doctor
left, they were grouped around the table. The potato bowl was

empty, nothing left of the eggs but the shells, and the biscuit plate had one solitary biscuit left on it.

Corinna looked at them in astonishment. "My stars! I plumb fergot them young'uns hadn't eat! I reckon they was about half starved!"

Tara stood. "I'd say they were completely starved from the way they ate. But I'll guarantee they're full now. There's not much left for you, though."

"Oh, I'll make out. But you needn't of went to the trouble, Cap'n. I'm obliged to you, though."

Tara untied the apron that the children had giggled at and handed it to Corinna. "I'm glad to give you back your property, Mrs. Jones. As a cook I leave much to be desired."

"He done good," the oldest girl said, suddenly defending him. "Hit all tasted real good."

Jory had looked on, laughing. "You'd make a right good family man, Cap'n. Of course," he drawled, "when you run out of milk and potatoes and eggs, you might come up against a problem."

"You shut up," Tara growled. "Are we ready to go now?"

"Just about." Jory turned to the woman. "Corinna, let us know if you need us. And one of us will come next week to take you to the Gap to start the shots. Ferdy ought to be all right by then."

Corinna fumbled the apron in her hands. "I owe you a heap, Jory. I reckon you know I'm obliged to you."

"You owe us nothing. If we can help, let us know."

"We'll be fine now. Me an' the oldest uns kin make out."

When they were down the road a piece, Tara turned to Jory. "Where do you get that 'us' stuff? 'Let us know!' 'We'll be glad to help out!' We . . . us! You sure make fine promises without asking a guy! Haven't we got our hands full already with Hattie?"

Jory chuckled and eased the old car through a mudhole. "We can stretch 'em if need be."

"Not me. You can just count me out of the Jones mess! Just count me out!"

Jory looked at him and grinned. Tara answered the look and found he was compelled to grin also. But he repeated: "Not me! Just count me out!"

CHAPTER

11

B UT of course he wasn't counted out. He was counted very much in the middle of "the Jones mess."

The days were so full now that neither Tara nor Jory knew where they found the time to do all that must be done. There was the work at Hattie's, the regular, daily tasks to be done first, and then for more than a week one or the other of them went daily to Ferdy's place. This was usually Tara's job in order that a professional eye might be kept on his progress.

Tara rose early now and climbed the ridge to help Jory. In the afternoon he settled Hattie in her chair by the fire and read to her. Her days were full of pain. The sedatives Tara gave her eased her for so short a time, and the clutching, clawing thing that was eating her life away seldom gave her respite. She was thinner, her eyes circled and hollowed, and the pain left her face pinched and drawn.

Hod came every day as soon as his chores at home were done. Mary came often, Miss Willie, others. But inevitably the heaviest burden fell on Jory and Tara, for they were the only ones free to give themselves over completely to the needs and the demands of the household. Increasingly Hattie needed help. Tom was beside her faithfully, and Jory and Tara shouldered the rest of the work between them.

When Ferdy was able to be up and around again, they began the trips with the family to the nurse at the Gap for the shots, and then for three weeks they had barely time to sit down for meals.

The day came for the last of the shots and both Tara and Jory went. They had been taking the family in two sections, but today, with the sun shining and the air crisply cold, today with the last shots coming up, they piled the whole family in at once, tumbling them into the back on top of each other and holding the rest between them and on them in front. It was by way of a celebration today!

"We'll have ice cream when the nurse finishes," Tara promised the youngest who straddled his knees.

"I . . . scream!" the child squealed, and he burrowed his head into Tara's stomach. Tara rubbed the child's scarred little legs. Not all the sores were gone. But they were going . . . the remaining ones were drying up and dwindling. He looked like a different child these days. Tara pulled the overalls down over the scars and snuggled him closer. He was a smart youngster, he thought. Just as smart as they came!

When they let the family out at their own home later, Ferdy tried to thank them. He looked different too, Tara thought. He was still gaunt and stringy, still swallowing his Adam's apple convulsively, still bean-poled into his clothes, but with health returned the hangdog look in his eyes had gone and his chin, which had quavered dangerously, looked more firm.

Jory turned off his thanks lightly. "Don't mention it, Ferdy," he said. "You'll be able to get your crops in this spring now. You can do a man's work again."

Wistfully Ferdy looked across his overgrown fields. "I reckon," he said, and then he laughed. "I ain't much of a farmer at best. Don't seem to take to farmin' like others. Hit don't never seem to turn out right fer me."

"Don't you like farming?" Tara asked.

"Well, I don't to say think about it much one way or the other. Man can't exactly have his likes, I reckon. I've allus wisht I could try my hand at carpenterin'. Used to be right handy with it. But a feller's got a family has got to do what's handiest. Wisht you'd let me pay you a little somethin' on the gas, Jory. Corinna sold her calf the other day an' we got a little cash money right now."

"Keep it," Jory said. "You'll need it. We've not run out of gas yet."

"Well, much obliged. To you too, Cap'n. We'd not of got along withouten the both of you."

They were washing the supper dishes at Hattie's that night, Jory washing, Tara wiping. "Cap'n," Jory said suddenly, "we've got to get Ferdy a job."

Tara wiped a plate industriously. Round and round. He began to whistle, off key and out of tune. Jory stuck his tongue in his cheek and glanced cornerwise at him. "You needn't to act like you never heard me."

"I heard you. I thought you'd get around to something like this. I've been waiting for it. Some more of this 'we' business!" He laid the plate on the shelf and took up another one. "Now, listen, Jory. It doesn't work to go interfering with people's lives. Help, yes. In an emergency such as Ferdy's family has just faced. But we've done all we can do for Ferdy Jones and his family. Ferdy is just plain shiftless and no good. It won't help a bit to get him a job. There's nothing he can do, in the first place. And in the second, even if you got him some kind of job, he'd just get drunk and lose it. You can't change that kind of guy!"

"Oh, yes, you can!"

"Oh, no, you can't!"

They left it at that. Nothing more was said about it for several days. Then a few mornings later they were separating the milk. "I've been thinking about the carpentering angle," Tara said.

Jory threw his head back and shouted. "Some more of this 'we' business! I'll bet you've already got a job figured out for him!"

Tara laughed too, ruefully. "No, I haven't. That's the tough part. If the only thing he can do is carpentering, it makes it kind of rough. That kind of work is so seasonal and uncertain. What we've got to think of is something steady. Something every day, day in and day out."

"And something that he likes to do! You know, Cap'n, I figure one thing's been wrong with Ferdy is, he's been a round peg in a square hole. Must make a man feel kind of hopeless, plowing and sweating day after day with no heart in it. Not liking it. Maybe even hating it. And prodded all the time with more kids coming. More mouths to feed. Not seeing any way out at all. You can't honestly blame him for taking to drink."

"No. Maybe not. I don't put too much faith in this job business, Jory. I'd feel a lot better about it if he showed enough initiative to get out and get it for himself."

"Cap'n, look. You take a guy that's all his life farmed. Maybe he don't like it. Say he don't, anyway. But it's what he's used to. He don't know anything else to do. He's just got a hankering. Just a hankering to go on. Take a guy like that and grind him down with a big bunch of kids. He's caught, see. Caught like a rat in a trap. And then, besides, say he don't have the right kind of food. Lot of these folks are shiftless just because they can't eat right. No energy. No ambition. No nothing. Bone-tired all the time and not knowing why. How can you expect a guy like that to have any initiative!"

"You can't, I guess. There's probably a lot in what you say. Enough, anyhow, so that if you can think of something for him, I'll string along. If," he grinned, "for no other reason than to see what happens!"

In the days that followed, when some of the ridge folks were there to spell them with Hattie, they took to driving to town . . . to both towns, Campbellsville and Columbia. They went to see people. They saw a lumber dealer. "Can your man figure lumber?" he asked.

They didn't know. They doubted if he could. But he could probably learn. The dealer shook his head. "I couldn't use him."

They talked with several carpenters. "Work's not too good right now," they were told. One man said: "I'm between jobs myself. But there's a new building going up pretty soon and I expect to get on."

"How much experience have you had?" they asked him.

"Twenty years," came the reply, and they figured that, short of carrying a hod and doing odd jobs as a day laborer, Ferdy was past the age of making a start in that trade.

They even saw the owner of a sawmill. But when they learned that the mill was located in another county, they had to count that out. It wouldn't do to have Ferdy off alone a hundred miles from home.

One by one they reduced the possibilities, and they were beginning to feel that they were few and far between for a man of indeterminate skills. They scraped up one chance for him . . . in a warehouse, handling feed, loading trucks, but when they talked it over, they decided the work was too heavy for a man of Ferdy's years. "It'd break him down," Jory said. And they still wanted to find something he would take joy in doing.

They were in Columbia one day, the county seat town. They had been to see the foreman of a construction company. He had said he could use Ferdy, but he hadn't been able to promise anything more than the roughest sort of work. Building scaffolds, tearing them down, moving them, rebuilding them. But the bridge job the company was working on would last a year anyhow, and they thought this might be the best chance they'd have. They turned toward home, talking it over. "I reckon that's about the best we can do," Jory said.

"It looks like it," Tara agreed.

About five miles out of town they passed a small furniture shop. The man was noted for his handmade chairs and tables, chests and beds. From as far as Louisville his customers came to order fine, hand-turned cherry and walnut furniture. Often Tara had meant to stop there and visit the place. He liked period furniture, and he had a little ability himself with a lathe and turning saw. He glanced at the building as they passed. Then, "Jory, stop!" he yelled suddenly.

Jory slammed on the brakes so fast that Tara had to catch at the windshield to brace himself. "That furniture place," he said, piling out of the car. "See that sign in the window!"

A neatly lettered sign was propped in one of the front windows. "Helper wanted," it said.

"By George!" Jory said, crawling out on his side. "Have we been passing that sign every time we've been over this way?"

"I don't think so. I think it's been put there since we went into town. I always look at that place every time we pass, and I'd have seen it, I'm sure. The job's still open, I'll bet."

The man was a stooped, frail old white-haired fellow with spectacles perched on the end of his nose, over which he peered at them. "Well, yes," he said, "I need a helper. I'm not too strong any more."

"Would he have to be experienced?" Tara asked.

"I'd rather he would be," the old man confessed. "It would make it easier for me. But I can't pay much, and I'd count it lucky if I could get a dependable fellow who was willing to learn. A good furniture man's hard to find. Would expect good pay and would have a right to expect it. So I don't count on it."

Without leaving out any of the details then, they told him about Ferdy. Told him the whole story. "We couldn't even promise you he'd be dependable," Tara admitted. "We don't know whether he would or not. And he's not been in the past. We," he grinned, "are just sort of going around playing God in a man's life. Just trying to make a chance for him."

"He's not ever had much of a chance, though," Jory took it up, "not a real chance to do something he likes to do. We don't even know whether he'd actually like this kind of work when he got into it. You'd be taking a big chance to give him the job, of course. But if you did, and if it worked . . . well, you'd be helping ten people out. Him, his wife, and eight children. And they need it."

The old man rubbed his chin and looked at them. Then he walked around his shop, handling his tools, feeling the satiny woods all ready for his hands, creasing his forehead and thinking. Tara and Jory waited.

He came to a stop in front of them. "All right," he said. "You been square about him. I'll give him a chance," and he turned and took the sign out of the window. "It's the woman and children get me," he said, turning back to look at them, as if trying to excuse some softness in himself. "But, mind," he said, shaking his finger at them, "you mind now, if he starts drinking, he's through! My tools are too valuable, my wood is too expensive, to risk with some drunken fool!"

"If he starts drinking again, don't put up with him a minute," Tara urged. "This is an experiment. We're frank to admit it. It may not work. If it does, fine. If it doesn't, we've done our best and you've done your best. Between us, we're seeing he gets his chance. The rest is up to him."

"It's a pretty good chance," the old man said. "If he's any good, I'd like to train him so as to turn over most of the work to him. If he likes wood, likes to work with it, it's a good job. We'll see," he said, shaking hands with them. "We'll see."

Back in the car Tara was thinking. "You know," he said, "we'd better be pretty careful how we go about telling Ferdy about this."

"How you mean?"

"You'd better go over to his place by yourself. Just tell him you know where he can get a job if he wants one. Tell him you talked to the old guy, but he'll have to cinch the job himself. If he thinks he got the job on his own, he's likely to want it more and work harder to keep it."

"You're right, of course. He's going to have to figure out a way to get back and forth to work too."

"Well, leave that to him. If he wants the job bad enough, he'll take care of it."

"He can ride the milk truck a few weeks, and then he ought to be able to pick up an old car for a little or nothing."

"He'll figure it out. If he wants to."

So they left it.

Hattie didn't think much of their scheme when they told her about it that evening. "Like as not he'll not even go to see about it," she snorted. "Someone's allus had to do fer Ferdy Jones, ever sincet I kin remember. First his ma done it, till she died. Then his oldest sister takened it over till she died. An' they've made out a pore way ever sincet then. They ain't nothin' to Ferdy Jones an' they never will be. Jist take my word fer it!"

But Jory drove away to tell Ferdy about the job and Tara settled down to read to Hattie. His mind was not on the reading. He kept listening for Jory's car, wondering what Ferdy had said, worrying whether they'd handled it the best way. And he kept thinking of that youngest boy, the smart little fellow, and what a difference it would make for him. He thought about all the youngsters, and in his mind clothed them adequately with Ferdy's pay, and put good food before them, and filled out the hollows and the angles of their scrawny bodies. He thought about Corinna and what it would be like for her with a regular income. How much easier she could rest in such security. If only Ferdy will take the job, he thought. If only he'll take it and keep sober and work. And he realized that his thoughts were just this side of prayer that Ferdy would take the job and keep sober and work. Just a fraction this side of prayer, and maybe not even that much.

He heard the car before it turned the bend in the road, and he laid the book aside and waited tensely. Jory walked into the house with springs in his heels. "He was tickled to death!" he said jubilantly, "just tickled pink! Said he'd go over first thing in the morning and see about it! Said he'd give his right arm for a chance to have a job like that!"

Something unkinked inside of Tara. "Good," he said. "Good!"

Hattie humphed. "He'd better not give his right arm. He'll be needin' it, if he lasts long enough on the job."

"Hattie," scolded Tara, "you're just jealous, that's all! You don't want Jory and me thinking about anybody but you. You're getting spoiled."

He was surprised when tears filled her eyes, and he put his hand gently over hers. "Why, Hattie! You're the love of our hearts, don't you know that? We're trying to help Ferdy and Corinna, but it's you we love. Why, you're our girl! You're our own best lady love!"

She clung to his hand. "Ain't it a sight!" She sniffed her tears away and stuck her nose in the air. "Me, jealous! They ain't a jealous bone in my body! Little I keer whether you come or go, Cap'n Cochrane! Or Jory Clark, neither! I kin git along without both of you!"

"Oh, sure," Jory growled. "We're just the hired help around here. Come on, Cap'n. Let's pack and get out."

"Don't you dare!"

And the three of them broke into laughter. "Tie me a red bow in my hair tonight, Cap'n," Hattie begged. "I feel awful gay tonight."

CHAPTER

12

IT WAS the middle of February when the snow came, blowing up late one evening just as Tara started home. It came out of the north, from a black and blustery-looking cloud, and the air seethed with the wind and the snow. He fought it all the way home from the ridge, groping his way between the trees, almost blinded by the sleety, stinging particles and almost breathless from the force of the wind. He was numb from the cold when he stamped into the house. "That wind," he told Hod, "is fierce!"

"Tail end of winter, I reckon," Hod said. "One more good lick at us."

"Had supper yet, Tara?" Mary asked. Sometimes he ate at Hattie's before coming home. Sometimes he waited to eat with Mary and Hod.

"Yes," he said. "We ate early on account of the storm. Jory and Tom were going to get things bedded down early. I thought Hod might need some help."

"Done got it done," Hod told him. "I had the same idea Pa and Jory did."

Tara was glad these days not to be around Mary too much. He couldn't look at her, or talk to her, without remembering. And remembering brought such a torment of emotions that he couldn't face it often. It was a relief to be away from her so much, and yet he never came into a room where she was that her nearness didn't assail him with the longing to stay where she was. Just to see her sitting by the fire, Jeems on her lap, or to see her moving quickly, still, about the kitchen comforted him even as it hurt him. It was the old story of biting on a sore tooth, to relieve one kind of pain with another, perhaps sharper one. He didn't do it too often. He'd got used to the sore tooth in a way, and he preferred its familiar ache.

"Keeps this up all night," Hod said, "it'll be pretty deep tomorrow. Was the snow sticking?"

"Pretty much. In spite of the wind. There's just so everlasting much of it some of it's got to stick."

"Might be good enough to go rabbit-hunting tomorrow."

"Hey, that's an idea! I'd sure like to go!" Tara laughed. "Remember those rabbits in France?"

"Man, do I? Those were the biggest rabbits I ever saw! First one I saw, thought it was a deer!"

"Remember that time you and Jenkins went rabbit-hunting with a machine gun?"

"I remember you ate us out when we got back! But you also cleaned up your part of the stew! I remember that too!"

Remembering, they both sobered for a moment. Jenkins had been the first sergeant until he got killed. And he had been killed when their outfit bridged the Roer that spring. Well, Jenkins had been one who hadn't come back. That had happened to a lot of guys. But they'd come back. And here they were. Going rabbit-hunting again. That's the way life was. It sobered them and each one thought his own thoughts. But the embarrassment that lies between all men kept each of them silent. The embarrassment that keeps men from saying what they're thinking, lest it be thought uncommonplace, emotional, stuffy, and soft. The embarrassment of being considered, perhaps, sentimental. The possible embarrassment of being thought, even, spiritual.

So they went back to the weather and known facts, and the evening passed, until Tara said good night and went to his room.

The next morning was clear and the snow lay a good six inches on the ground. "Just right," Hod said.

"I'll meet you up the hollow," Tara told him. "I'll have to go up and tell Jory I'm slacking off this morning."

Hod waited for him at the head of the hollow and they took off, guns slanted across their shoulders, over the next ridge. Hod had brought only one dog, Coon. "Only good rabbit dog in the bunch," he said.

The dog strung out ahead of them now, jumping high in the snow and wallowing through the deep places. He hadn't settled down to business yet. The whole thing was still a lark to him. "Come on, Coon," Hod called, "let's get going!"

But for all the snow, the rabbits were scarce. The men plodded down the ridge and into the next hollow without seeing so much as a track. Out of a brush heap, then, Coon sniffed out one lone rabbit, which took off up the hillside, the dog yipping sharply behind it. But it was lost before either of the men could come up with the dog. "Some winters, warm and wet like this one's been," Hod said, "rabbits are scarcer than hen's teeth. I'd like to get just one, though. Ma would like a rabbit stew for a change. She always did like rabbit meat."

Slowly they raked the hollow from one side to the other, and then Tara got a shot. The rabbit jumped from behind a down log into the open, and he cracked down on it at about forty yards. "There's Hattie's rabbit stew!" he shouted.

He went to pick the rabbit up. Beyond it, almost hidden by a fall of rocks and a thicket of dried hazelnut bushes, a small ravine opened. It was narrow, its sides steep and sharp. The only way you could enter was up the floor of the stream, which trickled down sluggishly, almost icebound. "Hey, Hod," he called. There was something familiar about this place. "Isn't this where we went that night we were hunting? Look! We waded up a stream like that. It was narrow too. Remember?"

"By golly, it does look like it!" Hod looked around at the opening. "No wonder you can't tell this place is here. Look at those rocks! And that thicket of hazelnut bushes! They make a solid wall!"

Tara pushed the close-hanging limbs aside. "This is it, Hod. I'm sure it is. Come on, let's have a look at it in daylight."

Hod shoved in behind him. But the dog wouldn't come. He sat on his haunches on the other side of the thicket, and whimpered. "Look at that dog!" Hod said.

Coon sat in the snow and shivered and whined. Tara stared at him. Then he laughed. "Even in daylight they don't like this place."

"Well, he'll go home. Wonder . . ."

Tara looked at Hod. "Wondering if we'll hear the bell today?"

Hod grinned. "Well, I'm a heap braver about it today than I was the last time."

They climbed up the stream bed, sliding on the ice, holding by the bushes that lined the walls of the narrow canyon. The ascent was steep, and always narrow. The ravine was dark even at this hour of the day. Shadowy and dim.

They came finally to the fall of rocks over which they had clambered that night, into the level clearing. "This is where we heard the bell first," Hod said.

They stopped to breathe. And they listened. They listened hard, almost checking their breathing to hear better. But the silence was unbroken. A twig snapped over on the other side and they whirled to look. "Cold, I guess," Tara said when they saw nothing.

"Yeah."

Sheepishly they grinned at each other.

"How much farther up does this hollow go?" Tara asked.

"I don't know. Not much farther, though, I'd guess, from the way it's running out. It looks pretty tangled the rest of the way, doesn't it, and steep. Want to go on?"

Tara looked up at the rugged climb ahead. "Looks like solid rock to me just up there." He shook his head. "Nope. Not unless you want to scramble up that cliff. I guess I just wanted to see if we'd hear the bell in the daytime."

They started back down. The snow was deep in the clearing where its fall had been unobstructed, but beyond the rock fall, and below it, it was thin and scattered. The brush and heavy growth of trees had screened the floor of the ravine. They slid over the icy rock fall and began to descend. It was treacherous underfoot, and Tara clutched at a handhold with every step. Hod went ahead more surely.

Tara had reached for a clump of bushes leaning over the stream bed when he noticed a piece of newspaper blown into their thickly massed roots. He pulled it out. It was about a fourth of a page torn from a Louisville paper. The date line was November 24. The section contained one or two ads, and several short articles. One of them, he noticed, was an A.P. release from a town in West Virginia. An old man hunt was being revived. After twenty years, the news item said. Some fellow had murdered his wife. Or rather she had died after a peculiar accident. Suspicion had been aroused at the time, but nothing could be proved. Now, new evidence had come to light. The fellow they were looking for was named Carson. He had left West Virginia shortly after his wife had died.

The paper was soggy and had been crumpled and wind-blown. Funny, Tara thought, how debris gets blown around. Doubtless someone had thrown a paper away, perhaps up on the old road along the ridge, and a part of it had been caught and blown in a downdraft into this ravine. Still holding the paper, he followed Hod on down the canyon and came up with him when they came out into the main hollow.

"What you got there?" Hod asked, nodding at the paper.

"Piece of paper I found in a clump of bushes. Look at this news item."

He pointed it out and Hod read it. "Funny, isn't it," he said then, "how things can be stirred up again after such a long time? I'll bet that guy that killed his wife has been feeling the long arm of the law reaching out for him all these years. And now it's really reaching!"

Hod said nothing, but he looked thoughtfully back up the ravine. Then he folded the paper. "You mind if I keep this?"

Tara looked at him, surprised. "Why, no. You think it means anything?"

"I don't know. Funny, though, that that paper should be in this hollow."

They moved off down the main hollow and Tara picked up his rabbit.

"You remember the date we came here that night?" Hod asked after a time.

Tara thought. "Right after the first of December. I know it was a week or ten days after Thanksgiving."

"Yeah. That's the way I remember it."

Tara stared at him. "What's on your mind?"

"Nothing much. A little coincidence."

They walked homeward silently then. And it wasn't until they came out in the lower pasture that Hod spoke again. "Jory's pa came here from West Virginia."

Tara went to read to Hattie as usual that afternoon. A bright sun was melting the snow fast and it was slushy underfoot. His boots were gummy with it by the time he reached the house. He scraped them off carefully before going inside. "Jory's pa came from West Virginia!" He couldn't get Hod's words out of his mind.

Well, there were a lot of people from West Virginia! That didn't mean anything. But not here on Piney Ridge, his mind insisted. And he kept thinking about that scrap of paper. Someone had torn that news item out. And someone had had it in his possession somewhere near that narrow, hidden ravine. And a sheep bell had rung ominously when they had stumbled into the ravine by accident. Sure, it could all be coincidence. Probably was, he told himself. But he had a cold feeling that something was threatening, and he couldn't shake it off. It made him feel uneasy and more than a little scared. It was so ghostly! So tenuous and unreal.

He made himself put it out of his mind, though. Hod would decide, he thought. Leave it in Hod's hands. He's got a steady head on his shoulders. He'll know what to do. Just keep your mouth shut and forget it.

So he opened the book and read to Hattie, and the afternoon passed. Jory went to meet Sarah and they had supper. The rabbit stew delighted Hattie, although she ate only a tiny bit of it. "Hit's good, though," she said stoutly, "hit's awful good. But seems like I jist can't git no appetite fer nothin' nowadays."

Tara was thinking of going home then. But when the dishes were done, instead of going to her room, Sarah got her guitar from the chimney corner. "Can you help me restring my gittar, Cap'n?" she asked timidly. "I wouldn't ask, but you know about strings and such things. And I've got to do a piece on it tomorrow for the program."

"I don't know much about a guitar, Sarah," he said, "but I'll try."

She got the strings and they sat down together to the task. She knew more about the job than Tara, but her hands were too small and she lacked the strength to tighten the strings once they were in place. But she showed him, and he, following her instructions, got them strung and tightened. Then he ran his fingers over them and tuned them. "I've always wanted to play a guitar," he said. "Sarah, show me!"

"Why, if you can play a fiddle, Cap'n, you can surely pick a gittar!"

"Yeah, but there's six strings on this thing, Sarah. I don't know what to do with those two extra strings!"

Laughing, she moved around by his side and showed him with her own hands the position for the G-chord. "It's easy. Here, and here, and here. Ain't but three positions to keep in mind. That one is G. This one's B-flat. See?"

He caught on, of course, quickly, shifting from one chord to another. "What are the words of that 'foggy, foggy dew' song? I want to learn it."

To his accompaniment, and laughing over his mistakes, she sang it for him. He picked up the words and followed her. "Hod's always singing one about a crawdad hole. You know that one?" he asked.

"Oh, sure. Ever'body knows that one. It's in C. Here," and she showed him.

They sang the one about the crawdad hole, and then all the others he could remember, and some he'd never heard of that Sarah suggested. She had never been so friendly and at ease with him. Always she was awkward and timid and shy with him. But tonight she was different. Music is the charm, he thought. When she plays and sings, she forgets to be shy.

"They's another good one we've not sung," she said, then.

"One more, then. Just one more and I've got to go."

"It's in F."

"Now I don't know that one. Here, you take it this time."

She settled the guitar across her lap and picked a light, experimental chord or two from the strings. Then her voice gently and sweetly moved into a slow, minor tune. Tara did not try to sing with her. It was too beautiful to mar with his own bumbling efforts. The child really had a good voice, he thought again. An unusually good voice. And she used it well, under Mary's coaching. With just a little training something might be done with it.

"Black is the color of my true love's hair," Sarah sang. "Black, black, black . . . And if he on earth no more I see," her head was bent over the guitar and her voice had softened sadly, "If he on earth no more I see, My life will quickly fade away."

The last note held a moment, then faded, and Sarah laid her palm across the trembling strings. She did not lift her head.

Jory, standing in the door, looked at the bent head, and then slowly he looked at Tara. "Black is the color of my true love's hair. Black, black, black." And Tara's hair was as black as night. And ridge girls know their mind early. And Sarah was a ridge girl.

"Thank you, Sarah," Tara said quietly. "Thank you. That was lovely."

Without speaking, Sarah twisted from her chair and fled in confusion from the room.

CHAPTER

13

TARA felt a compulsion to see Jory's father. He didn't know why. He had felt no curiosity about him before. Hod had told him how shiftless the old man was, how filthy and dirty and crowded the house was, and how the family made out with what little work the old man could do, plus the meager welfare allotment he drew for the schooling of his children, which he never used to send his children to school. But now, his mind troubled, bothered by the news item and by what Hod had said, he wanted to see the old man for himself. Not, he admitted, that it would lead anywhere. He just wanted to see.

Without saying anything to Hod, and certainly not to Jory, he climbed the ridge the next morning and took the road down the other way past Gault's place. There was no mistaking the old tenant house in which Gault allowed the Clarks to live. Across a field grown up in broom sedge, which was now flattened and dried, a slatternly frame house leaned drunkenly on perilously inadequate foundation stones. Its windows yawned with missing panes, and rags stuffed in the holes fringed their edges like torn flags. A post was gone from the porch and a green sapling, untrimmed, propped the sagging roof. The porch floor gaped where planks had been ripped up for firewood, and the hogs rooted uneasily under what re-

mained. A crumbling chimney swayed outward from one end
of the house, with a crazy look of not having yet made up its
mind which way to fall. The yard was cluttered with broken
tools, old tires and wagon rims, a dilapidated iron bedstead and
springs, and an unbelievable litter of tin cans and glass bottles
and junk.

A brood of slovenly children gathered around the doorstep
when he came up. He had no idea where they had come from.
One minute he was walking through the cluttered yard alone.
The next he was faced with a swarm of kids. And their sour
smell—that smell that comes only from the never-washed
human body—their dirty clothing, their matted, uncut hair, and
their greasy, grimy faces made his nose quiver in spite of himself.

At about the same time the youngsters swarmed around him,
nine hound dogs—he counted them—sprang up and began a
hysterical and bloodcurdling uproar. For one endless moment
he thought that if he got out of the yard at all, it would be over
the dead bodies of nine hound dogs, and probably a few of the
children! The yard had sprouted dogs and kids like a baby
suddenly cutting teeth!

He yelled. Mamie answered his call. Mamie, he knew, was
old man Clark's third wife. She was a tall, rawboned woman,
her hair braided down her back, one eye squinting vacantly at
him, and her snuff stick crowding the corner of her mouth.

"Mr. Clark at home?" Tara asked. He could barely make himself heard over the clamor of the dogs.

"Shaddup!" Mamie shouted, and picking up a stick of stove
wood she clouted the nearest one. "Git them dawgs around to
the back," she told the children. "An' git thar yerselves!" Then
she turned back to Tara. "Yeah," she said, "he's on the bed.
You want to see him?" She scratched at her armpit and gulped
to keep from spilling snuff spittle down her chin. She didn't

ask him in. She waited, and Tara knew he would have to give his reason for seeing the old man.

"Hod wanted him to help him get some wood sawed up," he told her, using the first logical thing that came to mind.

She grunted. "He ain't got none of his own sawed up. I misdoubt he'll have the time."

"Well, Hod told me to ask."

She stepped inside, and in a moment the old man came to the door, buttoning his shirt as he came. He poked his shirttail inside his overalls and adjusted the suspenders over his shoulders. The overalls were slick with dirt and grease, and ragged and patched. The old man was short and thin, but there was no look of age about him. There was no suggestion of feebleness or frailty. Rather, there was a look of endurance, of stout doggedness, of ancient strength, like that of an old oak tree. Neither was there anything mean, shifty, or ugly-looking about the old man. The expression on his face was mildly interested and more pleasant than otherwise. "What you want?" he asked.

Tara repeated his story.

"You tell Hod I ain't feelin' so good right now. I don't know's I could make out to he'p him none. Ary other time I would. But I been feelin' right puny of late."

"Touch of flu, maybe," Tara said casually.

The old man bit off a chunk of cut plug and stowed it in his cheek. "Rheumatiz, more'n likely."

"Well, I'll tell Hod. The two of us can manage I guess." As if at random Tara threw out his next remark. "I hear you're from West Virginia. Mighty pretty country over that way. I've spent a little time there myself. What part you from?"

There was no change whatever in the old man's face. None, and Tara could swear it. "Mountains."

"Those mountains are mighty pretty. How long since you left?"

"Several years."

Well. This was it. He saw he wasn't getting anywhere, and never would. He turned to go. "Hope the worst of the winter is over."

"I kindly doubt it."

As he walked back down the road, he felt helplessly frustrated. He didn't know what he had gone for. Didn't know what he had expected. But one thing was sure. If that old man . . . if he was the one . . . by golly, that old guy would be a tough customer!

No one had asked him to come in. No one had said good-by when he left. There had been merely the silent, concerted, heavy-fastened look of all the Clarks, for the kids had milled around the door again as he left. And he had been bayed from the yard by the nine hound dogs, unchastened in their hoarse and frantic clamor this time. Tara felt like a complete fool.

At home he told Hod what had happened. Hod shook his head. "Don't mean much," he said. "Most hill folks are like that with strangers. A furriner's a furriner down here, until they get to know you. You say anything to Jory last night?"

"No. Why?"

"I meant to tell you not to. Nor to anybody else. More than likely this is nothing. Just imagination. No use us trying to put two and two together."

Tara spread his hands to the fire. "No. It won't add up. But that wasn't any sheep bell that night, Hod."

Hod rubbed his chin reflectively. "I reckon it wasn't. I don't know . . ."

"It doesn't ring in the daytime, anyhow. We found that out."

Hod looked at him quizzically. "You willing to go back some night? Just the two of us?"

Tara grinned at him. "I'm not exactly willing, but I don't suppose it would be any worse than a night patrol, would it?"

Hod turned the knob on the door slowly. "Come full moon, then, we'll go."

CHAPTER

14

B UT SOMEONE else heard the bell before full moon.
It was only a day or two later. A Sunday. Ferdy Jones had
his car torn down working on the engine. He hadn't had it but
a week or two, and it was his special pride and joy. The fact
that it had over a hundred thousand miles on it didn't matter.
Neither did it bother Ferdy that all four tires were as slick as
pigskin. Nor did he care that all the paint had rusted off and
that none of the windows had glass in them. It was a car. The
engine worked all right. The four wheels turned over and over
down the road. And the glass being out of the windows only
made it easier for the kids to hang their heads out. The thing
was, it was his. Bought with his own money. It was the most
tangible evidence Ferdy could think of that he had come up a
notch in the world. He owned and drove a car, and he tinkered
with it endlessly.

It had been a bright and warm day for February and the
snow had almost gone. The sun set redly, eating up the last of
the cold and slush. At suppertime, Corinna felt the first pangs
of her labor, but she finished feeding her brood and did up the
dishes. She sent the children up the ladder to the loft room and
then she told Ferdy. "You better git the doctor."

Ferdy was washing down the last bite, being late with his

supper on account of working on the car. He looked at her. "Hit's time?"

"Hit's time," and she set about making ready.

"I never got the car fixed yit. Don't know as I kin make the trip. I was aimin' on ridin' the milk truck to work tomorrer."

"You better git the cap'n, then. An' don't be too long."

Ferdy pulled on his coat. "I'll cut acrost Bear Holler. Hit'll be shorter."

The main road wound around the ridge, following its curves and turns and staying well up on the saddle. But the sides of the ridge were constantly pierced with numerous narrow hollows and short spur ridges. One of these led into Bear Hollow and cut directly across the long, winding three-mile turn in the main ridge. Down this spur, long ago, there had been a small settlement called Bethel. A road had gone, once, to the settlement, but it had long since grown over and was little more now than a cow track. All that remained of Bethel was an empty house or two, the old chapel which was boarded up, and the cemetery in the chapel yard. It, too, was grown over and buried in weeds and bushes.

Ferdy followed this old road down the spur, thinking to cross Bear Hollow and come up the ridge again back of Tom Pierce's place. He allowed to go there first, looking for the captain. If he wasn't at Tom's, it could be Jory would take him down to Hod's. His lantern was the only light in the darkness, and in the February cold the woods which closed all around him were quiet. Too quiet. He didn't like this old road, even in the daytime. It was too spooky, too deserted. Nothing but a stray cow or sheep ever wandered over on this spur. But it would save him nearly an hour's time.

He hurried, stumbling occasionally over a rock or limb blown across the track, and as he drew near the churchyard, he hugged the far side of the path and flashed his lantern uneasily ahead of him. It had been a time and a time since he'd been over this way and he didn't want to miss the path down to the hollow.

It was on the far side of the cemetery, where the path cut down the steep side of the ridge, that he heard the bell. Faint at first, and tinkly. As if it was far off. He stopped and his heart ballooned into his throat. He set his lantern down, and with shaking hands tried to turn the wick higher. The bell tinkled again, nearer. *Hit's in the graveyard*, Ferdy thought, and a paralyzing fear took hold of him. *Hit's on the fur side the graveyard!*

It wasn't until he placed the sound that he remembered the old legend of the belled hant. "O my God! Old man Thomas is walkin' tonight, shore!"

He dropped the lantern and it rolled into the mud of the track and went out. Frantically he clawed around for it, choking on his own breath, his knees buckling under him. He found it finally, but his hands were shaking so that he couldn't get it lighted. Clutching it, unlighted, he started running back down the road in the direction from which he had come, crashing through the undergrowth, falling over rocks and limbs, scrambling on all fours when he fell.

The bell followed, its clear, silvery tinkle carrying lightly on the thin, cold air. It followed, sharp and distinct at first, then fading as he neared the ridge road. But Ferdy never knew when it stopped. He ran and ran, until he was reeling with exhaustion, wet with sweat and sobbing for breath. Only then did he slow down to a walk, and only then did he notice that he could no longer hear the bell. He leaned against a tree and waited until he could breathe more evenly, and then he went on, shaken, trembling, and scared of every sudden sound.

And it was of the bell that he spoke first when he stumbled up on Tom Pierce's porch and Jory opened the door to him. Tara had been making ready to go home and was just behind Jory. He thought Ferdy was drunk, so wild and haggard did he look. "Man, what's the matter with you!" Jory cried, helping him inside.

"I jist seen a ghost . . . heared one, I mean. I jist heared old man Thomas aringin' his bell! He chased me plumb down the road! Chased me ever' step, aringin' that there bell of his'n!"

"Where?" Tara's voice was sharp.

"Over by the graveyard. The Bethel graveyard."

"What were you doing over there?"

Ferdy sank into a chair and loosened his coat around his throat. Tom had come in from Hattie's room, and Sarah was standing in the door wide-eyed. "I'll tell you. Git me a drink of water, somebody. My throat's so dry from bein' skeered I can't swaller! Gentlemen, I want you to know hit's somethin' fierce to be chased by a ghost!"

Jory brought him a glass of water and he swallowed it down at a gulp. "Corinna's time is on her, an' I been workin' on my car an' got it all tore down. I was comin' fer the cap'n, seein' as we had to have somebody quick. An' I thought I'd save time cuttin' acrost Bear Holler. Jist as I got past the graveyard the bell commenced ringin'. Hit skeered me so I couldn't rightly place it fer a time, but directly I knowed hit was comin' from the fur side the graveyard. Hit kept comin' closter an' closter, an' I dropped my lantern an' hit went out, an' there I was in the cold dark, no light atall, an' that there bell comin' closter all the time. I lit a shuck back down the road where I come from, an' hit taken out right after me. I don't know how fur hit chased me, but I was a good piece up the main road 'fore I stopped runnin', an' I reckon hit had give up by then, fer I couldn't hear no bell. But I tell you, hit's mortally true old man Thomas walks that there graveyard by night an' rings his bell! I heared it as plain as day!"

Tara and Jory looked at each other, and Tara wet his lips. "Were you starting down a narrow little hollow?"

Ferdy shook his head. "No, they ain't no holler along there.

I was jist startin' down the path leads down to Bear Holler.
Hit's the only holler around there. You know that old path cuts
acrost to the Bethel road, Jory?"

Jory nodded and he shook his head at Tara. "Must have been
a stray sheep, Ferdy. You know ghosts don't walk."

"This here wasn't no sheep bell I heared, Jory Clark. An' you
needn't to try to tell me so! I reckon I'd know a sheep bell. Besides ain't no sheep goin' to chase me plumb down the ridge
road! This here was that there belled hant of old man Thomas!
I'm atellin' you! Hit's a warnin' to keep away from that graveyard, that's what it is! An' gentlemen, I'm aimin' on keepin'
away!"

Tara laughed. "You sure you've not had one drink too many,
Ferdy?"

"You kin laugh if you want to, Cap'n. You ain't jist been run
half to death by a hant! I heared what I heared! An' I've not
had a drink sincet I went to work at the furniture place! Not,"
he added, "that I wouldn't like to have one right now! Hit's
enough to shake a man's nerves plumb to pieces, bein' took out
after by a bell-ringin' hant! You kin laugh, but you've not
heared that bell!"

Oh, yes, I have, thought Tara. I certainly have! And you're
right. It's a warning to keep away from that churchyard. But
why? And who?

Then he remembered Corinna. "Great day," he yelled, "here
we stand jabbering about a bell-ringing ghost and Corinna is
waiting. Come on, Jory."

Some two hours later Tara delivered Corinna of a son.
Corinna was an old hand at the business of birthing a baby and
gave him no trouble. When it was over, she said, shyly: "Yer a
knowin' kind of doctor, Cap'n Cochrane. Gentle-like and easy.
I'm much obliged to you. Hit was good you was handy."

She would have got along all right without him, he knew. All

else failing, one of the neighbors would have come in. More
children had been born on this ridge without a doctor than
with one, but Tara was glad he had been handy. It had felt
good to be at work, and he was proud of the husky boy he'd
helped Corinna birth. "You're welcome, Corinna," he told her.
"What are you going to name him?"

Corinna looked at him slyly. "I had kind of fixed on Cap'n
Jory."

Tara shouted with laughter. "My sakes, Corinna, what a name
to tack onto the little fellow!"

"Yessir. I kind of liked it, though."

Tara chuckled over the name all the way home. But he was
pleased, just the same.

When he got home around midnight he went sleepily and
tiredly to the kitchen to find a bite to eat. Hod heard him and
called, "That you, Cap'n?"

"Me."

"Where you been?"

"Getting us a namesake."

There was a silence and then Hod appeared in the doorway,
clutching his robe around him. "Ferdy's?" he said.

Tara nodded. "Big boy. Weighs close to ten pounds, I'd say.
Hod, Ferdy heard the bell tonight."

"Ferdy did?"

"Yeah. He was cutting across by the Bethel churchyard to
get me, and the bell chased him down to the main road."

Hod sat down at the breakfast table. "Pour me a cup of that
coffee. Cap'n, something's going on up there. Something that
means trouble. We might as well find out."

"Tonight?"

"Tonight."

Tara finished his sandwich and Hod gulped his coffee down,
then went into his and Mary's room to dress. Tara went to his

own room, and, going directly to the clothes closet, took down his Army holster and forty-five. He buckled it around him.

Hod met him in the kitchen with his shotgun.

Mary had awakened and followed Hod into the kitchen. Her dark hair was loose and lay like a scarf, softly, around her shoulders. There was little yet to tell of the child on its way, except a deepening serenity on her face. A quiet sheen of content that glossed her cheeks and glowed in her skin. That, and a certain languor of movement. Tara felt the familiar stricture in his chest at the sight of her, and the swift dart of hurt. Out of all the world, why did he have to love this woman? And if he had to love her, why too late?

She moved slowly now, stretching her arms over her head. "What you two guys up to?"

"Tara thought he heard a fox down close to the barn. We're going to see. May ramble around a little. You go on back to bed."

"I'm hungry! But go on. I know what'll happen, though. You'll probably be gone the rest of the night if you get on a fox trail!"

"Well, I've been wanting to go fox hunting," Tara said, "and this may be my best chance."

They made their way up the hollow, leaving the dogs at home. "We'll douse the light when we get to the mouth of the ravine," Hod said. "Don't want to warn him."

"It's going to be one devil of a job getting up that canyon in the dark," Tara said.

"Yeah, he'll probably hear us. But we'll do the best we can."

When they came abreast of the wall of thicket and rock, Hod flicked off his flashlight and cautiously they climbed around the now familiar stream bed. "Lucky the ice has melted," Tara whispered, "it's slick enough the way it is."

They made their way carefully up the stream, inching along

from one handhold to the next, crawling from one foothold to another, sliding, slipping, making as little noise as possible, but inevitably making some. "Just like that time in the hedgerows in France," Hod said softly.

"Yeah. Only the hedgerows sprouted guns!"

Hod laughed noiselessly. "That ain't exactly one dozen roses you got strapped around your belt now, is it?"

When they came to the fall of rock which rose nearly shoulder-high above them, Hod went first, stuffing the flashlight in his hip pocket, laying his gun on the ground above. He went up feeling his way with his hands, easing gently, careful not to dislodge any small stones. Tara waited tensely.

Hod had one knee over the top of the fall when the flashlight, pinched by the tightening of his pants when he raised his knee, clattered onto the rocks and went bounding off down the stream bed. Both he and Tara froze.

There was nothing but silence. Still, cold, dark silence. Then Hod whispered, "Can you find that light?"

"No! It's halfway down the hollow by now! You might as well have blown a horn to let him know we're coming!"

Hod swore under his breath and Tara started up over the rock. It was then that they heard the bell. Faraway-sounding as before, and faint, and yet clear and strong. Thin, silvery, light. Tara scrambled up, heedless of the noise. It was pitch dark, and up on the level he stretched out his hand to locate Hod. "Here," Hod said, guiding him.

Tara moved over by him. Silently they waited. The bell tinkled once more, and then was still. As if it were waiting too. There was no sound at all in the night. Nothing to give away movement of any sort. Tara loosened his gun. "What next?"

"Let's wait a minute. Don't make any noise."

They held themselves rigid, tense, and Tara felt his ears point with the effort of listening. Listening, he wondered, for what?

Five . . . ten minutes passed. It seemed longer. Tara eased his muscles restlessly. "Could you tell where it came from?"

"On up the hollow somewhere. It's up above us."

"Let's try to get up there."

Cautiously they moved. It was difficult in the dark. They could see scarcely a foot ahead of them, and they had to feel their way with both hands and feet. They slid along, making headway by inches, and then Tara's feet tangled in a tree lap, dry and brittle. The branches broke with a sharp, snapping sound. Instantly the bell warned them. Nearer and louder. It tinkled three times and then paused. Three times again, and paused. Three times . . . and then it was still. They waited. "He's listening for us," Hod warned.

"How far away is he?"

"Hard to tell. He's either nearer, or he deliberately muffles the bell at first to make you think he's farther away than he is."

They moved on. And then the ravine pinched out before the solid wall of rock. Hod ran his hand over it as high as he could reach. "This is that cliff," he said. "That's why there's no sign of a hollow at this end. It goes straight up as high as I can reach."

The bell sounded again, this time from their rear. They whirled around. "He's got in back of us," Tara said.

"Yeah, but he's up on the ridge yet. He's not down in the hollow."

"Can we get out that way? We don't want to get trapped in here!"

"I don't know. We better go back to that rockfall and try to climb out there."

They found their way back, the bell leading them. It was steady now, tinkling three times and pausing regularly. But the sound remained above them, and came no nearer. Tara shivered. "It's spooky. Even if you know it's a human. No wonder Ferdy was scared out of his wits!"

Hod said nothing. They came back to the level place above

the rockfall and Hod veered to the left. "Seems to me he's up on this side."

The side of the canyon was very steep, precipitate, strewn with loose rocks and boulders. It was impossible to climb in the dark without making a great deal of noise. The bell receded, jangling frantically, as if in sudden alarm. They climbed on, sliding, slipping, the rocks rattling under their feet. "How much farther?" Tara panted.

"Can't tell."

Then the dark was split by a stab of flame and the night exploded in the sharp report of a gun. Twice, three times, it fired. "Rifle," Hod muttered.

Tara aimed at the points of flame and fired. The forty-five made a terrific noise among the rocks of the canyon, going off like a small cannon. The sound echoed and reverberated, dying off in the distance like the rumblings of thunder.

He fired again, and then they charged the rim of the ridge, coming out suddenly on top. There was nothing. Not even the bell. Not a thing now. They waited. There was only stillness. Not a twig snapped. "We couldn't find him in a hundred years in this darkness," Hod said.

Tara holstered his gun. "One thing is sure. That guy means business!"

"Yeah. But what is he doing up here? Where does he stay? What's it all about?"

"You think it might just be a moonshiner?"

"Might be," Hod admitted. "Might easily be. But where would his still be hidden? We've been up that little hollow now. There's no place he could hide out there."

"What about up here on this ridge?"

"This is the Bethel spur. No place up here . . . except the old church."

"Maybe that's it."

Hod was quiet. "It could be . . . it could be. But we can't

do anything tonight. We'll have to come over to the church in the daytime."

In the darkness Tara grinned. "Brother, I just hope we can advance under cover when we do! Even in the dark that guy's shooting is too good for comfort!"

"You can say that again!" Hod seconded fervently, and he led the way down the side of the ridge.

The next day they went back to the Bethel spur. They went this time by the path that ascended the ridge from Bear Hollow. When they came to the churchyard, they waited a moment in the woods, and then circled cautiously, keeping an eye on the building. It looked deserted and abandoned. There seemed no sign of life. But they had to make sure. "Best way's to come up from the back," Hod said, "where all that tangle of stuff has grown right up the church. We can keep under cover that way."

They dropped to all fours and crawled warily through the mass of dried vines and broom sedge. Stopping occasionally to listen, they could hear nothing. Except for the rustling noise of their own progress, the silence was unbroken. They inched on and came, finally, to the back door of the building. Tara let out his breath explosively. "Well, so far, so good. I guess that door's locked, isn't it?"

Hod looked at it. "Nailed shut, I'd reckon. What you think of sneaking a look through one of the windows first?"

"I'd think right highly of it."

They edged around the corner of the building. The windows were boarded, but there were wide cracks between the boards. They crawled to the nearest window and straightened up cautiously. Hod glued his eye to the first crack. Then he laughed. "Not a thing in there. Come on."

Abandoning caution, they went back to the door and tried it. Surprisingly, it opened immediately. It was neither locked nor

nailed. Inside, the building was desolate and lifeless. The floor
was rotten and had broken through in places. Cobwebs hung
dustily in all the corners, and the walls gaped where pieces of
the boarding had been broken off. An old stove sat in the
middle of the room, and Hod flipped the door open. It was full
of ashes. Tara kicked at an empty whisky bottle. "Looks as if
somebody's done some drinking in here."

"Yeah, but not lately. These ashes are old. Well. There's
nobody hiding out in here. Reckon we're on a cold trail. Let's
take a look at the churchyard."

They walked over the churchyard, trying to examine it. But
the mat of blackberry vines, old grape runners, dried weeds,
and sedge had covered it for so many years that they could
hardly find the grave markers. It was hopeless to look for anything there. Hod wandered off toward the back side. Here
there was a heavy and impenetrable growth of thorn and locust,
covered over rankly with grape vines. Even in the winter when
the foliage was gone, the hedge of bushes and sprouts was so
thick as to prove impassable. "That cliff is bound to sheer off
somewhere near," Hod said as Tara came up.

"Probably on the other side of that hedge," Tara answered.
"Doesn't seem to be any path."

"If we had a sickle, we might cut our way through."

Hod laughed. "Man, you'd need a bulldozer to get through
that stuff!"

They stood and considered. The whole thing was a weird and
crazy mystery. Somewhere around here someone with a bell
and a gun hid out at night. There was no path, nor any trail,
indicating any coming or going. The church was not being
used. The churchyard had not been disturbed. And yet Ferdy
had heard the bell from the far side of the churchyard. And it
had followed him down the spur road. They had heard the bell
down in the hollow, and up on the ridge. It didn't make sense!

"It beats me," Hod said finally. "I reckon we're not very good detectives."

"It's no moonshiner, anyhow," Tara said. "At least we've eliminated that possibility. And if it's . . . if it's . . ."

"If it's Jory's pa, maybe we'd better let well enough alone," Hod finished.

Tara looked at him quickly. "Maybe we had."

Both were thinking the same thing. But neither said it. If it was Jory's father, and if Jory's father were this Carson fellow, soon enough some real detectives would be trying to solve the mystery.

As they went back down the ridge to the hollow, it was Tara who put their unspoken uneasiness into words. "I hope Jory doesn't go messing around that hollow trying to figure out anything."

CHAPTER
15

THAT same day Ferdy Jones bought a bottle of moonshine and proceeded to get completely and thoroughly drunk. Not just happily, hilariously, wobbly drunk. Soused. Definitely and purposely, soused.

His nerves had been so shook up, he told himself, he had to steady them down someway. Man couldn't be expected to get up and go to work as if nothing at all had happened. Everybody knowed it was hard on a feller, his woman birthing a young'un. Made him feel uneasy-like, at best, and give him a queer notion he'd done wrong somehow. Not exactly wrong, for after all he'd only had his rights, but kind of queer and unsettled in his feelings. And as if that wasn't enough, there was this bell-ringing hant chasing him down the road. Made his bones turn to jelly just to think of it. It was a miracle his hair hadn't turned white overnight. Just a plumb miracle. Put 'em together and he was so frazzled he was a nervous wreck. He misdoubted he could steady his hands to work on a piece of wood.

So he made no pretense of going to work. Said he didn't feel like it. Corinna eyed him uneasily from her bed. And when he put on his coat and cap and left the house without further explanation, she turned her face to the wall and wept. It had been so nice. Ferdy working regular and not drinking. It had been so safe and good and nice. But she'd ought to have known it was too good to last. She'd ought to have known something so good wasn't for them. Now he'd get fired off his job and everything would be like it had always been. Scratching and scrabbling. Not enough to eat. Not enough firewood to keep warm. Not enough clothes to cover their nakedness. Not enough of nothing. So she wept hopelessly, and resignedly.

The oldest girl came in, frightened at her mother's weeping. "Ma," she pleaded, "Ma, don't."

"I can't he'p it. Yer pa'll git drunk now, an' he'll git fired offen his job, an' things'll be jist like they was. An' hit was so nice, havin' cash money along, an' him not gittin' drunk. I can't he'p but mourn!"

The girl studied her mother, and then she got up and put on her coat and cap.

"Where you goin'?" Corinna asked.

"I'm agoin' to git Jory an' the Cap'n. Pa may git drunk, but hit may be they kin he'p him from gittin' fired. We ain't goin' back like we was. Not if they's ary way to he'p it!"

She met Tara at Hattie's gate, just coming up on the ridge after his morning over at Bethel with Hod. "Hello there, Elsie," he said. "How's the new baby over at your house?"

"He's fine," Elsie said.

"Something wrong?"

She nodded her head. "Pa's out somewheres drunk."

"Didn't he go to work this morning?"

"No. Said he never felt like workin'. Then he lit out to git him somethin' to drink. Ma's afeared he'll git fired."

"Likely he will," Tara said. This was just about what he'd expected.

"Ma's acryin'."

Yes, Tara thought, she would be. And with good reason. The whole family would be plunged back into the same old hopeless and shiftless way of living. He looked at Elsie. She had on a new coat. A good, new, warm coat. And new shoes on her feet. And the rest of the kids, they had shoes now. And coats. And they had something besides beans and corn bread to eat. And Corinna had had something still more vital to human life. She had had hope. For a little while she had had hope.

"I was thinkin' mebbe you or Jory could he'p me find him," Elsie was saying, "an' git him to work someway."

"All right," Tara said. "We'll find him and take care of him. You and I'll find him. No need to bother Jory with it."

He called to the house. "Hattie, tell Jory I'm going to use the car for a while. I'm going to take Elsie to the Gap for some medicine."

When they had driven out of sight of the house, Tara turned to the girl. "Where would he be likely to go?"

"I've not got no idee, 'thout he'd head fer the store down on the pike. Seems like he allus heads down thataway."

"We'll try the store. Someone there may have seen him anyhow."

They went down the hill to the pike and to the small store which sat at the foot of the ridge where the road turned. Tara stopped the car, got out, and went in. The usual crowd of men were sitting clustered around the stove. "Any of you fellows seen Ferdy Jones this morning?" he asked.

The storekeeper laughed and motioned with his thumb toward the corner back of the stove. In the dimness Tara had not seen beyond the first few feet inside the door. There sat Ferdy. He was drunk, drunk as a boiled owl, but not out yet. Red-faced and weaving on the nail keg which served him as a seat, he was still expertly manipulating a cud of tobacco and hitting, with fair aim, the ash bucket in front of the stove when he spit. "Here I am," he yelled belligerently, "what you want with me?"

The captain looked at him and laughed. Ferdy looked like a thin, pin-plucked, scrawny-necked rooster sitting there on his nail keg, his eyes crossed in their effort to focus, his legs spraddled to balance him. "What you want with me?" he yelled.

"Come on, Ferdy. You gotta go to work."

"Naw. I ain't agoin' to work this mornin'. My nerves is all to pieces."

"We'll take care of your nerves. Come on."

"I ain't agoin' to work this mornin', I said! Ain't nobody kin make me, neither!"

"Oh, yes, there is!" And the captain strode rapidly over to Ferdy, and taking him by the scruff of the neck, hauled him onto his feet. For all he was tall, Ferdy was thin and slight, and he was helpless in Tara's grasp. He dangled on his toes and hit out with his fists and scrambled around for a foothold. Tara held onto him. "Where's the pump?" he asked the storekeeper.

"Out back."

Tara dragged Ferdy out the back door. Elsie, who had been standing in the door, followed. She started the pump going, wordlessly. Ferdy wrenched loose with the first gasp of cold water and hit out blindly at the captain. Tara knocked him down. Flat. He crawled up and crouched, more sober now, and ready to fight.

"All right," Tara said to him. "Come on, if that's the way you want it."

Ferdy tried, and kept on trying, but he was still weaving on his feet. With something of the feeling a parent has in punishing a child, with almost a loving feeling of this-hurts-me-more-than-it-does-you, Tara batted him down two or three times, trying not to hurt him too much. When Ferdy rolled over and groaned and failed, finally, to get up, Tara pulled him up and doused his head into the bucket of water Elsie had pumped. Holding him by the hair he plunged him up and down three or four times, until Ferdy was spluttering and choking for breath.

Then he handed him his handkerchief. "Now dry your face off and get in the car. You're going to work."

Ferdy wiped his face and hands and shook the water off his wet head. He looked at the captain. Tara stood there, feet astraddle, his breath blowing through his nose. Ferdy laughed. "By grannies, Cap'n, when you git goin' you're a regular windstorm! I misdoubt I'd have much of a chancet with you, sober!"

"I misdoubt it too. But every time you get drunk from now on, you can know what to expect. You're going to keep that job! Hear! It means too much to your family. And it means too much to Jory Clark. And, by golly, it ought to mean something to you! Jory thinks love and forbearance will hold you to the straight and narrow path. But I'm going to back it up with a little fist fighting when it's necessary. You're not going to let your family down, and you're not going to let Jory Clark down. Now, get in the car. Tell the old man your wife has a new baby. That's excuse enough for being late to work this morning. But you stay away from the bottle from now on!"

When they let Ferdy out in front of the furniture shop, he fumbled a minute with his cap. Then he grinned sheepishly at the captain. "Much obliged," he said, and he started shuffling across the yard. He turned halfway across and looked back. "But my nerves was awful shook up!"

Tara laughed. Personally, and privately, he didn't much blame Ferdy for hitting the bottle. No doubt his nerves had been "awful shook up!" But he couldn't be allowed to lose that job. Too much and too many depended on his holding it.

Tara looked at his skinned knuckles on the steering wheel. Getting to be quite a good little Samaritan, aren't you? he scoffed at himself. Almost as good as Jory! Getting to where the ridge can't run without you! Just full of good works, you! Just brimming over with loving your neighbor! Twelve hours a day you're running around butting into other people's affairs! Twelve hours a day you're just busy as a bee setting the world

to rights! Twelve hours a day you go around poking your nose
into things that are none of your business! Being your brother's
keeper!

But he still felt pretty good. Ferdy's job was saved. Corinna
and the kids would have another chance. And Jory could go on
believing in love and forbearance. He couldn't scoff himself
out of feeling pretty good about it.

Things come in threes, Tara told himself later. I might have
known something else would happen.

He went back to Hattie's after taking Ferdy to work and
taking Elsie home. Jory had dinner ready. "Corinna all right?"
he asked Tara.

"Fine," Tara said. "She needed some medicine, though." And
the medicine she had got was the best she could have had, he
thought.

They had eaten and Tara was settled with Hattie for the
afternoon reading when Tom came running into the house.
"Hey," he yelled, "they's a fire looks like down at Gaults'!
Smoke's jist abilin' out the roof!" And he went tearing down
the road.

Jory and Tara ran to the porch. Tom was right. The smoke,
black and heavy, was pouring from the roof around the chimney, and already flames were licking around the edges. "I'll go,"
Jory said. "You stay here with Hattie."

"No need," Hattie called. "I'll be all right. Both of you go."

"Take the car and get Hod," Jory said, struggling into his
coat. "Circle around then and pick up Wells. We'll need all the
men we can get."

But when Tara got back with Hod and Wells, the front of
the house was burning strongly. "Let it go!" Wells called, running toward the house. "Let it go! Try to save the back!"

Jory and Gault and Tom were trying feebly to wet down the

flames with water. Water, Tara remembered, brought up from the spring down in the hollow, one bucket at a time! "Let it go!" Wells yelled again. "Git hooks an' crowbars an' pull it down if we kin. Save the back room!"

They scattered in every direction, grabbing whatever tools they could find, but it was useless. The fire was so hot they couldn't get near it. They went back then to dabbing wet sacks onto the back roof, slapping buckets of water onto the side walls, trying to keep the fire from spreading. Hod and Tara toiled ceaselessly up and down the long hill to the spring, filling tubs and buckets and carrying all they could at one time. It was no good. "When a house gits afire here on the ridge," Gault said, "hit's jist gone. Ain't no way of checkin' it."

Becky stood with small Hannah in her arms watching. There had been little time to save anything in the front of the house. "See if you kin git my stove an' cabinet outen the kitchen," she told Gault, setting Hannah down. "We kin make out if we got a way to cook an' eat."

It was hot inside the kitchen, but not yet unbearable. The men lifted the heavy stove bodily and carried it out. In the same way they were able to get the cabinet out, and then Wells went back and gathered up all the china, pots and pans, and silver he could pile into a tub. "That's jist about it, Becky," he said then. "Hit's agittin' pow'ful hot in there."

Calmly Becky sat down on an upturned tub. "We'll make out," she said. "I'm jist thankful hit didn't come of a night an' mebbe burn us all to a cinder along with the house. Way it is, ain't nothin' lost but the house an' plunder."

Then she missed Hannah. In sudden panic she whirled around. "Where's Hannah? Where's Hannah at? I set her down right here jist a minnit ago! Oh, Lord love us, she's got away! She'll be in the fire! She'll be burnt up! Gault! Gault! He'p me find Hannah!"

Her fear was a frenzy which spread from her to all the rest. She shrieked and screamed at them to find her baby! She was frantic with fear, and her panic spread like an epidemic over all of them. Wells tried to go back in the house, and Hod caught him and held him. Gault took off his coat and wrapped it around his head, and it took Jory and Tom both to stop him from plunging back into the flame-eaten house. Tara was frozen and paralyzed, rooted to the ground with the horror of the moment. But it was he who found the child after all. One small corner of his mind was functioning clearly amidst all the panic. Hannah was a baby, but even a baby would not have gone into the house. Becky had been holding her until just a few minutes ago. The heat by that time was much too great for the child to have wandered in out of curiosity. The heat would have hurt, and even a baby avoided hurt. She couldn't be in the house! Where would a child, set down suddenly, freed, have gone? He had a small, mental picture of a child set down on her feet, loosed from restraining hands, and the child was running, running away from the people and the burning house. Out in the weeds and dried grass, maybe. But she would run. Use her feet.

He started looking in the fringes of weeds and grass around the yard. Wandered around the house, looked off into the back lot. And there was a little pink dab of apron, a small, white-diapered bottom turned up toward him. Hannah was stooped over the chicken trough in the back lot, happily and busily splashing herself with the water. Tara gathered her up and took her to Becky. Indignant at being disturbed, Hannah was howling mightily.

A great peace and weariness fell over them all when Hannah was found, and they stood and watched the walls of the house fall in, undisturbed by the tragedy of the burned house, relieved only that there had not been greater tragedy.

The next morning when Tara went up on the ridge a strange

truck stood in front of Hattie's house. "Whose truck?" he asked Jory.

"Jessie's, down at the store. Borrowed it to gather up the stuff."

"What stuff?"

"Why, stuff for Gault and Becky to get a new start with. Everybody'll want to give."

Tom stayed with Hattie and Tara went with Jory. They drove the full length of the ridge, stopping at every house. And at every house something more was added to the load that gradually piled up in the back of the truck. A bed here. Springs and mattress there. Quilts at another place. Sheets and pillow-cases. Chairs. Tables. Canned fruits and vegetables. Clothing. Dishes. Cooking utensils. The load mounted until it would hold no more. But Jory drove on until he had stopped at every house. No one would have wanted to be left out. Fire can come to anyone on the ridge. Had come to many. Most knew from experience what it was like to be burned out and left with nothing. And those who didn't know were well aware of their own constant peril. A faulty flue. A too hot fire. And an hour later, ashes and hot, cracked foundation stones, and blackened, fire-gutted ribs of what was once a home. No one wanted to be left out of the giving to Gault and Becky.

When they unloaded the truck in Becky's yard, she went over everything, appraising, noting, judging. "They's jist two things missin'," she told them happily. "Jist two things a body'd have to have. They ain't nobody give a teakittle, nor a wash-pan. Ain't it nice how they've thought of ever'thing, though? An' them clothes. My, I ain't had so many clothes in all my life! Two good coats. Jist look! An' more'n Hannah'll wear the next year. Look, I'll bet it was Corinna put them diapers in . . . asparin' 'em from her own young'un."

"Where will they live?" Tara asked Jory.

"They'll stay in that little cabin back of the house. The little log cabin Miss Willie lived in for a time. But it won't take long to raise a new house. Everybody'll help. We'll have to get busy felling trees, though."

"Will they build another log house?"

"I reckon."

"Looks as if it would be easier to build a frame house."

"Probably would. Only I doubt they've got the money. There's plenty of trees growing on Gault's place to be had for nothing."

"Except for the time and the work of everybody on the ridge to pitch in and help him get them cut."

"That doesn't matter."

"No. It doesn't seem to. It seems to be the business of everyone up here to be his brother's keeper."

Jory's smile lighted up his face gently. "That's just about it, Cap'n. And that's the way it ought to be."

Jory took the truck back to the store, and Tara went to meet Sarah. No one had had time to cook, so supper was a hurried affair of scrambled eggs and mush and milk. Then Sarah asked, "You ready for your music lesson, Cap'n?"

Every evening now when supper was over, Tara and Sarah played and sang together. They called it his music lesson, for he had bought himself a guitar. He had also sent to Louisville for books of old ballads, and gradually he was adding to Sarah's repertoire. He was teaching her as much as he knew, too, about voice training. He coached her in every song, developing her range, teaching her breath control, helping her interpret the meaning of the old songs. She was apt and interested, quickly learning and retaining what she learned. She was soon going to be ready for more than he could teach her, he knew. And from there on he didn't know what to do. She should go away to study. But he doubted if Hattie and Tom would ever let her go away from home.

When their hour of music was over, Jory walked down the

ridge with him. His car was out of repair. "You know, Cap'n," he said, "Hattie is getting worse."

"Yes, I know. There isn't much more time for Hattie."

"She needs a woman."

"Well, I've said all along she should have had a nurse."

"She wouldn't have been as happy. We . . . you've given her a lot of happiness these past months. That's counted for more than a nurse."

Tara said nothing. He too knew it had counted for more. If some prescience had made Hattie know that nothing could be done for her, she hadn't been wrong, he knew now, to want her last months at home, with folks she loved around her. And humbly he realized he was one of those Hattie loved.

"But she's more helpless now," Jory went on, "and a man, even as good as Tom or you, can't make out to do for her like a woman would. We've got to think of something."

"Couldn't Irma come home?"

Irma had gone to Indiana a few weeks before. Jory shook his head. "No. It may be Irma and John can get their problem worked out over there together. It wouldn't be good to separate them now."

They walked on, silent, thinking. "I've been thinking . . ." Jory began. He stopped and waited so long to go on that Tara asked, "Thinking what?"

"Well, I been wondering if Rose wouldn't come. Trouble is, I don't reckon she'd come if I asked her. Seems like I rub her the wrong way."

Tara laughed. "Now the woods are clear! Now I see where we're heading! Rose, huh? And *I'm* to ask Rose to come!"

"Would you?" Jory was laughing too, but his voice was eager.

Tara ran his arm through Jory's and he hitched into step with him. "Sure, I'll ask her. I've been every other kind of angel on this ridge. I might as well try my hand at being Cupid."

"Now, that's not what I . . ."

"Oh, I know. That's not what you were thinking. But it adds up to that in the long run. Sure, I'll ask her."

And he did. The next morning. She was raking leaves in the yard with Miss Willie and Taysie when he came up. He thought again how like a small hen partridge she was. Rounded, plump, brown. Beside Miss Willie's thin spareness she looked stocky and solid. He did not think her particularly attractive. But there was something homey and comfortable about her. And Jory was the one to be suited, not he.

"We should have done this last fall," Miss Willie explained, asking him in, "but the leaves kept falling and falling, so we put it off until we knew for sure they were through. No use doing our work a dozen times."

"Absolutely none," Tara agreed, "and don't stop. I have only a minute." And he came straight to the point. "Rose, can you come help with Hattie? She needs a woman now."

Miss Willie's glance was startled. "Is it that near?"

"We don't know, Miss Willie. It may be quite a while yet. But she's worse and she needs someone besides us men."

Rose looked questioningly at Miss Willie. Miss Willie nodded. "Of course, Rose. You must go. I'll look after Taysie."

"We'll bring you home every evening, Rose," Tara assured her. Jory will bring you home, he was thinking. I'll see to that. But he didn't say so. He didn't mention Jory at all. He was, indeed, very careful not to.

He walked home across the field. The sun was only feebly warm, and the wind blew fitfully in starts and spurts as if it could not make up its mind. It was a sad sort of day . . . broody and introspective.

Something of the sadness settled into Tara Cochrane. Jory and Rose Clark were poles apart now, perhaps. But he wished he had as good a chance to live out his life with the one he loved as Jory had. At least Rose was free. It only remained for Jory to convince her as to his way of believing. Nothing immovable and impassable stood between them. There was nothing hopeless between them . . . nothing like a perfectly happy marriage, for instance.

His thoughts saddled him wearily. And galled in the same old sore spots. What was he staying around here for? Don't stay too long, the doctor had said. And here he'd been most of the winter. A man with good sense would get out. But until Hattie died . . . and then something should be done about Sarah. And there was this bell-ringing hant too. So he ran out his thoughts, worried them, fretted them, and came to no decision. One day at a time, he thought. One day at a time now.

CHAPTER

16

AFTER February, March was a long, slow pause between winter and spring. The hardest month of the year to get through, Hattie said, sitting in her big chair by the window, watching the rain and the wind beat against the trees. "Hit's a mournful time," she said. "A body's allus so wearied out with winter, time March comes, hit don't seem like spring could git here fast enough."

But for all the dark, rainy days, there were also dry, windy ones that were quick-flashing, nervous, mercurial. And there were warm, sunny ones, lazy with sunlight, slow-moving through the hours. March was a prophet, bearded with winter, but promising spring.

Rose came every day to Hattie's now. Usually Wells brought her early in the morning, and she rarely came empty-handed. Miss Willie constantly sent good dishes by her . . . custards, soups, jellies . . . the only things Hattie could eat. Once it was a house plant, brightly potted, for her window. Another time it was a new book. Still again it was a stack of magazines with gay-colored illustrations to while away the long, weary hours.

But if Rose had brought nothing, she still was welcome. Hattie liked her. She was a Pierce. Home folks. Womenfolks. And

Hattie got along well with her. Tara, watching Rose with Hattie, noticed her gentleness, her slowness, which was restful, and her never-failing patience. She took time with Hattie, cheerfully, never minding the extra steps, the bending and stooping, the lifting and straightening. She knew ways to make Hattie comfortable, tucking a small pillow against the curves of the tired back, sliding a hot water bottle under the blanket to warm her always cold feet, turning her mattress frequently and changing the linens to keep the bed from getting tiresome. And she told Hattie all the news each day, laughing with her over it, talking easily and comfortably, recounting little things Taysie had said and done, telling how Miss Willie spoiled her. She remembered all the things that happened in the settlement and told them to Hattie. Gossip and rumor and fact. Jory and Tara, being men, had not drawn upon that resource. Rose told Hattie the news and kept her from thinking too much about herself and her pain. She knew how to rub Hattie's back and ease it, and she learned quickly to give the injections Hattie needed increasingly. She's a good nurse, Tara thought. She's just naturally a good nurse.

In the evening, Jory drove her home. Tara managed that by having his music lesson with Sarah. He never asked Jory if those drives alone together brought them closer. And Jory never spoke of them. But of course Tara wondered. Often he wondered. Sometimes he thought Rose was easier with Jory. Sometimes not. She was never actually unkind to him, but she still needled him occasionally about the White Caps. Tara couldn't tell about her. He thought she was a fool for passing up a man like Jory, but that was something he had to keep to himself.

With Rose there, neither Jory nor Tara went regularly in the mornings now. Jory moved back to his cabin, and he still went to do the heaviest work, and occasionally Tara went with him. But they were helping fell logs for Becky's new house, and while Tara still went to read to Hattie in the afternoons, he gave his mornings mostly to the tree-felling.

They worked in pairs. Gault's woods were heavy with tall, straight oak and poplar trees, and he himself marked the trees to be felled. The teams of men followed, working well apart in different sections of the woods. Tara found himself variously paired with Hod, Jory, or Wells. They were all good woodsmen, quick, wasting no motion or time. But he thought he worked best with Jory. Maybe it was that he was used to working with Jory. They made a good team together. But he thought Jory was just a little easier, just a little surer. And they accomplished more together.

They would come up to a tall poplar and Jory would look around at the lay of the land, always quickly but never hastily. "Better lay it across that low place," he'd say, and then he would ring the tree with a dozen strokes of the ax. Then came the saw. Cleanly, surely, it bit into the tree and ate its way through.

When he first came to the ridge, Tara Cochrane could no more have pulled his end of a crosscut saw without heaving for breath within five minutes than he could have sprouted wings and flown. Now he needed no more than the one breather Jory called halfway through the tree and he wasn't more blown than Jory when they stopped. He learned to watch with Jory when they were nearly through, watch for that first crack, that first groaning shudder that shivered down the entire length of the tree, watch and step back quickly, as, slowly at first, then gathering momentum, the big poplar would crash against the side of the hill, laid exactly across the place Jory had marked.

Then they took axes and lopped off the limbs, stripped the bark free, and left a long log, peeled and slick, ready to be snaked back to the house site. Slowly the pile of logs mounted, but it took most of March to get through, working steadily day after day. When it rained too hard, they had to quit. But usually they were able to make a little showing each day.

It was around the middle of April that the house was raised. The logs were piled and ready. Hod, Wells, Jory, Tom, and Gault had set the foundation. And word was passed around that Gault's house was ready to be raised. The womenfolks made ready for a big dinner, settling long tables in the yard, digging pits for cooking fires in the open, culling the cellars and the smokehouses for good things to eat.

When the day came, the folks from all over Piney Ridge came, and from Sawtooth, from Persimmon, from Wandering Creek and Little Lost Creek, from Coon Hollow and Bear Hollow, and even from the foot of Lo and Behold. From everywhere they came to help raise Gault's house. It had been a time and a time since a log house had been raised in these parts. Barns, yes. There were lots of log barns. But only an old-timer like Gault Pierce would be raising a log house.

Time was when it would have been an infare, lasting two or three days, given over to work, to singing, to dancing, drinking, eating, and making merry. But ways had changed and the ridge religion frowned on drinking and dancing now. Only the very young dared risk even the old singing games, now fast dying out. There had been some talk of the home demonstration lady reviving the old square dances. Not on Piney Ridge she wouldn't! She'd have had to pack up and light a shuck mighty quick, had she tried such on Piney Ridge.

The last time the ridge had seen the old singing games had been at Miss Willie's school opening party a couple of years ago. And Hod and Wells had been the ones who started that, and not everyone had thought they should have.

Mary thought it was a shame to let the old ways die out. She had told Tara: "There's so little for the young people to do. Just meeting on Saturday night. No parties. No fun. No wonder there are so many shotgun weddings! But fun and parties are sinful, and that's the end of it."

"What will they do at the house-raising?" Tara asked.

"They'll raise the house, swap jokes, eat, and enjoy being together, and then they'll go home."

And that was about the way the day went. The house went up surprisingly fast, with the men working in teams. When the women called them to dinner, the walls had already risen shoulder high. After dinner they took time to rest a spell, sprawling under the trees, chewing tobacco, spitting, and whittling.

There were three or four old men there, from Sawtooth and Persimmon ridges, gray-bearded old men with gnarled hands that whittled unsteadily. They were there merely to lean on their hickory sticks and give advice. It was freely given too. They gathered around Gault after dinner and talked about the weather, the condition of the roads, county politics, and a dozen other small, related topics.

Finally they got around to talking of fishing and hunting, and there was a general complaining about the scarcity of game. It was agreed that times were not like they used to be. Used to be, they said, a man could take his gun and go out into the woods and kill himself a mess of squirrels in less than an hour. Nowadays he could hunt all day long and count himself lucky if he got two or three measly squirrels. They shook their heads.

"No sir," Gault complained, "hit's been a time an' a time sincet they was ary game to speak of in these parts. Not like the olden days when the deer an' the turkey an' the bear was so thick . . . like in my grandpap's days. Why, I've heared him tell . . ." he shifted the stick he was whittling and let a shaving fall slowly to the ground, and he told long-winded and tirelessly how his grandpap had settled the ridge. One story followed another then, the old patriarchs mumbling them into their long, gray beards.

"Oncet," Gault picked up the theme, when it was his turn again, "oncet Grandpap was goin' out to the barn to milk late of an evenin'. Lived over yon way from Sawtooth. Reckon you mind where it was at, Jim." The old man he spoke to nodded. Gault spat and wiped his mouth. "Hit was late of an evenin', like I said, of a showery day which had wetted down ever'thing considerable. Grandpap, he was walkin' along the path to the barn, thinkin' about nothin' in pertickler, when all at oncet he seed a big old tom turkey raise his head beyondst the waterin' trough. Biggest old tom turkey he'd ever seed, he said. A plumb monstrous old feller. He raised his head an' then ducked down agin. Grandpap eased his milk bucket to the ground an' looked around fer somethin' to throw at him. Knowed he wouldn't have time to go back to the house fer his gun. So he looked around fer somethin' . . . a rock or chunk of wood. But they wasn't ary sign of a rock nor nothin' to be seed nowheres clost. All they was was a litter of corncobs where he'd fed the hogs all winter, an' they was turrible waterlogged. But he felt around till he got him a purty big 'un, an' then he takened his stance to wait fer the old tom to raise up agin." Gault paused, and there was a respectful silence. Tara waited impatiently for him to go on.

"The old tom, he poked his head over the trough real keerful-like, an' Grandpap drew back to let 'er fly. But the tom, he ducked down agin jist as Grandpap takened aim. Grandpap waited fer him agin, still as a stone, his right hand drawed back all ready. The tom takened his time, clucked a few times, an' then poked his head up oncet more. Grandpap went into a swing, but before he could turn loose the cob, the old tom ducked down agin. Hit was might' nigh more'n a mortal could stand, bein' so tormented. But Grandpap stood his ground an' waited."

Gault shifted his tobacco and spat, wiped his mouth, and whittled a few shavings carefully. Tara wished he would get on with his story. He hitched himself impatiently on the ground. No one interrupted. No one asked any questions.

Then Gault went on again. "The old tom then, I reckon, figgered hit was safe, an' he eased hisself around the end of the trough an' commenced awalkin' acrost the barnyard. Hit was too purty to be true! Hit was just sich a clean shot as a man would give his right arm fer, an' Grandpap drawed back, balanced his weight, takened keerful aim, an' let fly with that there corncob with all his might!"

The old man stopped again and spat. The whole circle of men around him eyed the ground studiedly and waited. Tara waited too. Seconds passed and then Tara couldn't stand it any longer. "Did he hit him?" he asked eagerly.

The old man puckered his mouth and squinted his eye at the peg he was whittling. "Why," he said softly, "he missed him slicker'n a whistle."

A shout went up from the crowd and Tara grinned shamefacedly. He'd really been taken in! The men heehawed and slapped each other on the back and jeered at him. "Hook, line, and sinker!" they yelled. "Man, you really takened that one in!"

"Sucker!" they shouted.

"One born ever' minnit!"

He knew then that the whole story had been told for his benefit. Doubtless the others had heard it over and over again. He should have known. But in a way he was glad he hadn't. They'd have been so disappointed if he hadn't fallen for it. He looked at Hod and Hod winked at him. And he felt a spurt of sheer pleasure. Pleasure in the telling of the tale, which had been masterly. Pleasure in the old man who had told it. Pleasure in the laughter at his own expense. Pleasure in everything . . . the house-raising, the gathering of folks, the work and the eating and the laughing together. This didn't happen in very many

parts of the country any more. It was dying out. A few years
more and even here on Piney Ridge it would be gone, for the
young men were not following in the ways of the old. And
the old stories and the old tales, told with that beautiful touch
that only an old-timer could manage, would be a thing of the
past.

He laughed with the others. "Hook, line, and sinker. I really
took 'em all, didn't I?"

Gault chuckled and leaned forward to put his hand on Tara's
shoulder. "Hit would of been awful flat ifen you hadn't of," he
confessed, "an' fer a time I was afeared you wasn't goin' to."

Tara shook his head. "Not me. I bite every time."

When the folks hitched up and went home that evening,
Becky's log house was raised, finished except for the roof, windows, and doors. Gault would also have to add the chimney.
But the house was up, and with summer coming on there was
time aplenty to complete it. Becky stood and looked at it.
"Ain't a new log house a sightly thing? Hit smells so good an'
looks so clean! We're obliged," she said to the folks, "to all of
you fer comin'. An' come when you kin an' hit's handy. You'll
allus be welcome."

Tara and Hod were doing up the night work that evening,
late because of the house-raising. By flashlight they were feeding, milking, winding up the day, when Rufe and his dog came
into the barn lot. "What you doing out so late, boy? I saw you
and Jupe sneak away from the house-raising this afternoon.
Where you been?" Hod teased.

Rufe was excited. "Oh, me'n Jupe got tired of that old house-
raisin'. They's a little sang comin' up an' we went up the holler
lookin' fer some. An' you know somethin', Hod! You know
they's a little cove up there I hadn't never seen before! We was
over in Bear Holler, an' we follered the branch up this little
holler, an' clumb clean to the top, an' you know! They's a cave

up there under a clift, an' hit's all fixed out like somebody was livin' in it! They was a heap of canned stuff stacked around, an' blankets an' quilts, an' a lantern, an' they was a kind of stove in there, an' the ashes wasn't cold, neither! Who you reckon's hidin' out up there? You reckon somebody's stillin' back in the holler an' sleepin' in that cave?"

Hod looked at Tara and his head jerked in a faint gesture of silence. "Well, now! What do you know! A cave! Where'd you say it was?"

Rufe gestured largely. "Right over beyond Bear Holler. They's this little cove runs back up a piece. Hit comes out at that old graveyard over there. This here cave is right under that old graveyard. Never would know it was there, savin' you happened to crawl up that clift."

"Reckon it takes a boy like you that can climb like a monkey to get up that cliff."

"No, hit don't! They's steps like, cut in the rock. Hit's all growed over, but when you git through the bushes hit's there. Hit's rough, gittin' up, but anybody could do it. What you think, Hod?"

Hod put his hand on the boy's shoulder. "I think maybe you're right, Rufe. But I wouldn't say much about it. Anybody's holed up there, it's his own business. I'd stay away from there, too."

Rufe shivered. "You reckon hit's a moonshiner?"

"It could be."

"Hit shore is a good place to hide out. Don't reckon the law could ever find him up there."

"No. It might be pretty hard for them. But you stay away. You never can tell. You don't want to be caught up there in the middle of a raid."

"Criminy, no! But, Hod, a feller with a gun up there could hold off a whole army! He could jist mow 'em down comin' up that holler! I wouldn't want to tackle him, if I was the law!"

Dryly Hod said: "Reckon that's what he's counting on. Just keep it to yourself, Rufe. You stumbled on something you weren't supposed to know. Might get you into trouble to go talking it around. And mind, you stay away."

Rufe whistled to his dog. "Yeah, I will. If I didn't git caught in a raid, I might git potted by whoever is hidin' out up there. But I'll bet they's trouble in that cove some of these days."

"I'll bet so too."

When the boy had gone, Hod turned back to forking down the hay. Tara picked up his fork also. "What you think?"

"I think it's adding up."

"Jory's father?"

Hod shrugged. "Looks like it."

Tara swore and let out a deep breath. "What do we do?"

"We don't do anything. Man, it's the law! If it's what we think it is, they're after him for murder! What *can* we do?"

"Oughtn't we go see that cave?"

"Why? We know it's there now. And we've got a good idea what for. What do we want to go messing around the cave for?"

He pitched a forkful of hay into the stall. "There's not a thing we can do. Nothing but try to keep Jory out of it. There's going to be shooting up that little hollow one of these days. That's what the old man is holing up for. When they come, he'll hide out up there. I reckon he's been ringing that sheep bell to scare folks off finding it. Keep 'em from wandering around up there. Right smart old cuss, isn't he?"

"No. He's a fool!"

"Sure. But that's the way a fool's head works when he thinks he's being smart."

Tara looked up toward the head of the hollow where the hills pinched together. Peaceful, it looked. Still, and as old as time. Placid and unmoved. The eternal hills. The rim of the ridge stood against the wisteria sky sharp and clean, cut blackly against it, standing clear of it, like a paper hill against a paper sky. Wrinkled, peaceful hills. Only they weren't. They had known blood and violence before. Since the time of their settlement they had known them. Dark-skinned men had skulked through these hills and hollows, sending their war whoops echoing through them, bringing fear and terror to the hearts of the white settlers. And when that era had passed and the red men were gone, the settlers had warred between themselves . . . the great civil war, the minor wars of feuds between families, the war between moonshiners and revenuers, the war between the tobacco growers and the combine. Blood, violence, war! These hills had seen them time and again. And there was nothing in their peace, nor in their antiquity, to guarantee they would not see them again.

Tara shivered. The hills looked ominous, and the night was settling in. The air was damp and chill.

CHAPTER

17

IF TARA Cochrane noticed how good Rose was with Hattie, Rose herself could not help seeing the greater goodness of Jory as she worked beside him day after day. She saw it, she used it, and she relied on it. She saw also that it was the expression of his love for her. She could not help seeing that. He never said a word to her about loving her. But it was evident in everything that he did. In the way that he guarded her from the heaviest work. In the way that he seemed to sense when she needed him about the place and was always there. In the way that he shared his chuckling, quiet jokes with her. In the way that he tenderly talked and played with Taysie when Rose brought her with her to Hattie's. It was thrown all around her, shelteringly, every day.

And she was not insensitive to it. She was even attracted to Jory in many ways. There was no hurdle to get over because he was Tay's brother. For he did not even remotely resemble Tay. But when she was most attracted to him, when practically and sensibly she thought of his goodness and his gentleness, she felt a lack in him. Then she felt a quick impatience with him. For what, she did not know. She did not know with what other qualities she would have imbued him. She only knew that Tay had been so reckless and swaggering, so wildly handsome

and so complete a lover, that he had filled all her heart. Not all
her needs, for there had been little comfort in loving and being
married to Tay. Even when she had loved him most she had
known, uneasily, that her love was not sufficient for him. But
she would not have traded the wild passionate interludes with
him for all the safety and comfort in the world with another
man. Whatever Tay's faults, and they had been many, he had
given her in the few brief months of their marriage some moments of such high, fulfilled happiness that their remembrance
still had the power to shake her and bring her tremblingly
awake in the night. How could another man ever take his
place? How could Jory, with all his goodness, with all his
patience, with all his tenderness, give her anything to compare
with what Tay had given her?

Not that Rose thought about these things consciously, weigh-
ing and balancing them. She didn't. She simply felt, instinctively, as perhaps all women do, the charm, the attraction of
the black sheep, the wayward, the reckless, the restless, even
the cruel man. It may be that no woman understands this in
herself. This preference of such a man to a good, upright,
gentle man. But illogically, impractically, unsensibly, a great
many women will cast their lot with the man most certain to
bring them to unhappiness in the end. Perhaps it's the adven-
ture . . . the very uncertainty itself. Perhaps it's the swagger,
the recklessness, the extravagance. Perhaps it's an inherent
sense of romance buried deep in women that makes them rebel
against routine, passiveness, submissiveness.

Without thinking deeply about it, Rose still felt she had had
the best of love. And yet she was young and restless under its
buried death. She didn't think of that, either. She only knew
that there were days in her life that were dull and flat, stretching endlessly before her, and that there were nights when it
was hard to sleep. She would have said she was still grieving

for Tay. And she was. But at the same time she was grieving for love.

She did not analyze or think too clearly about her growing nearness to Jory. They were thrown together day after day in circumstances greatly resembling the relationships within a family circle. They were constantly together, making choices, deciding things, sharing work and responsibilities. There grew up between them a store of common interests, jokes and laughter shared, anxieties joined, concerns knitted. Gradually their relationship became almost that of husband and wife in its friendly, easy companionship, in its undercurrent of affection and fond good humor. They were like a husband and wife who had been married long years, lacking only the background of an early, shared passion that had quieted.

If Jory was restive under this, he gave no sign of it. Not, that is, until a day in May when he was taking Rose home one evening. He was troubled. "Soon I'll have to be giving time to the Bible schools, Rose," he said. "I've not been neglecting my work at the church all this time I've been at Hattie's. It's been possible to get away to take care of things. But I've been able to pick my times, kind of. But we have the Bible schools this time of year, and I have my part to do, and I'll have to be gone day after day for several weeks. I'm afraid it will leave a lot for you to do."

"An' do you think we can't git along without you!" Rose laughed. "Go on to yer Bible schools! We'll make out jist fine!"

"I'll see if I can get the captain to come in the mornings again to help. He can do the heaviest work."

"Me an' Tom kin manage. You jist go on amongst yer White Caps."

"I'll have to."

"Well, don't be mindin' us." She laughed teasingly. "When you goin' to marry one of them women wears a little white cap on her head, Jory?"

Anger at her, as sudden as it was unreasonable, shot through Jory. Anger that was as vicious, boiling, and blinding as any he had ever felt in his life. She had hit out at him so often this way. And he felt an overpowering need to hit back. A need to hurt her as she had so often hurt him. He stopped the car, and, turning to her, he pulled her hard against him with a tense strength. Every thought left his mind but this great, fierce need to hurt. He had no idea what he meant to do . . . shake her, slap her, yell at her. Something violent. Something hateful, hurtful, rough, harsh. Something that would relieve all the hurts she had given him. Cancel them out. Make her sorry.

He certainly had no intention of doing what he did do! But when she was close against him, he bent his head quickly and kissed her. And his mouth was hot and hard in its sudden, flaming longing. It pressed down and down, having thirsted so long, and it gathered fire and would not be quenched, and he would not release her. Rose's mouth went soft beneath it, her arms which had pushed against him at first, went slack and then tightened about him. Her bones melted weakly and went jelly-soft in her body. She shivered and gave him back all the hungriness of his mouth.

When Jory let her go, she looked at him strangely, and wonderingly. So . . . he was kin to Tay after all!

"That's for you to remember while I'm gone," he muttered, mixed up with feeling ashamed of himself and not feeling ashamed of himself. A man's a man, even if he is a preacher!

Rose sat on her side of the seat and looked at him. Tall, thin, angular, brown, looking nothing like Tay. Still . . . there was that fire. So she decided. She laughed and took a deep breath. Then she touched her head. "They's a white cap on my head, Jory," she said, simply.

He didn't understand her. He looked blankly at her head. "See," she said, "ain't it pretty?"

When he tried to say something, his voice wouldn't come. He

swallowed and croaked hoarsely: "Rose! Rose, you mean it?"

"I mean it."

"But you've never acted like you . . ."

"You never kissed me before, neither! Love's more'n jist lookin' at a body!"

Jory stared at her, and then he threw back his head and laughed. Laughed with such freeing joy that the tears streamed down his face, and after a moment Rose joined him. She leaned against him and laid her head on his shoulder, and his laughter shook through them both. "I bet you never expected to convert me by kissin' me, did you?" she asked when she could talk again.

He put his forehead against her cheek and held her tightly. "I'll bet I didn't either! But the ways of the Lord are mysterious . . . and I'm not going to question them. But don't you ever tell this, Rose! This way of winning a convert is strictly between us! It's not in the book!"

Rose straightened. "Well, I should hope hit's between us, Jory Clark! You a White Cap preacher . . ."

"Now, Rose . . ."

Rose softened and put her arms about his neck. "Jory, you tease so easy. I never meant it." She kissed him sweetly and lightly. "Me, a preacher's wife! I never thought of sich! Oh, but I have to be a White Cap first! Oh, me, Jory! Reckon they'll have me? I've talked such a heap."

Jory assured her they would, but he was grave when he asked her, "Rose, you sure?"

Rose's face sobered at his tone. "I'm sure about you, Jory. An' I'll learn about the White Caps, an' I'll try to be the faithfullest White Cap was ever converted."

Jory cupped her face in his hands and laid his cheek against her hair. "Then I'm not worried. If you'll just be happy. And the white cap is going to look more beautiful on you than on any other woman in the world."

Rose was quiet and Jory raised his head to look at her. "What is it?"

"I was jist thinkin' how quare hit's goin' to be."

"Rose . . ."

"If you'll jist not hurry me none, Jory. We've not been in no hurry until now . . ."

"I've been. I've been in a hurry. Inside of me, I've been in a hurry for a long, long time. Longer than you think."

She reached her hand up to his face. "How long, Jory?"

She could barely hear his voice when it came. "Since the first time I saw you. You came with Tay to spend the day at Pa's when I first came home. You stood there in the door, and the sun was shining on your face. And your eyes crinkled at the corners when you looked at me. And you were my brother's wife." He lifted his head and looked at her. "It was a sin, Rose. A sin. But I couldn't have helped it if my soul was everlastingly damned. I couldn't help the way I felt."

"You never let on."

"No. That's what I *could* help. I *could* help showing it."

"An' you done so. Fer I never guessed. Hit wasn't no sin, then. An' that's done past now, Jory."

"Yes . . . but I reckon I'll be in a hurry until . . ." He stopped. "When you reckon will be time enough?"

"Jist fergit I said that, Jory. Now's time enough. Would next month be soon enough?"

"Next month!"

"Look, Jory. Hit's plumb night. We've got to git on. Miss Willie'll be aworryin'."

About the time Jory and Rose were talking thus, Mary Pierce entered her labor. She felt its first pangs as she set the table for supper, and her eyes went to the clock to time the frequency of the pains. Ten minutes. Time enough yet, so she went on preparing the meal. Hod was still at the barn. Tara would not be home until later. She must send Jeems to Miss Willie. Her bag was already packed for the trip to the hospital and arrangements were all made. As soon as supper was over they must start.

Hod brought the night's milk in. Mary looked up at him. "Willie Belle has started," she said.

He splashed the milk over the side of the bucket as he set it down. Mary might be calm about this business. but it scared the daylights out of him! "You sure?"

"Sure."

"When do we go?"

Mary laughed. "There's time to eat supper. Then you take Jeems to Miss Willie's, while I dress."

Mary fed the child but ate little herself. Then she dressed him, filled suddenly with loneliness for him. The thing she minded most about this was having to be separated from Jeems even for a few days. The new baby was not yet an identity to her. Jeems was her own, her very own. She hugged him to her and then set him down on his feet. "In a few days, Sonny," she promised him, "just a few days, and I'll be back with your little sister."

The child looked up at her and squinted his eyes at her. He was learning to repeat words and phrases. "Few days," he said solemnly, nodding his head, "few days." Satisfied, he ran away from her into the other room and Hod picked him up and carried him out to the car.

When he came back from taking Jeems, Mary was waiting. As they went to the car Tara came up. "Going somewhere?" he asked.

Mary climbed into the car before answering. "To the hospital," she said then. "Willie Belle's on the way."

Something like an icy wind blew over Tara's face and fear sank its ugly fangs into him. Something might happen to her! She might not come back! Things did happen! Women did die!

And he had never told her. He had never touched her. Not the
least little bit had she ever belonged to him.

He wanted to fling himself in the car and go along. To be
there and to know. Wait for her. Be near. And he had no right!
None at all. He was the outsider. The friend out on the edge.
There wasn't any place for him with her. He might love her, but
he had no right to tell her so. He had to stay outside. Hod was
to go with her and wait. To be allowed to stay near and to be
told, finally. Hod would know whether he had a son or a
daughter! Not he! Not Tara Cochrane!

The car drew away from him and he had not found one
word to say.

He went in the house and went straight to a piece of luggage
in his closet that he had never unpacked. There was nothing
in it but odds and ends of things, and a fifth of bourbon which
he had bought in Louisville, but which he had never opened.
He had almost forgotten he had it. Now he remembered it.
Now he wanted it!

He took it to the kitchen, found a glass, poured a drink, and
took it down straight. Then, taking the glass with him into the
living room, he filled it half full. He did not let it stay empty
after that. Steadily he kept filling it. The hours wore on and the
level in the bottle lowered. He did not think nor care how
drunk he was getting. He only knew this was one way to numb
the fear and hurt of this night. And even with the whisky there
remained too much of both. He could see too clearly into that
hospital room where Mary lay by now. He'd been in too many
of them, and as if he were there now, he could see. Only this
would be Mary. Mary's face, white against the pillow, drawn
with pain, her hair black around her white face. He could see
her hands knotted into fists, dragging at something to hold onto.
He wanted to be there! He wanted the right to be there! He
pounded his fists on the table in a fury of helplessness, and then
in defeat he buried his head in his arms, overturning the glass

at his elbow and not knowing when the liquid ran into his hair.

Jory found him like that.

It was late. "I came to see if there was any news," he said, walking in without knocking. "I met Hod as I went home after taking Rose. He was taking Jeems to Miss Willie. I didn't know but what you went with them to town. But I've not been able to sleep, and I saw your light . . . Cap'n!" He had seen the overturned glass, the bottle, and as he came closer he smelled the fumes which had soaked into Tara's hair and blew sourly from his mouth. "Cap'n," he said again, putting his hand on Tara's shoulder.

Tara shook it off and roused sluggishly. "Go away," he said thickly, "go away . . . preacher! I'm drunk and you've come to preach me a sermon. Preach me no sermon! Preach me no sermon now!" He turned slowly in the chair and blinked owlishly at Jory. "I'm drunk! Sure, I'm drunk! But I'm sick, Jory Clark! I'm sick with love!" He reached for the glass and the bottle and poured another drink unsteadily. He held the glass up to the light and peered dully at it. " 'Stay me with flagons,' Jory. 'Comfort me with apples: for I am sick of love. . . . Behold, thou art fair, my love; behold, thou art fair'! That's from your Bible too, preacher! But you never use that for a text! My love is a 'lily among thorns. . . . A bundle of myrrh is my well-beloved'! For my love is the wife of another man! Preach me from that text, preacher! Comfort me with those apples! My love is the wife of another man. And she has gone to give him another child!"

Jory stood very still. And it was as if his heart split wide open with pity and with love for this man. Cap'n, Cap'n, it cried. And he would have reached out and cradled the whisky-soaked head against him and hushed his crying and eased his hurt. All the captain's hurt came over and went inside him and became his own years of hurt again. He had no sermon for this man. He had only the same bleeding inside him.

He watched the captain down his drink and then he took the glass from him. "Cap'n," he said, "come on. You don't want Hod to find you here like this when he comes home. Let's put these things away and you come home with me."

"Why not let Hod find me here like this when he comes home? Why not? Why shouldn't he know? He isn't good enough for her! She deserves finer things than marriage to a Kentucky hillbilly! She ought to have the best of life! She should be surrounded by beauty! Here she is . . . settled for life in Wishful Hollow! Wishful! What a wonderful name for it! Live here and wish you could get out! I'm going to take her out!"

"No, Cap'n."

"I say yes! There's money enough to give her everything. And I love her, Jory."

"All your money and all your love can't give Mary Pierce a thing, Cap'n. Don't you know that?"

"Why can't it?"

"Because she's already got everything."

The brutality of it sank into Tara's whiskyed mind. Nothing he could give her. Nothing. Not even love. She had it. All. His mouth quivered and he swayed on his feet. Jory took his arm. "Come on, Cap'n." And he went with Jory without protest.

He did not wake until noon the next day. His head was as big as a bucket, his mouth full of cotton. Jory laughed at him when he tried to get up. "Made a real fool of myself, didn't I?" he mumbled.

Jory handed him a cup of black coffee. "I wouldn't say that."

Tara drained the cup and handed it back. He walked over to the window and looked up the hollow. "What am I going to do, Jory?"

Jory came to stand by him and to look up the hollow with

him. "There's a little comfort in knowing she's happy, Cap'n. Not much, maybe. But when you love somebody real deep, it's good to know they're happy. Even if you aren't part of it. Rose wasn't, you know."

Tara took in a chestful of air. "That kind of sublimity is mighty hard to come by, preacher. Mighty hard to come by."

Jory pulled the curtain over the window. "Yes. But I'd think there'd be peace in it."

Tara shrugged. "And peace is better than nothing, I suppose. Well . . . thanks. Thanks again."

Jory looked at him. "Think you can take the rest?"

Tara's head came up. "Mary?"

"The baby came about midnight," Jory grinned. "Willie Belle. Mary's fine. Hod got in about daylight this morning, all tuckered out."

Ruefully Tara grinned back at him. "I'm a little tuckered myself."

"And me. Cap'n . . ."

"Yes?"

"I kind of hate to tell you now, but I wanted you to know first. That's really why I went looking for you last night. Rose is . . . Rose and me . . ."

The captain laughed. "Rose has said yes."

Jory nodded. "I don't believe it yet, myself."

Tara reached out suddenly and tousled Jory's thick, brown hair. "Son of a gun!" he said, "I'm glad! By golly, I'm glad. There ought to be a little happiness around this place! And it couldn't happen to a better guy! Congratulations!"

"I hated to spring it on you when you were so down yourself."

"I'll be all right. And your news has perked me up considerably. Are you going to be married soon?"

"We think by the last of June."

"Good! Good! You've waited long enough!"

"That's what we think."

When Tara left, he walked slowly up the hollow thinking of Jory and Rose. He was deeply glad for them. Especially for Jory. But he had his tongue in his cheek about Rose. Not that he didn't think she loved Jory. But he remembered those needling remarks so often about the white cap. Still, he thought, love should be able to wear the little white cap most gracefully.

And he was glad, deeply glad, that Jory had kept him from making a complete ass of himself last night.

M ARY was home in less than a week, beautiful, serene, happy
with the new baby. Willie Belle was a tiny, wrinkled
mite with lustrous yellow fuzz on her head and, surprisingly,
deep brown eyes. Tara had dreaded seeing her. Had dreaded
worse seeing Mary again. But Mary herself was so normal, her
pride in the baby so contagious, that Tara found himself relax-
ing in spite of himself and showing an interest in Willie Belle.
"Where'd she get those brown eyes?" he asked.

Mary shook her head. "Don't know. Must be a throwback."

When Tara held the baby, however, all the ache and pain
came back. Daughter of Mary, he thought. And, inevitably,
daughter of Hod. She curled against his shoulder, soft in the
palms of his hands, rounded, curved, knotted. He would have
given every hope of tomorrow . . . every promise of the future
. . . almost every breath of his life, if she had been his. He had
to put her down, away from him, where he couldn't feel her. So
much punishment and no more, could any man stand.

His hands were trembling. He shoved them in his pockets
and walked over to the window. "The apple trees are blooming," he said irrelevantly.

"Yes. They're early this year."

"I never thought to be here this long. I should be moving on.
When Hattie . . ."

"Why?"

He lifted his shoulders and dropped them. "I've about used it up, don't you think?"

Mary laughed. "You're not digging holes and putting the dirt back in now, are you?"

She was lying on the couch, the bright-colored afghan which always lay across its back covering her knees. Tara moved across the room to her, and for the first time, for the very first time, he touched her. He laid his cheek against her hair, and, strangely, the only emotion he felt as he did so was one of tenderness and gentleness. And one of gratitude. "My thanks," he said softly, "my deepest thanks, Mary."

He went with Jory when Jory took Rose to the superintendent for preparation for church membership. Jory could have conducted her examination, but he didn't want to. "I don't think I could," he told Rose. "When I look at you and remember we're to be married, I forget my duties. It would be more seemly for the superintendent to conduct your instruction."

So he took her to the superintendent, Tara going along. Rose was nervous. "No need to be," Jory told her. "This is just so you'll know what we believe."

The superintendent was kind. Seeing Rose was nervous, he talked along at random for a few moments to give her time to get herself in hand. Tara and Jory sat nearby, and for all his assurance of Rose, Jory was more fidgety than she. Tara nudged him and Jory made his hands lie quietly along the arms of his chair.

When the superintendent turned, finally, to the instruction in doctrines and practices, Rose listened carefully. Because she was not only coming into the fellowship of the church, but was also to be a minister's wife, the superintendent instructed her also in the duties of an official's wife. This was not a time, he told her, of actual dedication or of admission. It was simply that she might know, without error, what it meant to be a fellow of the Church of the Brethren in Christ, and, further, that she might understand fully what it meant to be the wife of a minister of that Church. Rose nodded her head. "I understand," she said, "an' I'm ready."

The superintendent smiled and took her hand. "Then, Brother Clark," he said, "I think we may proceed to lay the matter before the officials of your congregation."

"How do you feel about all of this?" Tara asked Mary.

"I think it's wonderful," Mary replied. "I think it's the most beautiful thing I ever saw happen!"

If Miss Willie and Wells Pierce had any doubts as to the wisdom of Rose's course, they did not mention them. "Rose will make a good wife for Jory," Miss Willie said. "She has an outgoing personality, loves people, and is wonderfully healthy and strong. She can do her share of bearing the burdens with him."

And Wells said, "I never thought on one of my own joinin' the White Caps, but if Rose is happier amongst 'em, I'd not put a stone in her way."

As far as the rest of the ridge was concerned, everyone was glad. Everyone thought it was fine. Jory and Rose. They'd make out fine together. They'd be suited to one another. They'd do good.

A week later Rose was received into the Church. Jory asked Tara to bring her to the service, since he would need to be there earlier, and Tara borrowed Hod's car for the occasion. "Are you scared, Rose?" he asked her as they drove down the ridge.

"No," she said, "I ain't to say skeered, Cap'n, but I'm some twitchy-like. I've studied that there book the man give me, an' I've had Jory explain it to me, till I know it by heart. I know better'n I ever done before the ways they believe. Hit was never made clear to me before. Hit's all in the Scriptures, Cap'n, an' I know hit's right. I ain't jist joinin' on account of Jory. Of course I wouldn't lie to say Jory was the main cause in the beginnin'. But I'm ready, now, to take my place alongside of him. An' I kin make my testimony today in my own name."

Tara wondered at the simplicity of heart and mind that had brought her to this point. She, whom he had thought ready to become a White Cap in order to marry Jory! He wondered at it, but he didn't doubt it. For there was no doubt Rose meant it. Today she would stand before a group of people and witness to her own personal faith. She had gone all the way in love, which had grown broader and deeper as she walked along its path. If she had started out with love for one man, the way had widened before her to include all men.

Tara sat at the back of the church, his own emotions confused, as he watched Rose at the end of the service go forward to meet Jory. He listened to her quiet voice answering the vows which Jory's voice so tremblingly charged her with. She was so much the calmer of the two. She stood quietly and with dignity in her cotton print dress, her flowered hat covering her brown hair. This was the last time she would wear such a dress and such a hat. Tomorrow she would put on the uniform of White Cap women, and tomorrow the lovely, sheer little white cap would grace her head. Mary had told Tara that Rose had been making her White Cap dresses, and that her prayer veiling was waiting, ready for her.

There was a sadness to Tara in this putting aside of all worldly things. A solemn sadness, for it was a dedication forever. It did not mean that Rose would be less gay, nor that she would, by donning the uniform dress, don a long-faced, dreary habit of life. But it could not be denied that it meant a separation for her, and there is always a moment of loneliness in separation. There is always a little of good-by, a little of farewell, a little of death. No matter what fullness lies beyond the separation, the partition itself has its moment of nostalgia.

But if Rose felt any of this, it was not evident. There was only confidence in her manner . . . confidence and certainty that where Jory led she could safely follow.

Now there remained her baptism, the marriage, and her dedication. The baptism was set for two weeks later.

Now it was June, and there was heavy shade along the ridge path when Tara climbed to Hattie's each afternoon. Shade and smell of small flowers blooming and wet dews that lingered on until noon. Smell of earth warming under the high-riding sun. Smell of grass, damped down and dusty. Smell of summer and blue skies and white, woolly clouds. "You should see the woods," he told Hattie one afternoon. "They're beautiful! Green and thick and heavy. The birds have gone crazy with excitement! And I saw a lizard and a hoptoad today."

"I wisht I could," Hattie said wistfully, "I shore wisht I could. Hit would pleasure me a heap."

"We'll take your chair outside today. Out in the yard, and we'll read out there," he promised.

He was always glad later that he had thought of it, for when he had padded her chair with pillows and lifted her into it, easily as he knew how so well, she had leaned her head against the back and drawn a deep breath. "Hit's fine . . . jist fine. Oh, hit is fair to see! I'm glad I was spared to see the summer."

"Why, Hattie! You'll see many a summer yet." He assured her, knowing he lied. "You've just started getting well."

She smiled at him and didn't contradict him. It was as if she knew he was lying, and knew he knew it too. But between them they would keep it a secret. They'd play a little game with one another. They wouldn't let another soul know.

"Shall I read now?" he asked, drawing up his own chair.

"I'd like it if you would. I kin listen an' look at the same time."

He picked up the book to begin, opened it to the marked page. But he never began. For the thing eating away inside her

chose that time to spurt forth its fountain of corruption again
. . . and the words on the page opened in Tara's hand went
red with Hattie's blood . . . sponged out by it, erased and
made illegible. On the book, Tara's hands were reddened with
it, and his clothes soaked it up. When he lifted her and carried
her into the house, a red path streamed behind him where he
walked.

The members of the family gathered. Hod and Mary. Miss
Willie and Wells. Becky and Gault. Irma and John were sent
for and came that night.

There was no talk of sending for a doctor. Hod spoke for
them. "We'd rather it was you stayed by," he told Tara. "She
loved you."

So Tara stayed by. Each time he came out of Hattie's room
they looked hopefully at his face, although they knew there
was no hope. It was a death watch they were keeping. But
some frail thread of life remained in Hattie, and so long as it
held, unsnapped, they watched Tara's face.

Irma and Mary prepared a meal late in the evening. Miss
Willie and Wells had gone by then, as had Gault and Becky.
Only the immediate family remained. Tom sat with Hattie
while they ate. Tara felt sick and exhausted. All his strength
had drained away. His hands shook and his head ached. He
was surprised at the depth of his feeling at the death of this
woman. He had felt pity for her from the first . . . pity and
compassion. And he had known a long time that this end lay
before her. But now that it was here, he was as unready for it
as the family. He knew that long ago the pity had turned to
something warmer, and that the hours spent with her had been
full of tenderness and love.

Shaken, he thought of her red hair bows, and the thin, clutching hands that had so often held onto him. He could feel her
frailty in his arms now, the shape of her had become so familiar
to him through lifting her into and out of bed. He could hear

her brittle laugh, deriding him for some clumsy attempt at cleaning or helping about the place. His mind formed words in her voice . . . "The Lord is my shepherd; I shall not want . . ." Her favorite psalm. She'd said it often from memory. He'd read it to her often—she liked to hear it in his voice.

And the words became real, and he realized that he had been saying them aloud, and that Irma and Jory were joining in repeating them at the table. "Surely goodness and mercy shall follow me all the days of my life . . ." It was a memorial to Hattie's faith and courage.

Irma wiped her eyes when they had finished. "I wisht they was somethin' we could do. Jory . . ."

Jory knew that she meant the healing. "Don't you know, Irma," he said, "that I've been having faith all along?"

"Yes," she murmured, bending her head.

John moved impatiently. "But death comes to all. Faith can't stop it!"

Jory's face was gentle when he looked at John, and he smiled. When he smiles, Tara thought, it's like a lamp being lighted. I never saw a smile so sweet . . . so loving. It's as if his whole big heart had opened up before you.

"It doesn't try to, John," Jory said quietly. "Faith doesn't try to stop death. It only tries to keep death from being the victor. It only says, If this flesh can be useful to you longer, Lord, heal it and use it. If it has done its work, take it away."

"No . . ." Mary said, her face in her hands.

But Irma's face lifted calmly, and serenity passed over it. "Yes," she said. "Yes."

"What more beautiful way is there to think of death, Mary?" Jory asked. "There is no answer to it. No reason can fathom it. It is final. Inevitable. Universal. Can you make it any easier by denying it?"

"Do you believe in havin' the cap'n here with Hattie? He's a doctor. If you believe," John said, "in faith healin', don't you put yer whole faith in it?"

"I believe in faith healing. But I certainly believe also in having a doctor with Hattie. It's not for all, John. And sometimes we are powerless to use it even for our own closest and dearest. Sometimes, too, we must believe the doctor's way is the Lord's way. It isn't a doubt to use medicine and to call in the doctor! It isn't a lack of faith!"

"Then why depend on faith healin' at all? Why try it?"

"Because it's there to be used if we can. Because for some of us it has power. Because it is the ultimate trust of love. But there is room for all in what we believe, John. There's room for you. You don't have to accept divine healing. You don't have, ever, to try to make use of it. But there's room also for Irma. And there's no need for it to divide you. Side by side you can share the same house of faith, neither of you denying its sheltering roof, both of you accepting what you can of it, fully!"

John was silent. He looked at Irma. "You mean," he said at last, "that if Irma an' me was White Caps, she could believe like she wanted about this faith healin', an' I could believe what I wanted, an' we could both be in the same religion?"

"That's just exactly what I mean!"

"What about Susie? What about if Irma held out like she done when Johnnie was sick?"

Irma's head went down. "I wouldn't . . . not now. I never knowed it was like Jory says. I was thinkin' . . . I was thinkin' they was jist one way."

Tara went back to Hattie then. But he knew Jory had shown Irma and John a clear path their feet could take.

Hattie died within the hour, and when it was over, the family gathered in the fireplace room. "I'll take Mary home and come back," Hod said. "She's worn out."

"I'll stay," said Irma, leaning wearily against the mantel.

"You want I should see about Susie?" John asked.

"Yes. But come back, John. Come back quick as you kin."

When Tara went back into Hattie's room, he pulled the sheet down from her face and looked at her. In her illness the skin had drawn taut across the bones, but it had stayed smooth and fine. Now the bones stood forth, carved clean, shaped strongly. And the chin, under her mouth, was square and lean. The deep dimple was sunk even deeper, and for a moment Tara laid his finger against it. Then he covered the face again and turned and walked out of the house down the road to the path that led to Wishful Hollow.

The next day he would have stayed away, feeling that this time belonged to the family. But Jory came for him. "Sarah troubles me," he said. "Come stay near her."

So he went, and to occupy himself while the family made plans he packed the books he had brought to read to Hattie. Some were Miss Willie's. Some were Mary's. Some he had bought himself. He packed them all. All, that is, but the one he had been reading the day before. He couldn't find it. It was gone. He wandered around the room, thinking someone might have put it away.

Sarah touched his arm, appearing beside him quietly. "I've got it," she said softly. "I takened it. Can I keep it?"

He put his arm around her shoulders. "Of course, Sarah. If you like. I didn't know whether anyone would want to see it around."

She bent her head against his arm. "You'll not be comin' no more now, I reckon."

"Not so often," he said, smoothing the tangled curls. "But I'll come for my guitar lessons once in a while, just the same."

He felt her shoulders knotted and tense under his arm. "I'm sorry, Sarah," he said gently, "I'm so sorry."

She twisted away. "Don't be. She's through with all the hurtin' now. She's restin' easy."

"Of course."

Her hands rubbed fretfully together. "I ain't agrievin' about Ma none. Hit's best."

"Yes."

"An' Pa an' me'll make out."

Tara made no reply.

"Savin'," Sarah went on, her eyes looking past him out the window, "savin' it'll be sort of empty-like."

"Yes."

There was so little to be said. Nothing could fill the emptiness or comfort the loss. What Sarah felt now she must feel alone. No one could excuse her from it. No one could take it over for her.

She looked at him again. "You goin' to be leavin' out any time soon?"

"Leaving?"

"The ridge . . . the holler."

"Not for a while yet."

"But you will be . . . someday?"

"Someday . . . yes. I'll have to, Sarah."

She looked hopelessly at him . . . beseechingly. But she said nothing. She merely turned away and went into her own room. What would become of her now, he thought. What would the days hold for her?

The family gathered in the fireplace room. Hod took the initiative in planning. "Pa, you go with me to pick out the casket. Irma, you want to go too?"

"No. Whatever you do'll suit me. Jist git a real nice one."

"I will."

With Hod and Tom gone, Irma set about putting things to rights. She wept noiselessly as she decided on the dress Hattie should wear, and put the rest of her clothes away. She came across Hattie's small box of ribbons. "Would it be unseemly, Jory, you think," she asked, "to put a red bow in her hair? She loved them ribbons the captain give her so good."

Jory was to have the funeral. "Unseemly, Irma? It would be the most natural thing in the world."

Tara's stomach cramped suddenly. Almost carelessly he had bought all those ribbons. Thinking only to give Hattie some color, some brightness. Practice had taught him that invalids like their little private belongings, and almost without thinking at all he had got the ribbons for Hattie. Now she would wear one in her longest sleep.

John Walton came into the room. Irma looked up at him. He nodded at her. "Mebbe this is the best time fer us to talk to Jory," he said.

She put down the box of ribbons and came across the room to sit beside him. He took her hand, and while he talked he smoothed it. "Me an' Irma has been talkin' over what you said yesterday, Jory. We'd like to be baptized into the White Caps. Hit appears to be the way fer us. We kin go in together, like you said. Under one roof they's room fer the two of us, believin' a mite different, but allowin' fer the difference. We never knowed that before."

Jory's smile lighted his face. "Whenever you say, John."

"Let it be soon," Irma begged. "Soon. We've been drawed apart too long. Jory, hit's good to be together agin!"

A wetness stung Tara's eyes and he blinked it away. If Jory went pontifical now, he thought, he'd hit him! But he didn't, of course. Jory knew there was nothing he could add, and there was no need of further words. "Rose is to be baptized next week," he told them. "Will that be all right?"

"Hit'll be fine," they said.

So there were three who were baptized after all. Rose, Irma, and John. Three who knelt together in the water for the trine immersion in the name of the Father, of the Son, and of the Holy Ghost. And if it was a baptism of the flesh for all, it was a marriage of the spirit for two, for the yawning abyss of difference between Irma and John had been bridged, and under Jory's hand they walked across the bridge together.

It may have been wistfulness that Tara felt as he witnessed the baptism. A wistful yearning for the simplicity of such a faith. It may have been nostalgia . . . a homesickness for the intellectual innocence of another, less complicated, day and age. He did not know. But he did know that he and this present sophisticated generation were the losers. And he did feel grateful that somewhere in this complex, disillusioned world there still was a faith that was open to those of childlike hearts and believing minds. The truth appears to each man in its own guise, he thought, and each must receive it in the measure he is able.

CHAPTER

19

IT WAS a few days later that Mary handed Tara the book review section of the Sunday paper. "Have you seen this?" she asked.

Splashed across the page, given generous space, was a review of John Michael Cochrane's history of the Aztecs. "From the pen of an eminent scholar comes this brilliantly colorful book," the review read. "John Cochrane was not content to release this book until he had spent over fifteen years in research on it. And then he took five years to write it. The careful work of the historian is evident in it, but the book is more than history. It is a vivid, glowing pageant, brought swiftly and movingly alive by the sheer beauty of John Cochrane's words. The man is a poet as well as an historian."

Tara looked wonderingly at a small picture of his father at the top of the column. Either it was an old picture or his father had changed very little. To the boy Tara, his father had always seemed old. Suddenly he realized he was not an old man at all. He isn't over sixty, he thought, trying to remember. A lot of good years yet.

And suddenly he felt a sense of pride, and equally a great sense of loss. Twenty years to do one book! What discipline that had taken! What thoroughness and what dedication. If things had been different, how much he might have learned from his father.

He gave the paper back to Mary. "So he finally finished it. I must send for a copy." And that was all he could find to say.

Mary went to the piano. "Are you in the mood for some music? We haven't played in a long time."

Tara tuned his violin absently, his mind still turned backward to his father. He'd like to see him again. Like to talk with him.

They played for an hour, and when they had finished, Tara laid his violin on the piano and stretched loosely. "That was good," he said. "Good."

. He knew as he went into his own room that the day was come when he must make his own peace with his father. "What a pity," Mary had said that day he had told her the story of his life. "What a pity!" And his heart echoed it. A pity that the years had been so cankered and wasted. A pity that a father and son had thrown away their dearest treasure. A pity that a wall had been built between them. But it wasn't entirely too late yet. He could tear down a part of that wall, and, however his father received him, he could at least cleanse his own soul and set his own house in order. How could he not have known it sooner!

The week before the wedding was a busy time for everyone on the ridge. Jory went around in a state of somnambulant happiness. Tara laughed at him. "I have to go with him everywhere he goes," he told Hod and Mary. "He forgets what he's been sent for . . . where he's to go . . . whom he's to see! If ever I saw a man walking around in clouds, it's Jory!"

Rose's wedding dress was plain and simple. Made, of course, by the White Cap pattern. But Mary and Miss Willie saw to it that it was beautiful for her. They chose a pale ivory silk with tiny rosebuds scattered over it. There was no trimming. The small round neck fitted closely, lovingly, and the long, full sleeves gathered at her wrist in a neat band. Her cap was the sheerest, the whitest, the most beautiful organdy they could find.

Rose herself was busier than anyone else. Not with the wedding. She left that to the others. But she and Jory were to live in a small house near the church. It had been unoccupied for a long time, and was in disrepair. It must be scrubbed, cleaned, papered, varnished, and polished. This was Rose's joy, to prepare the little house for their coming. And Jory joined her there every day, cutting weeds, bricking up the foundation, mending the chimney, painting. Sometimes when Tara looked at the two of them he thought he had never seen such happiness as shone from their eyes. "Man, you'll not be any happier when you finally put the ring on her finger than you are right now!" he told Jory.

"There'll be no ring," Jory said.

"No ring?"

"We don't wear jewelry," Rose said simply.

"Not even a wedding ring?"

Rose and Jory looked at each other, and Jory smiled at Tara. "Especially not a wedding ring. We wouldn't want to make our marriage conform to the world like that."

Tara stared at them a moment and then he turned back to the fence he was mending. He didn't pretend to understand this. But he recognized integrity when he saw it. No worldly ornaments meant exactly that to Jory and Rose. No worldly ornaments, not even adorning their marriage.

When he got home that evening, Hod met him at the door. He motioned to Tara's room and, when they had closed the door behind them, handed Tara the morning paper. It was folded to an item dated that morning in Louisville.

The man Carson, wanted for murder in West Virginia, had been traced to Kentucky. More details of the murder were given. The man had been married about five years when his wife had been killed in the peculiar accident. She had fallen into an open well in the back yard and had broken her neck. Under question, Carson had said he had been cleaning out the well that day and had forgotten to put the cover back on. Water in the regular well was running low, he had said, and he had decided to clean out the old well. But his wife knew about it, he insisted. He had gone to bed that night, tired, and had gone straight to sleep. His wife, he said, must have gone outside for something. He didn't miss her until the next morning.

The well, the article said, gave evidence of having been worked in. Gravel, shale, dirt were piled to one side and fresh dirt showed in the bottom. Tools were lying near the opening of the well. The woman was crumpled in a shallow pool of water at the bottom.

There was no reason to suspect foul play. No reason at all. There was not even an autopsy. The coroner simply returned a quick verdict of death by accident. There was only one funny thing. A St. Christopher that the woman always wore on a thin chain about her neck was gone. But then women lose such things easily. Carson could not say when he had last noticed the little medal. She might have lost it a week or two before the accident. Or broken the link and put it away to be repaired. It was one of the sons who had called attention to the missing St. Christopher.

But people in the little community remembered things now. Now that a crowbar and a thin, greened silver chain with a broken St. Christopher still attached to it had been unearthed by a farmer plowing an old abandoned field. They remembered how quickly the man had married his wife's sister. And they remembered how suddenly the whole family had left. Left without saying where they were going. Left, never to come back, taking the man's children with them. A little boy about four who had been called Jory. A little boy about two whose name was Taylor. And a baby girl, Julie. The people remembered now. It had been the boy Jory who had cried when he saw his mother and who had said: "Her locket's gone! Mamma's locket is gone!"

The whole thing fell into place now! Tara looked at Hod. There was no doubt that old man Clark was Carson. The names of the children made that certain. And the long, tireless arm of the law was reaching close. The cave under the cliff would soon be needed. Tara laid the paper down and a heavy weight settled on him. Things were shaping up. He rubbed his hand over his eyes. It would come soon now. He hoped it would wait until Jory and Rose were married and had left on their honeymoon. They were going to Pennsylvania in the old car. To a church conference near Lancaster. If the law would just take it slow, now. Just wait another day or two. Then Jory would be safely out of the way.

"This is it, then," Tara said.

"Looks like it."

"What do we do?"

"Wait. Too many people saw this paper. The whole ridge'll know. It won't be long now. We'll wait. And watch out for Jory."

But that was not the way it was to be. The wheel was spinning rapidly now, and the finger of fate was pointing to its stopping place. When Tara went in to supper, Tom was there. A troubled, disturbed Tom. Hod turned to Tara. "Sarah's missing," he said grimly through set lips. "Tell him, Pa."

"They ain't much to tell," Tom said, his voice slow and heavy. "She was there at home durin' the day, like always. Cooked dinner fer us. Red up when she was through. I seen her walkin' down towards the holler some time in the afternoon. But she likes to go down to that little branch an' fish, times. I figgered that's where she was goin'. Never thought nothin' about it. She never come home, though, like she usual done. I waited awhile, then I went down to the branch myself. Hollered fer her. Never seen no sign of her, nor got no answer. Wasn't no way of tellin' whether she'd been there or not. Then I come on down here, fer hit was gittin' late, an' I allowed mebbe she'd come down to visit a spell with Mary. I misdoubt she's lost. She was raised in these here woods an' knows ever' crook an' turn of 'em. Hit's a puzzle to me."

Hod was getting his gun. "We'll take a turn around the ridge in the car. See if she's at any of the folks'." He turned to his father. "Pa," he said, "would you stay here with Mary?"

Tom hesitated.

Quickly Hod spoke again. "I know it'll be hard, anxious like you are. But there's reasons why I don't want Mary by herself tonight."

Without understanding, but knowing Hod had good reason for what he asked, Tom agreed immediately. "I'll stay," he said. Hod had spoken with a quiet, grim finality, so Tom knew there was more happening than he was aware of. And that a younger man must handle it.

Tara stepped into his room to get his gun. A clammy hand had laid hold of him, cold and chill with fear. Night was coming on, and Sarah was missing . . . and a murderer was loose in the night.

Mary's face whitened when she saw the guns. But she said nothing. She followed them to the car. Mutely she stood and watched them get in. Only then, when Hod started the motor, did she speak. And then all she said was, "Hod, be careful!"

Hod nodded and slid the gears into place, and the car slipped slowly away, leaving Mary standing alone. Tara had the feeling that there was something final about it. Something final, done with, finished. He felt like saying good-by. He looked back. Mary still stood there, growing smaller as the car put distance between them. And then they rounded the bend in the road and he could see her no more. He turned around and settled himself against the back of the seat. For what, he did not know. But there was foreboding in his veins. Farewell in his thoughts.

Sarah was not at Becky's, nor had she been there. She was not at Irma and John's. She was not at Ferdy Jones's. She was not at Miss Willie's. But there they found their clue. Rufe had seen her. "I seen her," he said, "early in the afternoon. She was over in Bear Holler. I was diggin' sang, an' she was too. We dug a little together, but she wanted to go on up the holler, an' I'd already been up that. I'd already got what they was, an' I told her so. But she wanted to see fer herself. Like I'd overlook a patch of sang. Me, that's been diggin' sang all my life!"

Hod's quick look met Tara's. "Thanks, Rufe," he told the boy.

"Want I should come with you?" Wells asked.

"Be glad if you would," Hod's answer was short. Wells got his gun and crawled into the back of the car. Rufe came running, with his new rifle. "Wait fer me," he yelled.

"Son," Wells leaned out to say, "we can't both go. A man's got to stay here with the wimmenfolks. We don't know what's on the loose tonight. I'd best go, I think. But you stay up an' watch out. Take keer of the place. Mind, an' be keerful of yerself, though. But don't let nothin' happen to Miss Willie an' Rose an' the baby. I'll be dependin' on you."

Rufe had stopped as Wells spoke to him, and at first his face had drawn down in disappointment. But as Wells gave him a full man's job to do, it brightened, and then it grew grave in determination. "They won't nary thing come botherin' around *this* house tonight!" he promised. "Not nary thing! You kin put yer dependence in that!"

"I know I kin," Wells told him. "Jist take keer."

Hod turned the car and headed for the pike.

"Aren't you going to take the car home?" Tara asked.

"No. It'd take us longer to walk over the ridge. We can go a piece up the hollow in the car from the lower end. Quicker that way. And time counts."

Tara, remembering that Bear Hollow lay over the next ridge
from Wishful Hollow, knew he was right. It would take over an
hour to walk from home. There was no need for them to say
what they were thinking. That there was a narrow, hidden
ravine opening off Bear Hollow. And that there was a cave
somewhere up that ravine, sheltered under a cliff, concealed
from all eyes. A cave that held quilts and food stores, lanterns
and guns. And a cave that held, perhaps, also a fearful, guilty
old man. If Sarah had stumbled onto his hiding place now . . .
now, when he most needed it, when the law was close and
reaching closer! But Tara's mind refused to thread that thought
out to its knotted end. Sanity lay in one thing at a time, he
thought. One thing at a time.

It was already growing dark when they left the car. Hod had
driven it as far up the hollow as he could, but the track finally
played out and became too rough for driving. From there they
must go on foot. Hod led the way. They all had flashlights and
they moved silently along the narrowing hollow, single file. The
floor of Bear Hollow was fairly smooth, but it had grown over
with sprouts and bushes since winter. They made their way
through them, keeping close to the watercourse.

When they came to the now familiar thicket that hid the
opening into the smaller ravine, Hod stopped. "Wells," he said,
"you better know what you're getting into." He flicked his light
off. There would be a moon later, but now, down in the floor of
the hollow, it was as dark as midnight. Hod told Wells then all
that he and Tara knew, and what they suspected. "This is
more, you see," he said, "than hunting for a lost girl. Somebody
may get hurt tonight."

"I seen yer guns," Wells said, "and I reckon you takened note
I brung mine."

Hod grunted. "Just wanted you to know. Ready, Cap'n?"

Tara hitched at his holster. "Ready."

They flicked their lights on again and shoved through the

thicket. "Right up the bed of the creek, Wells," Hod directed.

The creek was little more than a trickle now, for June had been dry, with no rains to swell the streams. But the bushes, young blackberry canes, and vines had grown thickly during the spring, and they now bent and tangled over the stream bed in a matted barrier through which they must claw and fight their way. It was hard going. It was always, Tara thought, hard going up this damned little hollow! The briers and brambles caught on their clothing, tore at their hands and faces, and held them to a slow crawl up the steep ravine. The night was close with heat, and down here in this narrow box it was as sticky and steamy as in a jungle. They sweated, and the sweat ran into their eyes and down their faces, keeping them swiping at it constantly, and it ran into the scratched places and stung like the bite of small bees. They mumbled their curses, but they kept climbing steadily.

As they climbed, Tara grew more tense. He wondered if Hod felt the same way, and if Hod were listening for the same sound. The bell should ring any time now! He kept thinking he heard it, thin, tinkly, light, distant and yet distinct. Any time now. But they climbed on, and there was no bell. Hod motioned for them to douse their lights. They climbed now in the dark. Any time now the bell would ring. They'd hear it.

But they never did. They came up to the fall of rocks, dry now in the heat, and they didn't hear any bell at all. They heard something else instead. Hod was in front. He laid his flashlight and gun on top of the barrier and hitched himself up and over. Pin-n-n-ng! Instantly the bullet sang over their heads, ominously close. Tara ducked instinctively. How he hated the sound of a high-powered rifle! "Pierce?" he whispered.

"O. K. I'm flat," Hod answered.

Tara chuckled. "Sniper in the hedgerow, Sergeant!"

Hod drawled in exasperation: "And me without no hand grenades!"

They waited a moment, and then Tara could hear Hod moving cautiously. All at once he was back in uniform . . . the captain. Pierce was there, in the dark, on his right. But he was responsible. This was his job. He was the captain. Smoothly, clearly, his mind functioned. Just a reconnaissance job. An unpleasant night job, but not particularly dangerous if you were careful. The map of the level place spread out before him in his mind. "To the right, Pierce," he whispered. "I'll take the left. Wells, you cover us here. Fire when you see his fire. But high. Keep it up there, man, we'll be out there in front of you!"

Hod chuckled. "That's an order, Wells!"

Wells grunted.

Neither had to say what they were going to look for. The rock steps had to be found.

Carefully Tara inched himself up over the rocks, one cautious movement at a time, trying not to dislodge any telltale gravel and stones. The night was full of quiet, and he felt every nerve in his body strained under the tension. Underneath, though, he felt elation and certainty. Just a night job. Just another patrol.

He gained the top of the barrier and crawled slowly to the left. The wall of the cliff was not more than fifty feet ahead. Once he got there, the old man would have to shoot straight down. But his map stopped there. Why hadn't they thought to ask Rufe where the steps went up the cliff? He could at least have told them right or left, and maybe identified some bush or tree or boulder. That's what too much hurry did. Made them slip up. Now they had to find those steps in this blackness, and it was going to be one more ticklish job with the old man up there potting away at them.

Carefully, noiselessly, he crawled along, sweating out every inch of the way. He felt as if the small soft sluff-sluff of his clothes against the ground made a noise that carried a mile. But when he stopped to listen, he could not hear Hod on the other side, so he knew that his own progress was as silent. Pi-n-n-ng!

The bullet sang, well over his head, and almost immediately Wells's answering shot rang out. Tara flattened.

His hand touched the sheer block of the cliff and he pulled himself up slowly, gingerly. Keep him shooting high, Wells, he thought. Keep him busy. He began edging his way toward the center, feeling every inch of the wall before him, pushing back every outgrowth of bush to feel behind it. Behind some bushes, Rufe had said. The ravine pinched in here and the cliff was not more than thirty feet wide. He heard the slide of Hod's shoe, and the next moment felt his shoulder rub against his own. "Now what?" Hod whispered.

"Any break on your side?"

"None."

"None here, either. What's the side wall like?"

"Straight up."

The old man's rifle sang out now, twice, three times. Tara and Hod crouched. But Wells's gun was silent.

"The steps are cut in a niche to the right, where the cliff runs into the ridge."

Tara swung around. "Jory!"

Incautiously he had spoken aloud, and the rifle above answered with a clattering fire, straight down. They hugged the cliff, spread-eagling themselves against it, while the rifle spatted venomously into the gravel around them. Tara slewed himself slowly to the right, away from the center. His hand touched someone's shoulder. "Jory?"

"Yes." Jory's whisper was careful.

"What are you doing here? How did you know about this?"

"You think I don't read the newspapers, Cap'n? An' when I went to see Rose tonight, Rufe told me. Told me about the cave, and Sarah being missing. You think I couldn't add it up, then?"

Tara pressed his shoulder. "It's too bad, Jory."

The rifle spurted loose stones around them. "Your old man can shoot, Jory."

"Yes." Jory's voice came from farther away.

"Where you going?"

"Up the ladder."

"Wait . . . wait, Jory!"

"This is my job."

And the small, soft, sliding sound of Jory's feet went steadily away from Tara.

For the space of one short, vanishing second Tara stood still and alone. But with the clarity and timelessness of a dream, he saw Jory climbing up those laddered steps in the niche of the cliff, steadily and certainly toward the flame of the old man's rifle. Jory, who did not believe in violence. Jory, whose whole faith rested in the doctrine of nonresistance. He was as sure as death that even now Jory did not have a gun. Would not have used one had they given it to him. And he was as sure as death that what waited for Jory at the top of the niched steps was violence that he would not even try to resist.

In a split second the whole scene laid itself bare before him. He saw Jory fall before the fire, and he knew Rose would be a widow before she was even a wife. And almost as quickly he rejected it and moved, forgetting caution, forgetting to move quietly, forgetting everything except the sudden necessity to get between Jory and what lay waiting up above.

He ran, conscious of the gun firing regularly down into the level place, conscious of Wells's answering fire high above them, conscious of all of it, but not caring. He had to stop Jory!

In the dark, split only by the flame of the guns, he came up sharply against someone. He laid hold of him. "Jory."

"Pierce," came Hod's reply.

Tara loosed him and felt around him. And then his hand touched Jory's feet, already shoulder high on the narrow steps cut in the crevice of the wall. He pulled at them, and Jory kicked loose. Tara got his own feet on the lowest step and braced his back against the wall. Then he wrapped his arms around Jory's knees and swung free, pulling Jory down with him as he fell. They rolled into an open space and Tara flung himself away from Jory. "Hold him, Hod!" he yelled. And at the same time he found the crevice again and started up the steps.

The noise had drawn fire, but here in this small, boxed, flat space Tara did not give himself time to think. He found the steps by feeling and went steadily up them. A sound behind him made him pause. "We're on your heels, Cap'n," came Hod's voice. "What made you think this was all your party?"

"Keep Jory back, Hod. Keep him there!"

"I'm ahead of Jory, Cap'n."

Tara felt a flash of the old companionship . . . the old comfort in his men . . . always there, right beside him. There to be counted on. There to steady him. It was good.

He went on up the steps, wondering now where they led. Did they come out in front of the old man, or within the cave itself? In front, likely. The old man wouldn't let his entrance trap him.

Up and up the steps went. Higher than he had thought, and almost straight, so steeply did they climb. And then Tara's hand reached for a step and felt flatness stretching under it. This is it, then. This is the top! He loosed his gun and kicked at Hod's shoulder to warn him. Inching his way, he pulled himself up and over the top. When his head was up, there was only darkness ahead of him. Darkness and silence. The gun was strangely quiet. And Tara knew why. He's heard us. He's heard us climbing. He's waiting. He's sitting over there, listening, waiting.

He drew his body over the edge of the last step. And then there came the swift flame of the gun, and the jolt of the bullet knocked him halfway round. It was as if a boulder had been bounced off his shoulder. Pain seared through his arm, and his gun dropped useless and clattering down the crevice behind him. He groaned and bent forward. But he felt a swift admiration for the way the old man knew his ground. He knew the head of those steps like it was the center of a target, and even in the dark he could hit it!

Another shot rang out, and a fine knife drew a line across his skull. His head went down and the sounds of the shots diminished slowly as consciousness ebbed. He felt rather than heard the sound that Hod and Jory made as they went by him. Felt rather than heard Hod's gun speaking. Felt, and had time to think, oddly, that the battle was in good hands. A company is no stronger than its top sergeant, he remembered. And Pierce was a good top sergeant. He would hold. He would stick. And then he relinquished his hold on consciousness and for Tara Cochrane the night and the battle were over.

CHAPTER

20

H<small>E HAD</small> no way of knowing the days of fever and delirium that lay between that last moment of consciousness and this waking moment. No way of knowing how hard the small staff of the little hospital had fought for his life. No way of knowing the long hours Jory and Hod had spent by his bedside. No way of knowing how often they had looked at each other in despair. It was all unknown to him, and when he waked, it was to look strangely at the walls around him and to think ruefully that they did right well by themselves in this field hospital. Under a roof, by golly! And with whole walls to the rooms. Where had they found a building this near the front in such good repair!

And then he saw Hod. "Did the line hold, Pierce?"

"The line held, Cap'n."

He frowned, and over his memories of a battle line grimly fought for, there gradually emerged, like gray ghosts, the more recent memories. The ravine, the rock fall, the rifle shots, the cliff, and the laddered steps. Like scenes seen through water they blurred and ran together, the merged edges blotted and indistinct. And then they came clear, photographed and sharp. "Hey!" he said, and shifted himself abruptly in the bed.

Hod was beside him instantly. "Take it easy, Cap'n. You're not out of the woods, yet."

"What happened?"

"Lay back there and be good and I'll tell you. Otherwise, no!"

Tara shook his head and the bandages rubbed against the pillow. He put up a hand to feel of them, and then he noticed that his other arm was in a cast. "Brother, I'm really a casualty, aren't I?"

Hod sucked in his breath. The last few days they had told him the captain was going to make it, but this moment of lucidity held a world of relief for him. Even knowing things were better, it had been pretty bad to sit here and watch him lying there unconscious. He had never before seen a man just lying there, day after day, unknowing and uncaring what went on around him. Just lying there, only his chest rising and falling to tell that he still lived. He'd got so that the captain's chest had been the only barometer of hope. He'd watched it when the fever drove it into a rapid, shallow movement, and then he'd watched it when the fever sank, and vitality had sunk with it, and the rise and fall had been slow and deep. The whole thing had scared him out of ten years' growth. And now the captain was awake. Awake and talking. Making sense.

A bullet had creased his skull, another had shattered the bones in his shoulder, and then, as if that weren't enough, he'd developed pneumonia. But he wanted to know what had happened. And he could grin over what a crock he was. Some guy, the captain!

To be safe he pushed the button for the nurse. When she came, he asked her to call the doctor and see if the captain could talk. "Tell him," he said, "he's come to."

When she came back, she shoved a thermometer into Tara's mouth. "He said," she told Hod, "if he didn't have any temperature he could talk ten minutes."

Tara grunted around the thermometer.

Not that day, nor even the next, did Tara hear all of the story. But little by little, one piece at a time, he learned it.

How Hod had stormed past him when he went down, his gun blazing, and how when he reached the mouth of the cave he found the old man crumpled over his own gun. No one could say whether it was Hod's shot that had got him, or a stray shot from Wells's gun. But the shot that had creased the captain's skull had been the old man's last shot. Hod and Jory found him dead.

And Sarah was in the cave. Frightened, her face streaked with tears, her wrists chafed from the ropes with which she was tied, and gagged, but otherwise unharmed. She had wandered up the narrow, boxed ravine and had surprised the old man at the foot of the cliff. He had not been unkind to her. He had simply told her that she must come with him, that he was sorry but he could not let her go back home now. She had not understood much of what followed and she was not afraid until night came on. Then she had begun to cry. The old man had fixed food and told her to eat. He had not tied her or gagged her until they heard the noise of the men's progress up the hollow. Then he was afraid she would scream or cry out. But he had put her far back in the cave where she wouldn't be hit.

"He said," she had sobbed against Hod's shoulder, "that the law was after him, an' that likely they'd come that night. But if they never, he said he'd let me go home in the mornin'."

Tara shuddered when Hod told him that. He knew as well as Hod that the old man could never have let the girl go free to tell of his hiding place. It was the merest stroke of luck that he had delayed the inevitable and that they had been in time.

"And she's all right now?" Tara asked.

"She's fine. Mary's got her at home with her."

A clearly defined path opened before Tara then. It was like coming on a well-beaten track after wandering around in the woods. He'd been wondering what was going to happen to Sarah. Well, now he knew. "Hod," he said, "I want to take Sarah east with me when I go. I want to see that her voice is trained and that she has an opportunity to use it. I want to do the most that can be done for her."

Hod was still; but Tara could see his throat working.

"Do you think Tom will let her go?" Tara went on.

"Cap'n," Hod said finally, "I reckon Sarah sort of belongs to you now. You've kind of earned an interest in her. Pa'll not stand in the way."

"You and Mary?"

"We'd be glad. It's more than we could ever have hoped for her."

"I think she'll want to go."

"I think she will."

And then Hod told him how the men from West Virginia had come. How Jory had identified his father and how the men had claimed him as Carson. "It was a bad time for Jory," Hod said, "but not as bad as it would have been if they'd taken him alive. Jory said it was best this way. He didn't figure his pa would have let 'em take him, anyway."

Jory himself added to that later. "It was clean-cut and over," he said, "no trial, no sentence, no imprisonment. Just the end of the road."

"Jory, didn't you remember any of it?"

"There was something there. Not much. I was too young. But I think I always knew something had gone wrong. I remembered seeing my mother after they brought her out of the well, and I can still remember how bare her throat looked without the chain."

"Didn't you remember that your name was Carson?"

"No. Kids as a rule don't think about their last names. Not at three or four, anyhow. I reckon it's when you start to school that your last name begins to have any meaning to you. And mine was Clark by then."

"What are you going to do about it now?"

"It's Carson, isn't it?"

If it disturbed Jory that he must accustom himself to a new and damaged name, it was not evident in his manner. Carson or Clark, he was still himself. And Tara knew he would invest the unfamiliar name with his own courage and dignity. Jory Clark . . . Jory Carson. It did not matter. The man himself was what counted.

"You shouldn't have done it, Cap'n." Jory's voice brought Tara back.

"Shouldn't have done what?"

"Shouldn't have put yourself in my place."

Tara was embarrassed. They were all making too much of this thing. "Did I?" he squirmed.

"Yes."

"Well, I couldn't let you be a hero all by yourself!"

Jory smiled, and, as always when he smiled, his face went young and sweet. A great hurt and sense of loss ran through Tara. He was going to miss this man. There was a brotherhood between them that he had never known with anyone before. And he had had time now to know why. Only when you can find something of yourself in another man do you really know him. There's always that screen, that thin, strong screen hanging between men. The kind of screen that is transparent only on one side. You are behind it, and if you peer long enough and hard enough you can see, vaguely, through the screen. But no one can see through to you, hidden behind it. Once in a while, once maybe in a whole lifetime, you catch a glimpse of yourself, mirrored, fixed, reflected before you. That image of yourself, the knowable self, is your brother, staring back at you through his own little screen. That's all you can ever know of him. What you know of yourself.

There was a lot of the saint in Jory Clark. And the only reason he could see it and recognize it was because there was a lot of the saint in himself. The saint he had never guessed was there. He knew, though, now that it lay in all men, beneath the surface somewhere, a little ashamed, a little embarrassed, a little uneasy. Pushed down because it was good, and goodness was softness, and softness was the denial of manliness. He had seen men in the Army covering an inherent gentleness in themselves with a swaggering and cruel toughness. Seen them rough over their impulses toward goodness, callous them, and pervert them. Seen it in life all around him, for that matter. Men veneered over with hardness, afraid to be good. Afraid of the saint in themselves. And he had done it too. Pushed it down. Been afraid of it.

He wished he could tell Jory how he felt. He'd like to tell him that because he'd seen and known a man who wasn't afraid to be good, he wasn't afraid any longer. Because the only reason he could see the goodness in him was because it was the image of his own most secret self. And he needn't be afraid, because now he knew the image of himself is in all men. He didn't need to look for it any longer. For he knew, because one man had loved him, that it was there, and therefore, because he had been loved, and one man had seen himself in him, he needn't go on looking any more.

He wished he could say those things . . . put them into words that didn't sound so confused. And then, as clearly as he had known what he was thinking, he knew that he needn't say the words. Jory already knew.

"We've waited for the wedding till you're home again," Jory said. "Both of us wanted you to be there."

Tara hitched himself up on the pillows. "Well, now, that was plumb nice of you," he drawled in a good imitation of the ridge speech. "I take that proudly, Jory Clark."

Jory punched the pillow near the bandaged head. "Don't take it too proudly! And don't try to horn in this time! I'll be the hero without any help!"

"I'll not even argue with you about that. You can face your own guns all by yourself that day."

And then soberly he approached another thing which had been growing in his thoughts as he had lain in the hospital bed with so much time to think. Another hard, narrow hospital bed . . . with no jitters this time. "Jory," he began, "you've been eating your heart out for a doctor here in the hills. I've found him for you."

"That's right nice of you, Cap'n," Jory said, grinning and unimpressed, "but I already found him."

Tara grinned back at him, glad of this closeness between them, for Jory must understand this now. Mustn't think he was just ratting on him. He was almost sure he would see it, though. "That wouldn't work, Jory," he said. "I know you've been beating a drum for me to stay here. I'm not blind . . . or deaf. But that's not the answer."

Jory's face sobered.

"We've said it would have to be a man who loved the ridge and who would be willing to live with the people. Someone who didn't care about money. Someone whose life would be dedicated to the people. It has to be someone more than that, Jory. It has to be someone the people love and trust. And it's been right in front of us all the time. You're the man, Jory."

"But I'm not a doctor!"

"But you can be! A few years of training and you can be!"

"I'm a preacher, Cap'n."

"You can be both. Don't you have medical missionaries in your Church? You don't have to quit being a preacher."

Tara gave him time, and Jory took it, looking at him steadily. Only the muscles of his jaw worked to show what he was thinking and feeling. "It's you and Rose, Jory," Tara said.

Jory got up then and went to the window. He stared out at the houses across the street from the hospital a long time. "I'm not too old?" he asked then, turning back to the bed.

"It won't be easy for you. I wouldn't promise you that. But you're not too old."

Jory's shoulders straightened. "And I reckon you're going to pay for it."

"I reckon I am."

"It'll take a right smart."

"I've got a right smart."

And that's all that was said about it. Tara had counted on Jory's understanding that the money was his part . . . the job was Jory's. And he'd been right.

Against the pillows his own shoulders straightened. His job was waiting for him . . . outside . . . back there where he'd left it.

It was another week before Tara went home from the hospital. And home, when he got there, was bedecked for the wedding. Because of him, it was to be at Mary's instead of Miss Willie's. They brought him out the morning before the wedding that night. The house was sweet-smelling with flowers, and brightly shining. "I missed out on the housecleaning this time," Tara jeered at Hod.

"Yeah, and you missed a heap too," Hod grumbled. "I had to *varnish* the floors this time. Wasn't enough just to wax and polish 'em! A wedding's extra-special!"

Tara walked gingerly across the room. "Mighty slick shine you got on 'em."

"Mighty slick," Hod agreed. "You walk easy on 'em."

It was good to be at home again. Tara looked around at the old log walls, the piano in the corner, the broad hearth, the old clock ticking gently on the mantel. It was the best of home he had ever known. And it had become a part of him, another man's though it might be. Here he had learned to love a woman, and here he had been hurt by his love. Here he had ravaged it in a drunken fit of anger, but here too he had struggled to live with it, control it, guard it. He thought it would always have the power to hurt. But it had its goodness too. Whatever hurt it held, it held also his knowledge, hard learned, that a man can find a certain measure of happiness in the happiness of the one he loves. It was far from joy, of course. But Jory had been right. There was a peace in it. And he was beginning to find it.

As if he were saying good-by already, he looked around the room. The time was almost through.

Mary fussed over him and mothered him.

"I'm all right," he protested, "don't make such a bother!"

"But you gave us such a scare!"

"Well, that's over. Now, I'm fine."

She reached out and rumpled his hair.

He caught her hand. "Good-by, Mary."

Her hand was still in his own. "Good-by?"

"I want to say it now."

"You're going away, then?"

"As soon as I can travel, yes."

"And you're taking Sarah with you?"

"Yes."

"Where are you going?"

"I thought you'd know."

"Your father's."

It was not a question. It was a confirmation.

"There, first. Then back to work."

Mary bent then and laid her cheek against his head. "Good-by, Tara Cochrane. But you'll come back to see us."

"I'll come back," he promised.

"Weddings are over so quickly." Miss Willie grieved that night after Jory and Rose had stood so briefly before the minister. "All the fuss and bother! All the getting ready! All the excitement! And for what? Five minutes. That's all it takes. Five short minutes and it's over!"

"But think what an eternity that five minutes leads to." Wells teased, coming up and slipping an arm around Miss Willie. "Man," he said, shaking Jory's hand, "hit don't take long fer the gates to open, but they're shore closed behind you a lifetime."

"That suits me," Jory grinned.

"Supper's ready," Sarah announced shyly, and then she slipped around to Tara's side and slid her hand possessively through his arm. "I'll help you," she promised, "I'll cut up yore chicken fer you, since yore arm's still stiff."

Tara looked down at her. There was a shine on Sarah's face these days. A radiant happiness that made her skin glow like a pink pearl. Heaven's own gate had opened up for Sarah. She was to go with the captain, and to live in his house with him, and to go to school, and to learn to sing the way he wanted her to! She smiled up at him. She would not have asked more of paradise! Tara patted her hand on his arm. "That'll be fine, Sarah."

When the wedding supper was over, there was music. Mary played and the whole group sang. Tara's arm was still too stiff to hold a bow, so they had to forego his violin. But he could join in the singing. It was a happy hour. And then Tara asked Sarah to sing.

"Can you play yore gittar?" she asked.

"Bring it and I'll see. I think maybe I can manage."

His fingers worked all right. It was just in the shoulder the muscles were still sore. He picked a chord or two, turned a key, listened, and was ready. "All right, Sarah."

"It's in F," she said.

He looked up at her. "F?"

"Yes."

He gave her an opening bar, and then her voice lifted softly over the room. As light and as sweet as peach down. As soft and as silvery as starlight. As steady and as true as time. Tara bent his head over his guitar and the lamplight caught its sooty shine. "Black, black, black," sang Sarah, ". . . black is the color of my true love's hair."

The little song whispered through the room, and then, like a sigh, the last note hung trembling, delicate. Like a sigh, breathed and forgotten, but part of the air forever. Sighed and forgotten and made part of time.

Tara laid his hands across the guitar strings, palmed them gently to still them. And they were quiet under his hands. "Black is the color of my true love's hair!" He looked across the room at Jory. And as if he knew already where this trail was leading, Jory smiled at him.